SECRET LEGACY

THE LEGACY SERIES, BOOK 3

JEN TALTY

JUPITER PRESS

This book is a work of fiction. Names, characters, places, and incidents are products of the author's imagination or used fictitiously. Any resemblance to actual events or locales or persons living or dead is entirely coincidental.

SECRET LEGACY

LEGACY SERIES, BOOK 3

USA Today Bestseller

JEN TALTY

PRAISE FOR JEN TALTY

"*Deadly Secrets* is the best of romance and suspense in one hot read!" *NYT Bestselling Author Jennifer Probst*

"A charming setting and a steamy couple heat up the pages in a suspenseful story I couldn't put down!" *NY Times and USA today Bestselling Author Donna Grant*

"Jen Talty's books will grab your attention and pull you into a world of relatable characters, strong personalities, humor, and believable storylines. You'll laugh, you'll cry, and you'll rush to get the next book she releases!" Natalie Ann USA Today Bestselling Author

"I positively loved *In Two Weeks*, and highly recommend it. The writing is wonderful, the story is fantastic, and the characters will keep you coming back for more. I can't wait to get my hands on future installments of the NYS Troopers series." *Long and Short Reviews*

"*In Two Weeks* hooks the reader from page one. This is a fast paced story where the development of the romance grabs you emotionally and the suspense keeps you sitting on the edge of your chair. Great characters, great writing, and a believable plot that can be a warning to all of us." *Desiree Holt, USA Today Bestseller*

"*Dark Water* delivers an engaging portrait of wounded hearts as the memorable characters take you on a healing journey of love. A mysterious death brings danger and intrigue into the drama, while sultry passions brew into a believable plot that melts the reader's heart. Jen Talty pens an entertaining romance that grips the heart as the colorful and dangerous story unfolds into a chilling ending." *Night Owl Reviews*

"This is not the typical love story, nor is it the typical mystery. The characters are well rounded and interesting." *You Gotta Read Reviews*

"Murder in Paradise Bay is a fast-paced romantic thriller with plenty of twists and turns to keep you guessing until the end. You won't want to miss this one..." *USA Today bestselling author Janice Maynard*

BOOK DESCRIPTION

She wanted to protect her brother...but she failed.
He'll do whatever it takes to protect Vivian, even if it means taking a bullet...
But will it be enough?

Vivian Rose thought she burned her family's dirty little secret the day she laid her father to rest. Only, years later, when her brother is found murdered, it seems that secret might have been the very thing that got her brother killed. Now, Vivian finds herself in the middle of an internet game that she doesn't understand and the target of a dangerous man who will stop at nothing to make her his.

Agent Cameron Thatcher has had his eyes on the sexy Vivian Rose for months. However, when his current case includes a sex club and her brother gets involved, he finds himself in a precarious situation. The more he digs, the more he uncovers, and the more he realizes that Vivian's in danger. He'll do whatever is necessary to protect her—including taking a bullet.

But will it be enough?

PROLOGUE

Vivian Rose took her little brother by the hand, terrified that he might fall into the grave—or worse, try to climb into the casket. Oliver was too young to understand. He was only ten years old, and he idolized their dad.

So had Vivian. Until the night before her father put a gun to his temple and pulled the trigger.

Everyone at the funeral looked at her with pity in their eyes for the poor little girl who'd lost her father.

Little did they know what he'd done. Or that the only reason he'd killed himself was because he got caught.

By his teenaged daughter.

Oliver glanced up at her with tears streaking down his face. "Why did Daddy have to die?"

"I don't know," she whispered, wishing she could comfort her little brother. She wanted to wrap him in a protective bubble and make sure nothing ever hurt him again.

Her mother stepped behind them. "Oliver, go with your Aunt Kiki."

Oliver swiped his pudgy hands across his face. He followed their father's sister across the cemetery toward the limo. He was such a sweet, innocent little boy and had a heart of gold. It sucked that not only would he grow up without a father, but he'd also forever wonder about why his father had ended his life.

But it was better than the alternative.

"How are you holding up?" Vivian's mother wrapped a loving arm around her shoulders.

Vivian was only fourteen, but she'd had to grow up real fast the past week. "I'm tired of pretending I'm sad he's dead when I'm not."

"Don't say that," her mother said with a stern tone. "If he were alive, no one would be speaking to us. The scandal he could have brought down on this family would have destroyed us, and we would be hiding out in shame. I'd rather people feel sorry for us this way than wonder if we knew what he was doing and turned a blind eye." She turned, cupping Vivian's face. "I'm sorry that you had to see your father doing those things with those women. I'm even more sorry that I knew about what he was doing for a while but didn't move fast enough to leave him. I wanted to protect you from ever knowing his dirty secret. But now, we both must protect Oliver. He never needs to know the shame your father caused. Can you help me do that?"

Vivian glanced over her shoulder. Ever since her dad had died, Oliver had been sleeping in her room. He'd often wake up in the middle of the night in a cold sweat, crying. If her father had been having an affair, that would have been heartbreaking. But it wouldn't have been overly scandalous, and it wouldn't have been the end of the world if Oliver ever found out.

But making homemade porn with prostitutes and loading it to the internet?

Why?

She shivered.

That really was a question she wasn't sure she ever wanted to be answered.

"Yes, Mom. I can do that."

"Good. As much as I'd like your father to suffer for what he did to our marriage and the fact that you had to see it, I love you and Oliver more. Giving the two of you as much of a normal childhood as possible is more important to me than anything."

Vivian knew her mother was right. There was no point in dragging her father through the mud. It would only bring shame on her mother and make things more difficult for her and Oliver. That was the last thing she wanted. She took in a long, slow breath.

She would not be defined by her father's secret legacy.

1

The last few weeks of school for any teacher were always bittersweet. Vivian Rose was ready for summer. She was ready to leave teaching in the classroom behind and move the education to the great outdoors. Her mother didn't understand why she still worked at Camp Lookout at her age. Her mom thought it was a job for college students, not professionals in their late twenties. Granted, Vivian was one of the older staff members, but she wasn't the oldest. And about five of them had all grown up at the camp together and weren't ready to give up that part of their youth yet.

However, if Vivian were totally honest with herself, the real reason she didn't want to give up her summers at Camp Lookout was because when she was a kid, it was the one place she could go and forget about her father and what he'd done. At camp, she wasn't the daughter of Lukas Rose, the man who'd blown his brains out. No. She was Vivian Rose, the girl who had no fear. The young woman who had hopes and dreams and wasn't about to let anyone stand in her way.

Vivian opened her desk drawer and lifted her cell. She'd texted her brother twice, but no answer.

She tapped the contacts app and pulled up his number.

It went straight to voicemail.

"Oliver. It's me, Vivian. It's not like you to ignore me. And now Mom's worried. What's going on? Call me, or I'm going to have to show up unannounced." She stuffed her cell into her purse and stood. She had one full week left of school and then a couple of days of exams. After that, it was back to the most special place on Earth.

She tossed her bag over her shoulder and headed for the parking lot. The place was empty except for the janitor in the hall, and a classroom filled with students being tutored for the AP history exam. She didn't normally stay at the high school this late, but she was meeting her best friend, Lilly, and her husband, Ethan, for dinner at the Boardwalk. Even though she lived just up the street, she didn't feel like going home.

It took all of ten minutes to drive from the high school into town. But it took nearly that long to find a parking spot afterward. She should have known that a beautiful night in the middle of June would make for a crowded village.

The second she entered the restaurant, her gaze locked on her Aunt Kiki. God, she hated running into her. And no matter how many times she did, it never got easier to ignore her father's sister.

Shit. And it seemed that Kiki wouldn't be ignored this time.

"Hello, Vivian," Kiki said. "You look well."

"We have nothing to say to each other." Vivian couldn't forgive her aunt for not being there when she'd needed her the most.

"Do you even know why you're mad at me?"

Vivian let out a dry laugh. "After my father's funeral, you walked away for over a year. You didn't return a single phone call. You basically abandoned me and my family. And then you came in like a wrecking ball, expecting some of his things? His money? Yeah. No. That's not how things work. Besides, you've never once apologized for that."

"I don't owe you anything," Kiki said, shaking her head. "Call me when you're ready to have a real conversation."

"That's never going to happen," Vivian said under her breath as she watched her aunt disappear into the sea of people.

Vivian scanned the room, looking for a friendly face, finding Cameron Thatcher on the other side of the bar. Butterflies filled her stomach. She hadn't had this kind of reaction to a man since Tommy Ricter asked her to the senior prom. It was a nice distraction from the negative sensations her aunt had created.

But Cameron lived in Albany, and while that was only an hour away, he was also a federal agent with the kind of lifestyle she wanted nothing to do with. She respected his badge and what he did to keep her and everyone else safe. However, she'd watched the struggles her friend Jacob Donovan had gone through when he was an FBI agent. Not to mention all the reasons his wife was a private investigator instead of law enforcement.

Jacob had gone back to being an assistant district attorney and was well on his way to being the next DA. He was a fair man and didn't always believe that prison was the answer. However, in his eyes, certain crimes were the only choice.

Vivian agreed.

Her mother had told her that her father's crimes had been buried with him. Except that wasn't entirely true. Vivian had to carry that darkness. It lurked in the corner of her soul, threatening to touch the very fiber of her being. It darkened her heart and made her frightened to allow anyone inside. She was terrified that someone would see her for who she really was. And while her therapist reminded her on a regular basis that she wasn't the sum of the parts of her father's legacy, that didn't change the biology.

Her counselor told her that was bullshit, too.

Cameron smiled.

She sucked in a deep breath and strolled across the room toward the bar. There was no need to be rude, especially when his surprise party was tomorrow.

While Vivian wasn't one of Cameron's closest friends, most times they ran into each other, he made it abundantly clear that he wanted to be more than friendly. He wasn't a nuisance about how he asked her out. No. He was actually quite sweet with his quick wit and subtle compliments that weren't over-the-top or only meant to be a pickup line. Often, he didn't even ask for a date but simply offered to spend time with her or lend her his ear—like a true friend would. He was genuine, and she appreciated the way he respected her need for space. She wondered how long she'd be able to keep saying no, though. Cameron was the real deal, and deep down, she knew that.

"Hey, Vivian." Cameron curled his fingers around her biceps and squeezed. "How are you?"

"I'm doing good. You?"

"Hanging tough," he said.

"What brings you up to Lake George?" She wondered if she should tell him happy birthday. She opted to say nothing for fear of ruining the surprise.

Cameron rubbed the back of his neck. "Unfortunately, it's not just pleasure. I'm working a case and had some things I needed to do here." He leaned against the bar and sipped his beer, looking all sexy in his sport coat. At least he'd loosened his tie. "Tomorrow, I'm going to hang with my old partner and do some catching up."

"Oh, my. Are you taking a day off?"

Cameron laughed. "Not a full day. I have an interview in the morning. And then over to Jacob's house."

"Are you staying in Lake George?"

He nodded. "I got a room at the Heritage Inn. I love that place. And Reese and his family are amazing."

"That they are," she said.

"You went to school with Patty, Reese's wife, and Katie and Jacob, too?"

"Actually, not really," Vivian said. "Katie moved when we were little, and Jacob and Patty are both about eight years older than me. But our families are friendly, and Jacob did babysit me a few times."

"I struggle with the concept of Jacob as the neighborhood child whisperer."

Vivian laughed. "He was my little brother's favorite. Jacob was so good with Oliver and always so attentive. Even when I was old enough to take care of my brother but was busy with some school activity, Jacob was always happy to swing by and take Oliver out for some ice cream or to the park if he was in town."

"Well, he's certainly an excellent father."

"You won't get an argument from me on that point."

"So, what brings you out tonight? And can I buy you a drink?"

Vivian liked Cameron. A lot. Maybe if she weren't running off to camp for the summer, she'd consider taking him up on his numerous offers to go out for a bite to eat. According to her best friend Lilly, Vivian only went to Camp Lookout to hide from life. It was the same reason she coached the dance team and taught dance at a local studio on the weekends.

The thing was, Lilly was right. But Vivian wasn't about to admit that because she had no idea what she was hiding from. Her life was amazing. She had everything she'd ever wanted. The perfect career. A nice place to live, right on the lake.

Life was good.

But not great.

And she was afraid to venture out into the real world.

Her cell vibrated in her pocket. She pulled it out and glanced down.

Lilly, not her brother.

She sighed. Of course, Lilly and Ethan would be late. They were always late. Lilly had been twenty minutes late to her wedding. But that hadn't been the best part. Ethan had been twenty-two minutes late. And they'd laughed their asses off about it while everyone in the church held a grudge.

"Is something wrong?" Cameron gently tapped his index finger on her temple. "You're scrunching your forehead."

"Well, for starters, my best friend is running late. But I was hoping to hear from my brother. However, it appears *he's* ghosting me for no reason."

"That doesn't sound like Oliver." Cameron had met Oliver a few times. For whatever reason, Oliver didn't like Cameron, and that annoyed Vivian.

Everything about Oliver lately bothered her because he hadn't been acting like her sweet, kind, loving little brother. No. He'd been cold, distant, and secretive.

And now, he had some girlfriend that he wouldn't bring around to meet anyone, which seemed odd.

"Tell me about it. Although we did have words about this new girl he's seeing." She shouldn't be saying a damn thing about her brother to anyone. Especially not someone she didn't know all that well. However, Cameron had this weird ability to make her feel at ease. Every single time she was in his company, it was as if protective bubble wrap engulfed her, and she found her safe place to release whatever demons were present at the moment.

That was a weird sensation, and one she didn't trust.

The last person who made her feel that way had betrayed her.

"He's seeing someone? I didn't know that," Cameron said with an arched brow. "Who is she?"

"I don't know. He hasn't introduced me to her. But ever since they started dating, he's been acting weird."

"Do you have a name?"

"Emma. But that's it. Why?" She quirked her eyebrow and smiled.

"Oh, my God. I'm so sorry." He shook his head. "I'm acting like a federal agent again, aren't I?"

"Pretty much," she said. "But I am worried about him." Ever since Oliver came back from his trip to South Carolina where their father's family lived, he hadn't been the same. And Vivian had to wonder if the secret she'd thought buried with her dad had somehow managed to resurface.

But how?

The only people that knew were her mother, whoever her father had been screwing, and Vivian.

Okay, so that was potentially a lot of people who knew that her father was a cheater and a homemade porn star. But if anyone did know, they never said a single word.

"I can check in on him if you'd like. I can also see what I can find out about this Emma girl."

She curled her fingers around Cameron's biceps.

Wow. She shouldn't have done that.

"Thanks. But I'm not that concerned. Yet. If I get there, I know who to call."

"I'm more than happy to help." Cameron patted her hand. "Are you sure I can't buy you a drink?"

"I appreciate it, but no," she said. "I'm going to go put my name in for a table and wait for my friends."

"Maybe next time." He leaned in and pressed his lips to her cheek.

She held her breath for a moment. The kiss lingered longer than a friendly peck normally would, and she savored every second.

If she were any other woman, she'd snatch him up in a heartbeat.

"See you around." It took a few moments for her to catch her breath as she made way through the crowd of people back to the hostess station, where the young woman led her to a table outside on the patio near the waterfront.

It was a perfect evening to eat under the stars and listen to the water gently lapping against the breakwall while the music echoed in the background like crickets.

She took a seat with her back to the water. Not because she didn't want to enjoy the view. Hell, no. But because Vivian wanted to see her friends when they walked through the door so she could wave them over, saving them the trouble of wandering through the entire restaurant.

Or at least that was the reason she told herself. If she dug deep and was honest, it had more to do with the way Ethan behaved when they went out. He just wasn't all that self-aware. And maybe if he had his back to the room and focused on the pretty view, he wouldn't annoy everyone who worked at this fine establishment.

Her cell buzzed. She pulled it out of her pocket, hoping it was from her brother.

Nope.

Her mom, wondering if she'd heard from Oliver.

Vivian quickly responded. If she didn't, not only would her mother likely freak out and call constantly, but she might also show up on Vivian's doorstep.

That was the last thing she wanted, especially when her mother went into overprotective mama-bear mode.

Understandably, though.

However, once, when her mom had gotten like that, she'd sat outside Vivian's dorm room for an entire weekend, waiting for her to return from a romantic getaway with her boyfriend. It had been totally embarrassing. Her mother had behaved as if Vivian had been kidnapped and treated Randell as if he was some kind of criminal. That relationship hadn't lasted too much longer after that incident.

Her mom's overbearing ways had toned down a lot over the years, but Oliver had been acting so strangely the last couple of months—especially with this new girlfriend he wouldn't let anyone meet. And their mother was fit to be tied. This time, Vivian had to take her mom's side.

But she couldn't have her mother pushing Oliver further away. He already had one foot out the door, and Vivian hadn't a fucking clue why. She blamed his new girlfriend.

Emma.

Fucking Emma with no last name.

Well, Vivian was sure she had one, but Oliver wouldn't give it up. And so far, there wasn't a single picture of the happy couple on social media, which wasn't like Oliver. Not that he spent a ton of time posting on the various sites, but he *was* addicted to his technology. For him not to post even a single random picture in a twenty-four-hour timeframe was unheard of. Not to announce to the world that he was in a relationship? Even stranger.

She pushed the negative thoughts from her brain, then smiled and waved to her friends, Lilly and Ethan.

Lilly had been her best friend since the sixth grade. They had bonded over sucking at the clarinet but being forced to continue with band and taking music lessons through eighth grade, when their parents finally agreed it would be okay for them to pursue other interests.

Lilly went on to star in the school plays while Vivian tried out for the dance team.

They'd both been wildly successful in their choices.

"Sorry we're late," Lilly said as she hung her purse on the side of the chair with a forced smile. "Per the usual, Ethan couldn't be pulled away from work."

"I had to finish that call, dear. I told you it was important."

Lilly rolled her eyes. "So important he locks himself in that home office. I mean, literally locks the door. Drives me crazy." Lilly sighed. "Anyway, so sorry."

"Not a problem." Vivian pulled her friend in for a long hug before giving Ethan a kiss on the cheek.

"I saw Cameron when we walked through the main bar." Lilly slipped into her seat and winked. "I don't understand why you and he aren't an item."

"I have to agree with my lovely bride," Ethan said.

"You always take her side." Vivian let her gaze wander into the restaurant, where it landed right on Cameron.

And, of course, they had to lock gazes.

He gave her a slight nod.

Her cheeks heated.

"It's obvious you're attracted to him." Ethan raised his hand and signaled to the server with a damn snap of his fingers.

Vivian kind of hated it when he did that, but only because he never gave the waitstaff a chance to make it to their table. It was as if Ethan expected them to drop everything and be at his beck and call. He didn't actually think that, and he was a nice man, but he'd been born with a shit ton of stupid money and was used to getting what he wanted, when he wanted it.

"And he's one of the good guys." Lilly leaned forward. "It's about time you started living a grown-up life. This has to be your last summer at camp."

Vivian laughed. "Thor, the waterfront director, is thirty, so I don't know what the hell you're talking about. Besides, it's better than teaching summer school or tutoring. Or worse, doing nothing at all. I love working with the kids and being outdoors. It's refreshing."

"Thor is weird. And we're talking about you and how you haven't really come to terms with your father's death."

"Stop right there." Vivian pinched her thigh. Lilly had no clue. The only person who had any idea about how she *truly* felt about her father's death was her mother, and that was a topic they barely discussed.

When they did, they were both in absolute agreement.

Her father had made their lives better by the choice he made. Only Oliver had been unexpected collateral damage. He struggled with demons and darkness because of their father's suicide. It had gotten so bad for him in high school that Vivian had worried Oliver might take his life, as well. But college had been Oliver's saving grace.

He'd thrived during his four years at Potsdam and now enjoyed an amazing career in sales.

Until a few months ago when Vivian noticed a major shift in Oliver's personality. He was only twenty-one and she worried about him living alone. He'd struggled with depression his entire life and being by himself and in his own headspace wasn't a good thing. He'd always had a roommate, but his best friend had recently gotten married, and no matter how hard Vivian pushed Oliver to find a new roomie, he wouldn't do it.

"Come on, Vivian. Camp has always been the one place you could go where you weren't the kid whose dad killed himself." Lilly waggled her finger. "You've told me that a million times. As a kid, you believed you could be yourself and that no one looked at you differently there. That no one pitied you or gave you a pass because of what your father did. I understood and supported you continuing with that shelter through college, but this is getting ridiculous. You're twenty-five freaking years old, and you're spending your summer managing a bunch of college students who only care about getting laid and trashed, and some high school students who aren't much better. Seriously, you get all bent out of shape over Oliver and his weirdness, but you're no better."

"Lilly," Ethan whispered. "You're raising your voice, and this isn't helping."

"Sorry, but I'm tired of holding back and walking on eggshells." Lilly reached across the table and tapped her fingernail. "You're my best friend, and I adore you to pieces. But you're letting life pass you by while still living in the shadow of what happened in the past."

Vivian's chest tightened. It felt as though her heart had stopped beating, even though she knew it had sped up.

Lilly was right.

Tears stung the corners of Vivian's eyes. She wasn't ready to admit to herself how much her father's legacy still hung over her head like a dark omen, much less to another human. She leaned back in her chair and folded her arms across her chest. "It's not that simple," she whispered.

"Yes, it is." Before Lilly could say another word, the waitress showed up and took their drink orders; only Ethan didn't really give anyone a chance to choose for themselves. Instead, he ordered a bottle of red wine for the table.

An expensive blend.

Only the best for Ethan.

He never understood that people sometimes didn't care about having the best. That choosing something inexpensive didn't make someone cheap. And didn't mean they didn't care about quality.

Vivian let out a long breath. Her obsession with Ethan and his desire for the finer things had nothing to do with the issue at hand and everything to do with her need for avoidance.

"Can you at least admit that your father's suicide still has a hold on your life, and that's why you still spend your summers hiding out at Camp Lookout as you let men like Cameron Thatcher slip through your fingers?"

For the last few months, Vivian had been having horrible nightmares and reliving the last few weeks of her father's life. It happened every year around the time of this death. It was worse this year, though, and she had no idea why. At first, she'd thought that maybe it was because her mother had finally gotten remarried.

But no.

It couldn't be that because Larry Ludwig was truly amazing. Her mother was finally happy, and Vivian wanted that for her mom. She'd been through so much. She deserved a slice of happiness.

It was Oliver and how he had pulled away and become almost confrontational that caused her new anxiety. Whatever was bothering Oliver had bled over into Vivian's life, and it was time to put a stop to it.

"Okay. So, you might be a little right in the sense that camp was always my safe place, but I do love my work there, and I'm not hiding."

"But you are," Ethan chimed in.

Vivian cocked her head. Ethan didn't usually make statements on this topic of conversation. "Excuse me?"

"I get that you love it there. And hell, I met my wife there. It's a great summer job—while in college. However, you throw yourself into your teaching and coaching during the school year and then immediately transfer your focus to Camp Lookout. You don't give yourself a break. You almost never take a vacation or a long weekend for yourself, much less do more than have a quick bite with us. You've always got an excuse whenever we want to fix you up with someone, or even when we just want to hang out sometimes. And the last few months, it's been worse. I'm tired of talking Lilly off the ledge every time she's worried about you. I'm worried."

Vivian's mouth dropped open. She had no idea

what to say or how to respond. She'd known Ethan for eight years. He'd been a good friend, and he was her best friend's husband. Vivian could count on Ethan, no matter what. But one thing Ethan had never done before was call it like he saw it.

He always kept his mouth closed, keeping most of his opinions to himself unless it had to do with major purchases—cars, investments, and things like that.

"I didn't mean to come in hot. I know that things have been weird with your brother. I've seen it first-hand. But I also know you thought about not going back to camp." Ethan raised his hand when she went to defend her late application, which would have been a total bullshit explanation.

She had seriously thought that maybe this would be her first summer enjoying what many teachers did—absolutely nothing. Only the thought had made her break out in hives. It meant that she had to be alone with her thoughts.

And then Oliver started acting funny, and that was the end of that.

"Look. We care about you," Ethan continued. "We want the best for you and hiding from life behind your career and at camp isn't the way to make the most out of life. If anything, it stifles you, and you can't even see that."

Vivian blew out a puff of air. She locked gazes with Lilly, who tilted her head and gave her a weak, compassionate smile.

They were right. There was no denying it. The

worst part was that, for the first time since their father died, Vivian worried she would be even less connected to her brother when she left for camp. They'd always been close, and she made sure that she was available no matter what, even through those angsty teenage years. Not to mention that Oliver had gone to the same camp all through high school and into his first two years of college until he found other passions.

Lilly scooted her chair closer and placed her hand on Vivian's shoulder. "I thought maybe Ethan was the cause of us growing apart a little, and I've tried to be a better friend. To be more present in your life. But I realized that I've always been here for you. In reality, it's you who's been slowly pulling away from me. I think it started after your father died. I've given you the space you needed to grieve. And I know it hasn't been easy. You were your dad's little girl, and he loved you. Everyone knew that."

Vivian swallowed hard and then pinched her lips closed. She'd been the apple of her father's eye. His baby girl. And he'd pranced her around like a little trophy.

Vivian had loved all the attention.

Her dad did the same thing with Oliver.

Maybe he *did* love his children, but that didn't change what he'd done or how he'd betrayed his family—his wife—in the worst way possible. There was no forgiveness for a man like Lukas.

"But your dad is gone, and he'd want you to live your life to its fullest." Ethan nodded toward a group of men. Cameron stood in the center. "We know you haven't had great luck with dating in the past."

"That's an understatement." Vivian had bad luck with men, but she'd never been honest about why most of her relationships either never really got off the ground at all, or ended after a year at most for the few that did. She'd tell Lilly and Ethan that there just wasn't a spark. Or that they didn't have enough in common.

However, the truth was that every time Vivian started having real feelings for a man, she'd remember what her father had done. She'd remember how much in love she'd thought her parents were. Her mother had definitely loved her dad, and it had taken her years to get over his lies. Everyone thought Eva was a grieving widow. And she was, only her anguish wasn't over her husband's death.

So, whenever a relationship got hot and heavy for Vivian, the memories of her childhood came crashing down on her like the house in *The Wizard of Oz*. She remembered the look on her father's face when she walked into his home office and saw the pornography on his computer screens. That, by itself, wasn't a problem. Who cared about a man watching a little sex? It wasn't that big of a deal. And she'd been about to turn away until she realized that her dad was watching himself.

With multiple women.

And not one of them was her mother.

To make matters worse, her dad was hurting those

girls, and they didn't look as though they were enjoying it.

Vivian blinked, forcing herself back to the present. She couldn't allow herself to go down that memory lane. It needed to be forever closed.

"Cameron's a pretty normal guy," Lilly said.

"He's an FBI agent. There's nothing *normal* about that." Vivian tried not to turn her head, but she couldn't help it. She locked gazes with Cameron again, and her heart dropped to the pit of her stomach like a jetliner falling from the sky. She felt the corners of her mouth tip up into an unwanted smile. Ever since she'd met him, she couldn't stop thinking about him, and that made her uncomfortable. Having deep emotions for any member of the opposite sex wasn't something she'd ever been able to handle.

Though not for lack of trying.

"It's obvious he's into you, and by that look on your face, you're into him," Lilly said with way too much excitement laced into every single syllable. "Go out on a date with him. Just one date to see how things go. I'll bet the two of you have a lot in common and are a match."

"I don't know." Vivian turned her head, forcing herself to stop gawking at the sexy agent.

"Will you promise me you'll say yes if he asks you out again?" Lilly leaned in and smiled. "Please? Going out with him isn't going to hurt."

Vivian laughed. That was exactly what she'd said to Lilly when she hemmed and hawed about going out with Ethan. "Fine. But you can't encourage him. He has to do it on his own."

Vivian stole one last glance at Cameron.

He lifted his beer and grinned.

"Looks like that's going to happen sooner rather than later." Lilly sat back in her chair. "Now, let's order some food. I'm starving."

2

Cameron rolled his SUV to a stop at his ex-partner's home at the end of Rockhurst Point, which had a panoramic view of Lake George. If Cameron didn't work in Albany, he'd live on the lake, but the commute was an hour drive, and the snow would be insane in the winter. Of course, his ex-partner's wife, Katie, and her business partner, Jackson, constantly tried to talk him into quitting the FBI and becoming a private investigator. He'd be lying if he hadn't entertained the idea.

He stuffed his keys into his pocket and made his way toward the garage entrance, wondering where all the cars were parked. Cameron had only been with the FBI for a little over a year now. He was not only green, he was also one of the youngest agents to be appointed lead on a baffling new case. He had been given the privilege because he was probably one of the smartest agents in the building. He wasn't being egotistical about it, but ever since Jacob Donovan retired a little over a year ago, someone had to step into his shoes. And that someone was Cameron.

He missed Jacob more than he cared to admit, and even though he suspected that this was supposed to be a birthday party, he had every intention of picking Jacob's brain about his most recent case. Though he'd wait until most of the guests left.

Rubbing the back of his neck, he glanced over his shoulder. He knew this was a surprise, but where were all the people?

Jacob and Katie lived on a dead-end point. There wasn't any place to hide cars. Not unless they were on a side street over on Cleverdale, which meant carting people around. Or maybe Cameron wasn't as smart as he thought and there was no party, after all, and this was just—shit. If Jacob and Katie were playing matchmaker with the sweet and sexy Vivian Rose, he'd have some choice words for his good friend. He could get his own dates. Though not with Vivian since she turned him down flat every time. She'd seemed different last night, however. As if she might actually say yes.

He banged on the door. He didn't want to make a big deal about his birthday. Twenty-six wasn't anything special, and he certainly wasn't old. He'd rather focus on his case. He'd worked hard to get where he was in his career. It had been all he'd wanted since he was sixteen years old. He'd even made sure he graduated from high school early and did his four years of college in three. Everything he'd ever done had been in an effort to be a Special Agent for the FBI, and he was still on that path. Only without Jacob as his partner, everything seemed different.

Jacob didn't believe that was the case at all. He thought Cameron had been so hyper-focused on one goal that he'd missed all the cues for what he really wanted along the way.

And that if Cameron took a moment to double back to his short stint as a New York state trooper, he might understand that it was more about the people and community and less about the alphabet agency.

The door rattled, and Jacob appeared, holding his little bundle of joy.

"Hey, man, happy birthday." Jacob waved him inside while his son, Jonathon, the fake shy little devil that he was, smiled as he snuggled his face into his father's neck.

"Thanks." Cameron patted Jonathon on the back. "I see he's still pretending to need time to warm up."

"He does that with everyone."

Cameron wiggled his fingers. "Are you going to come see me, or am I going to have to tickle you?"

Jonathon laughed as he lunged toward Cameron without a care in the world.

"Is the little tyke walking yet?" Cameron asked.

"Running is more like it," Jacob said. "And he says Mama, doggie, Grammy, Papa, but no Dada yet. I swear it's a conspiracy." Jacob led them through the family room and into the kitchen.

All the while, Jonathon pinched Cameron's cheeks and giggled.

Over the last year, Jacob and Katie had fully restored the Bateman Estate, though they'd made a lot of modern updates and a few changes to the original design. Cameron thought they'd done a bang-up job. The place looked fabulous. And from the lake, it had to be one of the most specular homes on the south end.

Jacob's mother-in-law, Grace, stood in front of the kitchen sink.

"I thought I heard someone at the door," Grace said. "You're looking handsome as ever."

"It's good to see you." Cameron handed her Jonathon, who smacked his lips on her cheek, yelling, "Grammy."

"And you look lovely as ever."

"I can't believe this boy is single." She smiled.

Cameron's mind wandered to the sexy but unattainable Vivian. He'd asked her out at least a half-dozen times and tried to get her to have *unofficial* dates a dozen others. She always let him down gently, saying that between her career as a high school English teacher and her position as the girls' unit director at summer camp, she didn't feel as though she had the time. He could understand that. A few years ago, his sole focus had been his career and moving up the chain of command to land this very job.

Now that he had exactly what he thought he wanted, though, he realized that his life was still incomplete.

He rubbed his temple. When he saw Vivian last night, he'd worried that if he *did* find himself having any alone time with her, he might end up asking pesky questions about her brother. Finding out that Oliver had been participating in an online porn website was disturbing, to say the least, especially when people associated with the site were dying.

The worst part was that Cameron couldn't tell Vivian that he planned to bring her brother in for questioning. And soon. And that made wanting to ask her out one last time something he probably shouldn't do.

Not until he wrapped up the case, or at least ruled out Oliver as someone having anything to do with the missing people or any of the deaths by suicide.

"He works too much." Jacob leaned in and kissed his son's forehead. "Come on. Katie is out on the patio enjoying some peace and quiet while Grammy here takes Jonathon to a play date."

"It was nice to see you again, Grace."

"You, too. And have a wonderful birthday," Grace said.

It was rare that Cameron read situations wrong, but it looked like this wouldn't be a surprise birthday party, after all. He meandered through the front living space and out onto the patio where an infinity pool overlooked the scenic waters of Lake George.

"Surprise!" A couple of dozen people or so popped out from behind the bushes and from around the side of the house. "Happy birthday!"

Cameron jumped. "Shit. You all scared me." He tapped his chest and stared at his old partner. "I told you I didn't want a party."

"Too bad. My wife and I needed adult company, and your birthday gave us just the excuse." Jacob slapped him on the back.

Katie came rushing toward Cameron with her arms wide and her red hair cascading over her shoulders. She wrapped them around him, giving him a big bear hug. "Look at you, all grown up and shit."

"It was bound to happen sometime." He squinted as the June sun beat down on his face. The temperatures weren't overly hot, and thankfully it wasn't humid—at least not yet. "This was really nice of you to do."

Katie palmed his cheek. "Anything for you. Now, there's a stocked bar, and we hired a bartender, so go get yourself a drink."

"Sounds great," Cameron said.

Katie looped her arm through Jacob's. "Can you help me put out some food trays?"

"Sure thing." Jacob nodded.

Cameron glanced around, looking for Vivian. He absolutely expected her to be at this party because Jacob and Katie knew how he felt about her.

But they also knew about the strange case that had come across his desk and how Oliver might be tied to it. Katie knew because Cameron had hired her PI firm, and Jacob knew because he was the ADA.

But now Cameron had found out about Oliver's new girlfriend, Emma. And so far, he'd been coming up blank there.

He stuffed his hands into his pockets and strolled across the patio toward his current partner, Stormi Swanson, who leaned against the bar, waving a shot of tequila. He shook his head. "The last time I drank that shit with you, I was sicker than a dog the next day. Not to mention, I have no idea how I ended up with a shaved chest." That had been at Jacob's bachelor party, a night that Cameron still couldn't completely piece together. He didn't think he'd ever been that drunk before, and he never planned on it happening again.

"That's because you're a lightweight and can't handle your liquor." She tossed her head back and downed the shot. "Give me two more." She held up two fingers and gave them a good waggle. "And you dared me to, dude."

The bartender nodded.

"And two beers," Cameron added. "I'm only doing one shot, and only because we're celebrating. Though if you ever come near my chest again, I'll tell your girlfriend you've got a thing for man nipples." He sucked in a deep breath and prepared himself for the burn. He took the small glass of tequila from the server and mentally counted to three before tossing it back. He swallowed the liquid and worried that he might cough it right back up. However, it was surprisingly smooth this time.

"Leslie knows better than that." Stormi slapped him on the back. "Besides, the last time we were drinking inexpensive booze. This shit is quality liquor."

"I could get used to that." He took a swig of his beer. "But not today. I got the go-ahead from Townsend to interview Oliver Rose. I tried calling him, but he didn't answer. And he wasn't home when I stopped by earlier, so I'll have to try again."

"I wouldn't say that name too loud. His sister is already here."

Cameron's heart dropped to the pit of his stomach. He scanned the yard. He hated that he'd spent the last twenty-four hours doing a deep-dive into her brother's life, which meant he'd learned more about *her* history, and that felt icky.

Those were the kinds of things he should be finding out from her, not from a police report, an old newspaper clipping, or having conversations with people from her brother's past.

And what the hell was her brother doing in the middle of an orgy that someone had uploaded to a porn site, where three people in the video were now dead?

More importantly, what did Oliver know about it?

"I ran into her last night. She mentioned that

Oliver had a girlfriend. Do you know anything about that?" he asked.

"No. Do you have a name?"

"Just a first name. Emma," he said. "Where's Vivian?"

"She's over there with Stacey."

"Sutten?"

"It's Tanner. Or have you forgotten she's married?"

Cameron laughed. "Just because a woman gets married, it doesn't mean she has to take her husband's name."

"That is so true." Stormi slapped him on his back. "I'll remind you of that when you get married."

"First, I have to find a woman willing to put up with me."

Stormi leaned closer. "If I weren't into women, I'd want a guy like you."

"I think that's the nicest thing you've ever said to me." Cameron had struck gold twice when it came to partners. He really enjoyed working with Stormi. She was smart, and he totally appreciated her sense of humor.

But she lacked the refinement that Jacob had, and sadly, she'd never learn that kind of finesse. She'd always be rough around the edges, no matter how long she worked for the federal government, and it would constantly get in her way.

"Don't look now, but Vivian is on her way over."

Stormi squeezed his biceps. "I'll catch you on the flip side."

Cameron leaned against the bar and nursed his beer as he soaked in Vivian's beauty.

She wore a pair of capri jeans that were high-waisted, and a crop top that didn't quite make it to the top of her pants, showing a little skin. She had her long, blond hair pulled back into a tight ponytail at the nape of her neck. Her lips were covered in bright red lipstick that showed off her porcelain skin, which practically glowed under the sun. Her long, thick lashes fluttered over her bright blue eyes.

His heart jumped to the back of his throat. He'd never describe himself as a man with much game. In high school, he'd spent most of his time either studying or playing hockey and golf. In college, it was studying and golf. He'd dated, but again, he had goals, and he wasn't about to let anything stand in his way.

"Hi, Vivian," he managed to croak out. "Did you have a nice night with Lilly and Ethan?"

"I did," she said. "Happy birthday. How old are we now?"

"Thank you. And I'm an old man at twenty-six." He smiled, contemplating if he should lean in and kiss her cheek, or do something he'd never done before and go for the lips. It was his birthday after all. Instead, he opted to gently touch her forearm and give it a little squeeze.

"A whole year older than me," she said. "It was

nice of Katie and Jacob to throw you this party. They both adore you. And so does Stacey. She had some interesting things to say about you."

Cameron shook his head. "I can only imagine." He'd worked four cases with Stacey. One as a state trooper, and the other three as an agent where she'd been a liaison. She was one hell of a cop. The FBI had tried to recruit her, but she wanted nothing to do with it. There were rumors about her retiring and becoming a PI, but she'd yet to pull the trigger.

He'd work with Stacey any day of the week.

"She says you're the best. Right next to Jacob and Katie."

"Stacey's not so bad herself," Cameron said. "Can I get you a drink?"

"I'd love a glass of white wine."

Cameron turned and waved to the bartender. He still had three-quarters of a beer left, and he really couldn't afford to even have too much of a buzz. Not if he wanted to interview Oliver later today.

Although Oliver wasn't the only one on Cameron's list.

Eight other people from that video were still alive and all potential suspects. At the very least, they were persons of interest.

Only, there wasn't a homicide, and Cameron was walking a fine line with his boss since the three dead people had all died by suicide. While that was a big coincidence, and it raised a huge red flag, it wasn't murder. And, therefore, it wasn't an actual case.

Yet.

What pulled it all together were the two unsolved cases from a year ago. Both women who'd been involved in sex videos.

Their murders had been captured on tape and loaded onto the dark web. Cameron was positive that those deaths were related to this current website, but he couldn't prove it.

All he had to go on were the similarities in the videos, and the fact that everyone had been involved in some kind of homemade pornography.

"Here you go, my lady." Cameron pushed all those work thoughts from his mind and handed Vivian the glass the bartender had given him. "Cheers." The bubbles tickled his throat. He swallowed, maintaining eye contact. "You look lovely today."

"You're sweet to say so."

"It's the truth." Cameron wanted so desperately to press his mouth against hers, but not when there were twenty or so people standing around watching. Not to mention, she might push him away. Or slap him. "You're a very pretty woman. Inside and out." Christ. He sounded like a fucking moron. He had no game whatsoever. It was like he'd never had a girlfriend before.

Well, he hadn't ever really been in a long-term relationship. Not a meaningful one, anyway. He'd had bed partners. And even those were few and far between.

How pathetic.

Vivian wasn't the kind of woman he'd consider having a fling with. She was so much more than that.

"Thank you." She pulled out her phone, glanced at the screen, and then frowned.

"Is everything okay?"

"I still haven't heard from my brother." She let out a long sigh and tucked her cell into her back pocket. "After the party, I'm going to stop by his place unannounced. He hates that, but if he's going to ghost me, then that's what's going to happen. He knows how I feel about him doing that."

"Sometimes, I take a day or two to get to my sister. It drives her nuts. She's the kind of person who expects an immediate response. Even if it's an *I'll get back to you tomorrow* kind of a response."

"I could live with that, but I've literally gotten nothing."

"If you want, I could go over with you," Cameron said. "For moral support."

"Thanks. I appreciate it, but I'll be fine."

A few long moments of silence slipped by as they sipped their drinks. He might as well go for it.

"I know I've asked this a million times, and you've shot me down every time, but I was hoping we could have dinner sometime."

"I'm going to be working a summer camp starting in a couple of weeks up here in Lake George, but I'd like to go out with you."

He gaped. He quickly snapped his mouth shut

and cleared his throat. He'd honestly expected to crash and burn. Now that she'd said yes, he needed a game plan. "How about tomorrow night?"

"It's a worknight for both of us."

"I'm staying up here for the next few days at the Heritage Inn," he said.

"Oh, really? Why?" She tilted her head and raised her hand. She pulled her hair from her ponytail over her shoulder and twisted it between her fingers. He noticed her short nails were painted red—almost the exact color as her lipstick.

Vivian was all lady when she needed to be. But he knew that she was the outdoorsy type, enjoying things like skiing in the winter and hiking and kayaking in the summer. She was exactly the type of person Cameron wanted as a partner in life. She was smart. Compassionate. Loved kids. And had similar interests.

But he saw pain behind those sweet, light blue eyes, and a lot of it. She'd built a wall around herself to protect from whatever had caused that anguish. It broke his heart to know that someone or something had put that hurt there.

"I have some interviews for a case I'm working, but I need to eat, and I'd really enjoy your company."

"Did you know I live right next to the Heritage Inn?" She brought her wine to her plump red lips and sipped.

He swallowed. "I knew you lived near there but didn't realize it was that close. Is it the cute cottage on the south side?"

She nodded. "I bought the place in February. I was so excited when I saw it go on the market. I was worried that Patty and Reese, the owners of the Heritage Inn, were going to snatch it up and expand, but they didn't want to, and I was really lucky that I didn't end up in some bidding war with anyone else."

"It's a beautiful piece of land, but doesn't it bother you being next to a hotel? Especially in the summer months when it's busy?"

"Not at all," she said with a beaming smile. "Mostly because I live at camp."

He arched a brow. "I forgot about that. While I enjoy camping, I don't think I'd like it with a bunch of teenagers."

She laughed. "This will be my last summer, but I don't actually sleep in the same cabin with the campers. Not anymore. I have my own all to myself, and it's very cozy. I grew up at Camp Lookout, and it's been hard to let it go. It's always been my happy place."

"I can understand that," he said. "When I first moved to Albany from Jacksonville, Florida, I thought I'd lose my mind. But I've come to really like it here, especially the snow."

Vivian covered her mouth and laughed. "Oh, that will change after a few more years."

"Well, I don't necessarily love the cold or driving in it, but I do love the change in seasons, and I've learned to snow ski and enjoy other winter sports."

"The winters can be beautiful, but it's much nicer up here than down in the capital."

"Oh. I know. I got stuck in a snowstorm once and had to spend a couple of days here with Jacob and Katie. Watching the snow fall from the sky and land in the lake under the lights was one of the most breathtaking things I've ever seen."

"Well, it's June, so can we enjoy the warm weather while it lasts?" she asked with the sweetest smile.

It melted his heart and reminded him of how his mom always looked at his father. They'd been married for nearly forty-two years, and they were still crazy in love. They were so goofy around each other that Cameron and his siblings were embarrassed half the time.

"Absolutely." Just as he was about to suggest that they go snag a couple of chaise lounge chairs by the pool, his cell vibrated in his back pocket. He pulled it out and glanced at the screen. "I'm sorry, I have to take this." He turned his body slightly to the right. "This is Agent Thatcher." Out of the corner of his eye, he noticed that his partner had her phone pressed to her ear, as well.

"It's Bradley Townsend," the Special Agent in Charge said in a dark tone. "We've got another death by suicide."

"Who?"

"Oliver Rose."

3

Vivian followed Cameron into the house. "What's going on? You're scaring me."

Cameron took her by the biceps and said nothing. He ran his hands up and down her arms tenderly. Gazing into his eyes only made things worse.

"You're really freaking me out." She clutched his hands.

He helped her onto the sofa where he knelt on the floor.

Katie and Jacob stepped into the living room with grim expressions that looked as though they'd just witnessed an execution.

"You better tell me what the hell is happening right now, or I'm going to lose my shit." Her heart pounded against her chest. Her hands shook. She rubbed them against her jeans. She had a bad feeling deep in her core. It had started yesterday, and it had only grown stronger. "Is it Oliver? Did something happen to my baby brother?"

Cameron barely blinked his eyes once, but that was all she needed.

Oliver was gone.

"I'm so sorry. One of Oliver's neighbors called 9-1-1 about forty-five minutes ago."

Vivian's throat went completely dry. She tried to swallow, but it felt as though a piece of sandpaper had gotten stuck on her tongue. She opened and closed her mouth at least a dozen times, except she couldn't form a single word. However, she managed a few grunts and groans.

Katie sat on the sofa and put her arm around Vivian's shoulders.

"He's dead," Vivian whispered. Her voice quivered. The reality of losing her brother had settled into her heart, shattering it into a million pieces. "How?"

"I don't have all the details." Cameron took her hands and squeezed. "I'm headed over to his apartment now. I need you to stay here with Katie and Jacob until I call."

"Are you going to be honest with me?" She knew that sounded like a weird question, but she remembered when her mother had found her father and how hushed the police had become. And then there were all the questions. Her mom worried they would find out about the videos and the disgusting website. The shame that something like that could bring was too much for her mother to bear, especially on top of the suicide. "Because if you're being called in as the FBI, this is something serious." She inhaled slowly, trying to stop the tears, but she couldn't. As she exhaled, her breath trembled.

"I will tell you everything I can," Cameron said. "Starting with: Oliver's home is an active crime scene."

"Was he murdered?" Vivian asked. "He's been acting so weird, and he wouldn't tell me much about this new girlfriend, which isn't like him. What about her? Do you know where she is? Could she have done this?"

Cameron brought her hands to his mouth and pressed his lips to her skin. "Like I said, I don't have all the details. However, from what I've been told, it's not a homicide."

"No. No. No," she said softly. "He wouldn't do what our father did. Please, tell me he didn't take his own life." She jerked her hands free and covered her face.

Cameron wrapped his strong arms around her body. "I promise I will give you as much information as I can without compromising the case."

"I might be able to do some digging where Cameron can't," Katie added. "I'll do it without upsetting the FBI."

"Just make sure you're working with me, not against me." Cameron continued rubbing his hand up and down Vivian's back.

Vivian took in deep breaths. She couldn't break

down. Not completely. Not yet. She pushed from Cameron's warm embrace. The last thing she needed was his comfort. It couldn't be trusted. He couldn't be trusted.

He cupped her face, staring intently into her eyes. "I've got to get going. I'll text you when I get there, and I'll call you as soon as I can."

"Do you promise?" She caved to her emotions. Cameron might be a man, but right now, he was all she had.

"Yes." He pressed his lips against hers in a short kiss.

She thought to pull away. It should feel inappropriate, but it didn't. "Thank you."

Cameron stood. "Katie, I need a huge favor."

"What's that?"

Vivian swiped her cheeks and did her best to focus on the conversation—the words that tumbled from her friend's mouths and not the emotions that seeped from her heart.

"After the initial shock wears off, make sure she hires you and Jackson to look into Oliver's death. That way, I can continue working with you on this." Cameron gave her a small smile.

Why would she need to hire Katie and Jackson? What had her brother gotten himself into? Nothing made sense. She rubbed her hands up and down her jeans. She wanted to bolt upright and scream at the top of her lungs. Or maybe grab Cameron by his shirt and shake him, begging him to take her with him to her brother's apartment.

But what would good would that do?

"You're going to have to clue me in a little more," Katie said.

"I will." Cameron reached down and squeezed Vivian's shoulder. "I need you to trust me, okay?"

Mindlessly, she nodded. Who else was she going to put her faith in? Cameron had proven to be one of the good guys.

Cameron turned and, in less than a minute, was gone.

Katie looped her arm around Vivian. "Stacey is sending everyone home."

"Do they all know what happened?" She couldn't stand the way everyone had looked at her when her father died. "Oh, God. I have to call my mom."

"I thought maybe you'd like to tell her in person," Jacob said. "So, my dad is going to her house and bringing her over here."

"She'll know something is going on." Vivian had to pull herself together if she were going to face her mother. She couldn't be a hot mess because her mom would crumble into a million pieces. Her mother relied on Vivian to be the strong one. To be the glue that held the family together.

And yet, she'd failed her brother in the worst way.

"But you'll be together, and you'll be the one to tell her. I think that's important." Jacob was no stranger to loss. His older brother had died in a house fire when he was a small boy. If anyone understood this kind of pain, Jacob did.

"You're right." Vivian tugged at her ponytail, setting her hair free. She twirled the ends. "I knew something was wrong. I could feel it, and yet I did nothing."

"That's not true," Katie said. "Don't go beating yourself up. This isn't your fault."

Vivian glared. "Yes. It is. I should have been more present in his life. I ignored the signs."

"That's not true, and you know it," Katie said. "You told me last week you were worried about him. And you also got in his face at your mom's garden party. So don't go putting any of this on yourself."

"You're a very giving person." Jacob pulled up the ottoman. "So much so that you forget to take care of yourself. I know this isn't going to help you feel any better, but I'm going to say it anyway. Cameron is the best agent I've ever met or worked with. Whatever is going on that has your brother tied to his caseload, he'll figure it out and give you closure."

She pressed her fist against her chest as if that would dislodge the pain. All she could think about was what her father had been doing for years before he died. The things she'd found on the external hard drives he'd hidden in his closet had been horrifying. She'd taken them when she and her mom had donated all his belongings. It'd taken her three years before she dared to take a peek, and she wished she hadn't.

It was bad enough that she and her mother had seen a handful of videos on his computer.

But dear old Dad had been creating them for a good two years, and he had quite the collection.

"If it's death by suicide, why is the FBI being called in?" She stared at Katie. "By the way, you're hired. Although, I'm not sure how I'm going to pay you or why I even require your services."

"Jackson is going to kill me, but you've got the friends and family mega discount." Katie tucked her red hair behind her ears. "Now, to answer your first question, Cameron has been working two unsolved murders from last year."

"How do you know that?" Vivian asked.

"One of the families hired Jackson and Katie to help find who killed their daughter," Jacob interjected.

"How is that related to Oliver's death?"

"I'd prefer to wait to hear from Cameron," Katie said. "I can't be sure, but the two cases he has open were both thought to be deaths by suicide at first glance. But they weren't."

"Oh, my God." Vivian choked on her breath. She didn't know what was worse. The idea that her brother had taken his life.

Or that someone else had.

Jacob took her hand. "We should have waited until Cameron texted or called to share that with you, but—"

"No. I'm glad you did." Vivian gathered up her

hair and wrapped the ponytail holder around it, tightening it at the nape of her neck.

"Hello?" a man's voice said. "Jacob? Katie?"

"In the living room, Dad." Jacob stood. "I think your mother is here. We'll give you some space."

Vivian sucked in a deep breath. Her pulse eerily slowed, much like it had when she went to her mother after finding her father in front of his computer. For a short period of time, she'd wondered if she'd made a mistake by telling her mom, but there was no way Vivian would have been able to look at either of her parents again if she hadn't.

"Vivian." Her mother raced through the house with her arms stretched wide. Mascara streaked down her cheeks. "It's Oliver, isn't it? He's dead. I can feel it in my bones."

"Yes, Mommy." Vivian grabbed her mom and held on for dear life. It was like she'd been catapulted back to when she was fourteen years old, only that death was all about shame. The grief they felt was for something they *thought* they had. They'd grieved the idea of the man they loved—only he wasn't *that* man at all.

This was so different.

Oliver was their light at the end of the tunnel.

Only now, there was complete darkness.

Cameron entered the third-floor, two-bedroom apartment and paused so he could scan the room, taking in the scene. He didn't need his training to tell him that even the most minor detail could become the thing that cracked the case.

Only, this technically wasn't his crime scene. The state police had only called in the FBI because they knew about Cameron's investigation and the connection to Oliver. His office and the local trooper office had a unique relationship, and they worked exceptionally well together.

Better than most local law enforcement agencies.

New York State Trooper Tristan Reid greeted Cameron at the door. "Looks like we might be working together."

"If this becomes a murder, we will be." Cameron squared his shoulders. In the last year, when dealing with other cops, especially more seasoned ones, Cameron received a lot of pushback.

He knew he was generally the youngest person in the room. When he first joined the FBI, it'd bothered him a great deal. Not because he lacked confidence, but because no one trusted his abilities because of his young age. Well, that wasn't true with Jacob. Nor was that the case with Tristan and many of the other state troopers. In part, because he'd been one for a brief time. But it was more than that.

Tristan's boss, Jared Blake, had a unique philosophy when it came to training anyone new who walked into his station. He also enjoyed working with some other agencies, though it all depended on the person.

But still, some thought Cameron had been given too much too quickly, and he had a lot to prove.

"Tell me what we have," Cameron said.

"I was the first on the scene, and it looked like death by suicide, but someone breached the front door, and that disturbed me."

"Was it open, or just unlocked?"

"It was damaged. As in kicked in."

"That's not good. What else?" Cameron glanced at the door and noted that the wood was cracked near the lock.

Tristan pointed to the overturned chair and the papers on the floor. "The neighbor that called it in said that he'd heard Oliver fighting with someone."

"Do we know who?"

"No. It was a phone call."

"Do you know anything about Oliver having a girlfriend? All I have is a first name. Emma."

"I'll check into that." Tristan shook his head. "As I made my way to the bedroom where they found the body, I had to think that maybe it *was* suicide."

"Why?" Cameron pulled out his cell and quickly sent a text to Vivian. He wanted to honor his promise. Not because of how he felt about her, but because it was the right thing to do. She deserved to be kept in the loop as much as possible. Right now, all he could give her was an update that he'd arrived and would contact her when he had more information.

He got a *Thank you* in response.

"He left a note to his sister and mom. And he was holding the gun that killed him," Tristan said.

"What did the note say?" Cameron would read it soon enough, but he wanted the CliffsNotes version to give him a better feel for the scene.

"It was a really short note. All he said was that he was sorry, and he just couldn't go on anymore."

Cameron had minored in psychology. Considering that Oliver's father had taken his life, Cameron would have thought Oliver would have had some kind of guilt for doing that to his mother and sister.

"There are some serious inconsistencies with death by suicide. Like he has marks on his neck and wrists as if someone held him down. There are also scratches on his face with fresh blood that are in line with a possible struggle. The other thing the medical examiner noticed was the angle of the bullet."

"What about it?"

"It was pointed down, which he said was odd. Typically, it would be straight or slightly upward. However, he's not saying it wasn't self-inflicted. He's just indicating that he needs to do an autopsy, and we need to cover all our bases."

Everything was inconclusive at this point, which wouldn't make meeting Vivian and her mother at the morgue any easier. He knew they'd want answers, and he couldn't give them any anytime soon.

"Oliver was a person of interest in two murders I'm investigating from last year."

"The orgy murders," Tristan said matter-of-factly.

Cameron did a double-take. There had only been two. It wasn't considered a serial killer, and the press hadn't been up his ass about either of them.

Yet.

The fact that the first two victims had been at the same sex party and had wound up dead couldn't be a coincidence.

Nor could the fact that a year later, Cameron had two deaths by suicide, and now another potential homicide, all from the same orgy that someone had loaded onto the dark web.

"Where did you hear that?" Cameron asked.

"You're forgetting that one of the murders happened right here in Lake George and that one of my buddies took the call."

"Who was that?"

"A trooper by the name of Jake Prichard."

"The one who owns the horse farm?"

"That's the one," Tristan said. "It got turned over to you because the victim crossed state lines."

"I remember." Cameron rubbed his temple as he eased toward the bedroom. He'd seen his share of dead bodies, but it never got easier. His stomach flipped. Then flopped. He inhaled sharply and did his best to clear his mind.

Especially any thoughts of Vivian. He couldn't have her clouding his judgment. Or making him more emotional than he already was, which wasn't a good thing considering this was his job.

A flash of light hit his eyes like a bolt of lightning. He blinked, doing his best to focus. He scanned Oliver's bedroom, looking at everything but Oliver.

He had a queen-sized bed pushed up under a window. In the far corner was a desk with a computer and a large monitor. A chair and an ottoman piled with clothing sat in the other corner.

Oliver's body was slumped on the floor at the foot of the bed. He wore only a pair of sweatpants. His right hand barely held the small-caliber weapon. Blood covered the side of his head.

But even Cameron noticed how the gunshot wound angled down. Which, based on the positioning of the body, didn't make sense.

"Where's the note? And where was it found?" Cameron asked as the New York State Trooper CSI team photographed and set up labels for possible evidence markers.

"It was on the desk." Tristan walked over to one of the CSI team members, who handed him a plastic baggie. "Here you go."

Cameron held it up.

Dear Mom and Vivian.

I'm sorry. I can't go on like this anymore. Please forgive me.

Love, Oliver.

"You've lived here for a while and know this family. What are your thoughts on that note?"

"I don't really know the family well. Stacey,

however, babysat for them. She might have a better assessment."

"I don't want that note shown to the family right away," Cameron said as he rubbed the back of his neck. He'd bring it up with Vivian in private. They had the right to know, but something about this entire scene, from the second that Cameron had walked through the front door, felt wrong. And that included the note. "When this turns out to be a murder, do you think you can talk Jared into a joint task force?"

"That won't be hard to do at all. What about your boss?"

Special Agent in Charge Bradley Townsend liked to pretend he was a hardass. He also acted like he hated working with other law enforcement agencies, but that was the furthest thing from the truth. He walked a fine line between being the head of the FBI's Albany office and having to answer to the federal government and doing what was morally in the best interests of the victims and their families.

Townsend was a good man. One of the best. He had a heart of gold, and he often struggled with the constraints the FBI placed on him, but he always rallied to the occasion.

This would be no different.

"You let me worry about Townsend," Cameron said. "Are you good to wrap this up?"

"I am." Tristan nodded. "We're going to need a positive ID from the family."

"I was just with his sister. I'll go get her and drive

her to the morgue myself." He pulled out his phone. He'd text Jacob and Katie first, and then Vivian. This case would be a bit unorthodox. But whatever. If it turned out to be death by suicide, he'd be there for Vivian and her family.

If it was murder...

He'd not only be there, he'd also make sure that whoever killed Oliver would go to prison for the rest of his or her life.

"It could be a while," Tristan said.

"I know. But Vivian is a friend of mine. Since I'm here as a courtesy right now, this is all yours. Unless there's something you really want me to do." Cameron had sent Stormi to find video footage from any street cameras or businesses in the area, in hopes of seeing anyone who might have entered the building and Oliver's apartment over the last forty-eight hours. Specifically, he wanted to get a handle on Oliver's girlfriend, Emma. If they found her, they might have a lead on what really happened to Oliver. Even though Cameron knew this would eventually be ruled a homicide and dumped in his lap, he had to follow protocol until then. To a point.

"I'll make sure everything here is taken care of and see that you're given copies of everything. I'll treat this as if we're working together because something tells me this isn't a death by suicide."

"I'm with you on that one." Cameron pointed to the medical examiner. "Make sure he knows to copy my—"

"I've got it," the medical examiner said. "I'll make this a priority, as well." He waved to one of his people. "We're ready to bag and transport unless either of you needs me to do anything else?"

"Can I bring the family down to identify?" Cameron rubbed the back of his neck.

"I'll need a little time to make him look presentable," the medical examiner said. "About three hours?"

Cameron nodded. "I want the computer, any external drives, his cell phone, and any other electronics to be logged and held until further notice."

"Already ordered." Tristan pointed to the trooper holding the camera. "Do you guys need anything else?"

"We got everything," the trooper said.

"This will remain an active crime scene with a uniform at the door until we get the autopsy back."

"Sounds good. I'll see you at the morgue with the family shortly for a formal identification." Cameron stretched out his arm, shook Tristan's hand, and then strolled out of the apartment, taking one last look around. He paused at the door. "Did you dust for prints?"

Tristan nodded. "I'm also checking the gun."

"Thanks." Cameron pulled his cell out of his pocket and tapped the screen as he jogged down the stairs.

Stormi answered on the second ring. "What's up?"

"Are you headed back to Albany tonight?"

"Yeah, why?"

"I'm staying up here at the Heritage, but I need the files on the death-by-suicide cases."

"They aren't ours at this point except for how they relate to the cybercrimes we're investigating, and the tightrope you're walking with those murders," Stormi said.

"Just get me the damn files."

"You want me to drive there now and bring them back up tonight?"

"Yup." He stepped out onto the sidewalk and squinted as the bright sun rays hit his face. "I'll get you and Leslie a room for the night."

"That's mighty generous of you, but something tells me you're also going to want me looking at those files—either with you or separately—so it's best if I leave her at home."

"Whatever makes you happy," he said. "I'll make sure you have a room. See you soon." He blew out a puff of air and contemplated whether to text or call Vivian. He needed to talk with her, but he didn't want her mother present. He was willing to break the rules a little for Vivian, but he couldn't with her mom.

He decided that texting was best.

Cameron: *On way back to Jacob's. Either you or your mom will need to make official identification. Or if you have trusted family, they can do it. We could put it off, but I think it's best if you do it now, for a lot of reasons. I'll drive you there.*

It was a long text, but it covered all the bases.

Before he had a chance to put his cell back into his pocket, it rang.

Vivian.

He snagged his car key and hit the unlock button. "Hi, Vivian," he said as he slipped behind the steering wheel of his SUV. "I just sent you a text."

"I know. That's why I'm calling." Her voice cracked and sounded weak. "Are you sure it's Oliver?" She sniffled.

Putting the vehicle in gear, he eased out onto the side street, doing a K-turn. He swallowed the thick lump of emotion that'd formed in his throat. For the last hour, he'd pushed down his personal feelings like he always did when he was working. He had to. It was the only way to stay sane.

"I'm sorry," he managed.

A sob filled his ears. "I know my mom will want to see him, and so do I."

"I'm in the car now."

"Okay," she whispered. "Cameron?"

"Yes?"

"Please don't lie to me or sugarcoat things."

He punched the gas. His stomach twisted into knots. "There are some things I can't tell you until we get the autopsy report back. Depending on how that goes, there might be other things I can't reveal. You're going to have to trust me."

"I guess I don't have any other choice."

4

Vivian sat in the middle of her family room, holding her mother while she cried once again. It had been almost twelve years since her father died, and during that time, she'd pretended, for the sake of her little brother, that Lukas Rose wasn't actually a thorn in her side.

"I can't believe he's gone," her mother said between sobs. "I've known something was bothering him for a month or so, but I had no idea it was so bad." She lifted her head. "Did we make a mistake by not telling him about your father?" she asked in a hushed voice.

Vivian leaned forward, making sure that Larry and Cameron were still in the kitchen. It appeared they were deep in conversation as they waited for the coffee to percolate. "No," Vivian said. "I don't think this has anything to do with Daddy."

"How can you be so sure? He did the exact same

thing, and if we'd been honest about why your father—"

"Mom. No. We gave him a truth."

"Oh, the shame over losing his job and putting us in debt. That's not a big deal," her mother said with a heavy dose of sarcasm.

"You know how proud Dad could be. So, yes. It was absolutely something that could have put him over the edge, but that's not my point." Vivian peered into the other room. "If you say a single word to Larry or anyone, Cameron could be in big trouble."

"What are you talking about?" Her mother swiped at her face, tucking her shoulder-length hair behind her ears.

Vivian's heart raced wildly out of control. She shouldn't have opened her big mouth. It was one thing for her to have a string of hope that her brother hadn't harmed himself. Not that the idea of him being murdered made any of this better, but it somehow meant that burying her father's secret had been the right thing to do. "I can't get into the details, mostly because Cameron hasn't told me much, but there is more to all of this than meets the eye."

"You're not making any sense."

"I know." She took her mother's hands and squeezed. "But trust me. We did the right thing. No one ever needs to know Dad's dirty little secret." Nor did her mother ever need to find out the extent of it.

Ever.

"Are you—?"

"Yes," Vivian said firmly. "No more talk of this. Especially around Cameron, okay?"

Her mother inhaled sharply and let it slowly as she wiped the mascara from under her eyes. "He seems like a nice young man. And I see how he looks at you. And I can tell you like him back."

Vivian's cheeks heated. "Not the time or place to have this conversation, Mother."

Her mom let out a slight chuckle. "I always know I hit a nerve when you call me that."

It wasn't so much that her mom had touched on a tender subject as it was that Vivian no longer knew how to compartmentalize her growing attraction and feelings for Cameron. She worried that the stirring she had in her gut that had worked its way to her heart was only because he'd been so compassionate with her and her mother through this entire process.

Or that he was willing to risk his job to make sure that she was as much in the loop as possible.

But it was more than that.

"He's different from all the other guys you've dated," her mother said. "You've got to stop holding back and open yourself up to love."

"First, we're not dating."

"Well, you should be." Her mother arched a brow. "If he wasn't interested in you, he'd be gone by now."

The sound of ceramic clanking caught her attention. She leaned over and glanced into the kitchen to see Larry pouring coffee while Cameron arranged stuff on a tray.

"I'm always afraid they'll be like dad," she whispered.

Her mother palmed her cheek. "It took me a long time to even think about dating. And then Larry came along. He showed me that not all men end up like your dad. But even so, I wouldn't erase those years because they gave me you and Oliver." A tear rolled down her mother's face. "I miss him so much already."

"I know. So do I." Vivian jumped when her phone vibrated in her back pocket. She pulled it out and groaned.

"What is it?"

"Aunt Kiki. She heard about Oliver," Vivian said. "I ran into her the other day, too. She's never once apologized to me for disappearing for an entire year or going after what little Dad left us with."

"She lost her brother. She was hurting, too."

"That's no excuse." Vivian would have given her aunt a pass if she'd acted as if she cared, just a little. But the woman didn't seem to have a kind bone in her body. Every time Vivian saw Kiki, she seemed to have a chip on her shoulder. Vivian sent the call right to voicemail. She wouldn't even bother listening to the message. It wasn't worth it.

Larry and Cameron appeared, front and center. Cameron set out a tray of nuts and pretzels, which was about all she had in the way of snack food, while Larry handed out a couple of mugs of coffee before racing back into the kitchen to get two more.

Once everyone had been served, her mother snuggled up against Larry on the other end of the sofa.

Cameron kept a safe distance by leaning against the wall near the front of the house that overlooked the lake. He seemed to understand when she needed him to hold her hand and when she didn't.

Only, right now, it would have been nice to be in someone's arms.

She raised the mug to her lips and stared at the tiny white things floating in what she'd thought was coffee. Turned out it was hot chocolate. One of her favorite things on a cool morning or evening—or anytime she wanted to have a few moments where nothing in the world mattered. She loved to grab a cup of cocoa and dunk a few marshmallows in it. If she was sitting by a campfire in front of the lake, even better. She shifted her gaze. "How did you know?"

"Know what?" Cameron asked.

"That I'd rather have this than coffee?" Vivian asked.

Her mother leaned over and investigated the mug.

"I didn't." Cameron shrugged. "Growing up, my mom always told me that while hot cocoa and marshmallows wouldn't solve my problems, it might make me feel just a tiny bit better in the time it took for me to drink it." He raised his mug. "When I saw that you had the fixings, I made us both a cup."

"I like the way your mother thinks." She couldn't hold back the smile if she tried. Whether he'd done some investigating and found out about her little decadent treat, or his story was real, it was about the nicest thing anyone had ever done for her in a long time.

"We really appreciate all you've done for us today," Larry said with a protective arm around her mother. "But I don't understand one thing."

"What's that?" Cameron pushed away from the wall and took a seat on the ottoman, which was so close to her end of the couch that his legs were mere inches from hers. He leaned forward, resting his elbows on his knees.

"Both the medical examiner and your friend, the state trooper, have avoided calling this a death by suicide," Larry said. "Why? Isn't it clear? What are we missing? Or is the question, what aren't you telling us?"

Vivian kept her gaze locked with Cameron's because if she looked at her mother, Cameron would know that she'd said something about what he'd told her on the ride to the morgue.

"I've told you everything I can." Cameron set his mug on the coffee table.

The last thing she wanted was for her stepfather and her—and Cameron—to get into an argument on the day her brother died. Emotions were high to begin with. Adding a heated discussion would only make things harder on her mother, who was already a ball of nerves.

"I'm sorry, son, but that's a bullshit answer," Larry said with a little too much animosity.

"Look." Cameron took Vivian's hand and ran his thumb over the back. "There were some inconsistencies at Oliver's apartment that the police want to look into, and the medical examiner has to do his job. In this type of situation, we never define the cause of death immediately. We have to go through the motions."

"It's true," Vivian's mother said. "I remember them doing this when Lukas took his life. Everyone knew what'd happened. Lukus's note explained it pretty well."

"But Oliver didn't leave a note," Larry said. "At least, not one that we know of."

"And that boy would have left one, and it would have been an interesting one," her mother added.

"What would he have said?" Cameron asked with a kind and gentle voice, but there was a sudden shift in the tone. He went from being in the background and helping her and her family out where he could, to needing to know information. It was subtle, but Vivian had seen him do it a few times.

"Does it matter?" Larry asked with a sense of indignance.

"I mean no disrespect, but it might help us understand a couple of things."

Vivian tugged her hand to her lap. "What are you talking about?" She had no right feeling this kind of anger toward Cameron. He'd warned her that he wouldn't be able to tell her everything. He'd said it a dozen times. Whatever he was keeping from her, he must have to because it meant his job. She knew that deep down, but part of her looked at him as if he were just another lying bastard like her father.

A secret keeper.

Like all men.

"If Oliver left a note, what do you think it would have said? Would it have been long with details, explaining his actions? Would it have been short and to the point? Would it have been angsty and full of blame?" Cameron raked a hand across the top of his head and stood, turning. He took a few steps toward the picture window, putting his back to Vivian. It appeared he stared out at the lake below.

"I thought I liked you," Larry stared. "Respected you. But I don't understand where this crap is coming from. I think you should leave."

"No," Vivian said firmly. She folded her arm against her stomach. Even though hot rage burned in her veins, she wanted to know why Cameron had asked the question. As gracefully as she could, she rose. Her legs felt like mush. They barely carried her across the room. She placed her hand on Cameron's shoulder.

He turned, catching her gaze.

"You asked me to trust you. And so far, you've given me no reason not to. It's not fair that you can't tell us whatever is going on, but I want answers. If that means I have to answer some really painful questions, then so be it."

"I don't want to hurt you or your family, and

when I know for sure what happened, you'll be the first to know. I promise you that."

"Tell me this, son," Larry interjected. "How will speculating what Oliver might have written in a note help you in determining anything about his death, which I think we can all agree was self-inflicted?"

"I'm not so sure it was," Cameron said matter-of-factly.

"Excuse me?" Larry's voice screeched a few octaves higher than normal.

Her mother gasped.

Vivian's throat went dry. "You shouldn't be giving them false hope," she whispered.

He reached out and squeezed her biceps. "Jacob has always told me to follow my instincts, no matter what. I might be young and still a bit green, but Jacob is the best I've ever worked with or trained under, and my gut is telling me that something doesn't add up. The more I know about Oliver, the faster I can figure out what the hell happened."

She sucked in a deep breath and let it out slowly. "Oliver went through some depression in high school. He worried he'd be just like our dad."

"How so?" Cameron asked.

"That he'd be a failure and kill himself," her mother said on a guttural sob. "I tried so hard to lift him up and tell him how proud I was of him, but if he got even a C in any subject, he went in a downward spiral. It wasn't until college that he turned things around. Where he found himself."

"He's been fine until the last two months or so," Vivian said. "Something happened to Oliver, and I think it has to do with his new girlfriend."

"Yes. You told me about Emma. We're looking for her," Cameron said. "But how would he write the note? I know I'm harping on this. But it's important."

"When Oliver was in high school and thought about hurting himself, he would call me, and we'd talk for hours about why he didn't need to be perfect. If he left us a note, I suspect it would be about how he came up short," Vivian said.

"Did you find something that you're not telling us about? Because we have the right to know," Larry said once again, his voice stern.

Vivian appreciated the way he embraced her mother, holding her tight, rubbing his hand up and down her arm. She felt the love he had for her all the way over on the other side of the room. She wished Larry had come into their life sooner. Oliver could have used a father figure.

"I'm having some of Oliver's sample writings analyzed," Cameron said.

Her mother bolted to a standing position. "He left a note, didn't he?"

"Things at Oliver's apartment aren't cut and dried. That's why the state police have been vague. Until they have gathered and analyzed everything, and I've had a chance to look it all over, Oliver's death will remain suspicious." Cameron pulled out his cell. "The reason we withheld this information from you."

He held up his hand. "And it was my call to do so because I don't believe Oliver wrote it. Or, if he did, it doesn't feel authentic."

Vivian tilted her head. "You didn't know my brother. How the hell can you make that kind of judgment?" She had half a mind to toss Cameron out the door on his ass. He should have told her about the note. At the very least, he shouldn't have sprung it on her in front of her mom and stepdad like it wouldn't be a big deal.

"Because it's my job." He pushed his cell under her nose. "This is the note. Does it look like Oliver's handwriting? Or is it something he would say?"

Vivian took the electronic device in her trembling hand. Her mother and Larry gathered behind her, peering over her shoulder. Her mom wrapped an arm around her waist while Larry squeezed her arm.

"Perhaps I could have brought this up differently." Cameron dropped his hand to his side. "I kept trying to find the right moment, but there never was one."

"When would you have done it in any other case?" Larry asked.

"I wouldn't be here if it were any other case. Because right now, it's in the hands of the state police. It's only mine if and when it becomes a murder." He pressed his finger over Vivian's lips when she opened her mouth. "And that's only because it's crossing over into something else I've been working on."

She blinked. When he told her that there were things he couldn't tell her, her mind couldn't imagine what it might be. Now, she wondered what the hell her brother might have gotten himself involved in. "Does this have to do with his new girlfriend, Emma?"

"He was so secretive about her," his mother said. "At first, he was happy and talked about her like she was great, but it was so new. And because he never really had a serious girlfriend, he didn't want to jinx it, so we didn't push."

"That didn't last very long," Larry added. "Every time we asked about when he was going to bring her around, he would tell us how busy she was, and he never did tell us her last name."

"He didn't even tell us how they met." Vivian tapped the screen. She re-read the note three times. It looked like his handwriting, but Cameron was right. "Oliver would have been more poetic with his words. He had a way with language, and he was seldom direct and to the point."

"Except in email or text messages," Larry interjected. "He'd been shortening everything even more lately."

"So you think he *could* have written something like that?" Cameron asked.

"The Oliver I know, yes." Larry nodded.

"I have to agree with my husband." Her mother took a step back and swiped at her cheeks. "He'd been withdrawn the last couple of months, and I too noticed a change in his communication habits."

Vivian couldn't deny that either.

"You mentioned Oliver's death and how it might be related to something else you're working on. How is it connected?" Larry asked.

Cameron took his cell and slipped it into his pocket. "I have two open murder cases that are way too similar to Oliver's death, and the people involved overlap. I can't believe that's a coincidence."

Vivian covered her mouth.

Her mother gasped.

"And you believe that Oliver could be another victim murdered by the same killer?" Vivian's voice trembled. Her stomach churned as if it had filled with sour milk.

"It's a theory based on what I saw at Oliver's apartment."

Vivian went straight for her mother and wrapped her arms around her, holding her tight. Neither cried, but the raw emotion filled the space like a thick, dark cloud ready to release its thunder and lightning. Not that having her brother murdered was any better than him taking his life. The pain that Oliver had worked through over what their father had done had taken courage, and he'd come so far in the last couple of years. To think that it had unraveled in just a few months was too much, and neither Vivian nor her mother could come up with any kind of reason that made sense.

Until recently, Oliver and Vivian spoke every couple of days, and he was always honest about his emotions and what he was going through. They'd made a pact after he hit his darkest point in high school that when he started having those feelings, he'd call.

And he always did.

So, these last few months had been hell.

"But you have nothing concrete," Larry said as more of a statement than a question. He folded his arms across his chest and glared. Larry meant well, and he loved her mother with all his heart and soul. If he could walk on water for Eva Ludwig, he would. However, he could also be overbearing.

Vivian understood that all he wanted was to protect his wife and help her through her grief. "I don't think that's the point." She kissed her mother's cheek and broke the physical contact, letting Larry take over.

Cameron reached out and curled his fingers around her biceps. "I can't imagine what all of you are going through right now. I'm doing my best to be as sensitive as possible. However, if what I believe is correct, someone else will be murdered, and I'd like to make sure that doesn't happen."

5

Cameron stepped from his cabin and inhaled the fresh scent of summer. A cool breeze rippled off the lake. A few fishing boats zipped up the shoreline, their lights still aglow as the morning light peeked out from the mountains. Sunrise was still forty-five minutes away.

He glanced to the south. Vivian's house stood tall between the trees. He'd hated leaving her alone last night, especially after her mother and Larry had left, but he had files to examine and phone calls to make. When all was said and done, it would have been a miracle if he'd gotten three hours of sleep.

And when he managed to close his eyes, his dreams were of Vivian. He needed to talk to her about what Oliver had been involved in. Cameron suspected that she hadn't a clue, and perhaps that was why Oliver had been ghosting her. That made sense. Cameron had seen it before. Especially if her brother had any feelings of shame or guilt over what he'd been doing.

The sound of the door opening behind him caught his attention.

"Good morning," Stormi said. "I can't believe this place had a two-bedroom available to rent."

"They had a cancelation, so they were able to move us. Otherwise, your sorry ass would have been up at the main hotel." He took the file Stormi handed him and made himself comfortable at the table. "Did you find anything interesting? Or is it still all exactly the same shit we've been looking at?" He opened the folder and spread out the papers. He missed working with Jacob, who had a unique way of analyzing paperwork.

Cameron had his own set of skills, and he had a bit of a photographic memory, but he hadn't quite the same abilities as Jacob. No matter how hard Cameron tried, he just didn't see things the same way.

He set the crime scene pictures on the far side of the table, organizing them by images of the room, the evidence, and the body. Next, he set the statements given by the family members, the neighbors, and the person who'd found the body. "We still have nothing on this Emma chick," he said, more to himself than to Stormi.

"Not exactly." Stormi set a second file on the table and flipped it open. "This is the name of everyone who was at that sex party." She handed him a piece of paper. "I cross-referenced with our two murders from a year ago and the sex orgy they were involved in, and we've got eight people who were at both."

"Keep talking." Cameron studied the list. He wasn't surprised that there was a crossover.

"There is an Emma Hoover who was at that party a year ago." Stormi pushed another piece of paper across the wooden table. It had a picture of a young woman, maybe twenty-five or thirty. She had reddish-brown hair and green eyes. "She doesn't show up anywhere in the orgy that Oliver was at, but the IT guys found some emails from an Emma M on Oliver's computer. They may or may not be related. There aren't many, but I asked for a warrant to see if we can retrieve any old, deleted ones."

"That was fast," Cameron said. "I want to see those emails."

"They're setting up a portal so we can have remote access to his computer from my laptop. But we're skating on thin ice until we have an official cause of death, and if Oliver's is officially ruled death by suicide, we're back to square one."

Cameron shuffled the papers, re-arranging them, using the techniques Jacob had taught him, tricking his brain into looking at everything from different perspectives. He added the names of the participants in both sex parties. As long as all parties were consenting adults, an orgy wasn't illegal.

Cameron took a sip of his high-octane coffee. "Okay. Oliver was at both orgies, so we know he's been into this shit for at least thirteen months. And this Emma Stone was at the first orgy, at least according to this." He tapped the paperwork. "But not the second one. If she's his girlfriend, why not?"

"I've been asking myself that question for the last twenty minutes." Stormi raised her mug. "I've also been wondering about these two emails, which I printed. They're from a *Simon Says*."

Cameron arched his brow. "Are you shitting me?" He took the papers and scanned the messages.

Oliver,

Simon says do it. Or else.

That was message one.

Oliver,

What are you waiting for? You know the game. When Simon says to do something, you're supposed to play along. It's not fair to the rest of the players. Get with the program and do it. Or else.

Simon Says.

"What the fuck does this mean?" Cameron re-read the emails a dozen times. "Are there any more?" He snagged the list of orgy participants.

No Simon.

"None that the IT department found in the inbox, sent box, or the deleted folder. But that doesn't mean there aren't." Stormi leaned back in her chair. "I think we need to ask a judge for a warrant to get emails from all the suicide victims and see if there are any from this Simon Says guy."

Cameron pinched the bridge of his nose. "I want the emails from the murders that were loaded to the dark web, as well. This has to be connected somehow. We also need to get email addresses for everyone at both parties and find out who else might be involved in this particular sex club. Because I'm sure there are more."

A picture formed in Cameron's brain. It was that of a spider web, and at the center was Simon Says. Whoever the guy was, he got off playing games.

There were two questions that Cameron had to figure out.

What was the game?

And what were the rules?

If he could answer those, he might be able to find out how and why Oliver was dead.

"I can head back to Albany this morning and get the ball rolling on all the warrants. Pull more files. But I think we need to set up a remote office here." She pulled out one more piece of paper. "If we include Oliver, two victims lived in the area. But both parties were held in Lake George. And all of the victims have ties to here." Stormi leaned forward, folding her hands on the table.

While she was no Jacob, she *was* smart, and she never kept her opinions to herself.

That was both good and bad.

Right now, it was excellent.

"You know Shannon Armstrong, right?"

"That's Jackson's wife. I know her pretty well since I've worked with her husband and Katie a few times."

"So, you know about what her father did to her?" Stormi lowered her chin.

Cameron nodded. No one really ever talked about what a horrible person Shannon's father was or the things he did to his daughter. But Cameron would be a fool if he hadn't seen the similarities. "No one's underage at these orgies. When we questioned the participants, it appeared that it was all consensual sex. Even the videos we watched didn't give us any reason to believe otherwise." He cringed at what he'd been forced to witness because of his job. He mostly loved what he did, but there were days that he wished he could unsee some things. "Do you think this could be a continuation of that group of men?"

"Probably not," Stormi said. "But it wouldn't hurt to have a conversation with Shannon."

Cameron had to agree. "All right. Why don't you head back now? Take care of all the red tape. If Townsend gives you a hard time, have him give me a call. Go to Judge Warren. He likes me, and tends to go hard on sex crimes. Then, get your ass back up here as soon as you can."

"What are you going to do?"

"I'm going to pay a visit to Shannon. Stop by the morgue. Call my buddy Tristan and visit a few names on this list to re-question them. Text me when you're on your way back, and we can re-group."

"Sounds like a plan." Stormi stood and knocked the table twice with her knuckles.

Cameron gathered all the papers and filed them

neatly in the folders. Before he did all those things he'd told Stormi he had planned for the day, he needed to go check on Vivian.

It was the least he could do.

Vivian made her way down to the waterfront. It wasn't the warmest of June mornings—cool enough that she felt the need to put on a sweatshirt, but she didn't need pants. Jean shorts were fine. She plopped herself into the Adirondack chair at the end of her boatless dock and stared out at the lake. She'd lived in Lake George for her entire life, and she couldn't imagine being anywhere else.

Lilly had been right about Vivian. She *had* been hiding from life. At first, she'd done it by being the perfect daughter to her mother and the best older sister to Oliver. Then she dove into her studies. Like Oliver, her grades were important, and she strove to be the best. The only difference was, she never felt the great fear of failure that Oliver had. For Vivian, it was more about keeping her mind and body occupied so she didn't stop and think.

As she got older, she found she needed to find ways to not only stay busy but also keep from becoming too entangled with any man. God forbid she have a real, deep, meaningful relationship.

Her career and the camp gave her freedom.

The dock vibrated under her feet. She glanced

over her shoulder, expecting to see Cameron. Her heart dropped to her stomach when Thor Myers, the waterfront director from camp, graced her vision. She swallowed. She'd known Thor since she was ten years old, and he was fifteen. She'd had a crush on him when he was her swim instructor.

Their age difference, while not that much now, had been worlds apart at camp and until she became staff. But by then, the crush had faded, and he'd never shown any interest in her other than friendship. That was until she'd taken her first teaching job at the local high school at the ripe old age of twenty-one.

The same school she'd attended as a kid.

Thor had grown up in Glens Falls, which was about twenty minutes south of Lake George, but had been working for the local school district for a couple of years. On her twenty-second birthday, they'd laughed at the fact that they'd gone from student-teacher type relationship to friends and colleagues. That was when he'd tried to kiss her. It had been clunky and awkward.

Three years had passed, and he'd made it perfectly clear numerous times that he was interested, but he hadn't been overly aggressive in his pursuit. He'd been relatively passive about it, basically accepting that he'd always be in the friend zone, though he did constantly make comments about how he was waiting in the wings if she ever changed her mind.

"What are you doing here?" she asked. She wasn't

used to people stopping by unannounced, and ever since she moved in, Thor had a horrible habit of doing it regularly.

She'd always been polite. Maybe too much so, because lately, he'd been doing it more often, and it was getting annoying. He often acted as if they were more than friends. Like he belonged wherever she was, and that the people around them shouldn't be surprised by his presence.

She'd made it clear that she wasn't interested in dating him—more than once. But he didn't give up. And it wasn't the same as it was with Cameron, where she felt as though she *encouraged* Cameron to flirt. She welcomed it and flirted back, even though she wasn't ready to go out with anyone. If she were, it would be Cameron, not Thor.

It was hard to ignore Thor, though, because they worked in the same school district. Actually, in the same building. He was head of the physical education department and the swim team coach. But other than faculty meetings, she barely had any contact with him.

Now, he had the audacity to pull up a chair and take her hand. "When I heard about Oliver, I had to come over. I couldn't just send a text or call." He brought her hand to his lips and pressed firmly. "I'm so sorry, Vivian. He was such a sweet soul. If there is anything I can help with. Please, let me know."

"Thank you. That's very kind." She gently pulled away, resisting the urge to scoot her chair back. She didn't normally feel this strange around him, and that bothered her.

He was only being nice. He'd always been a bit over-the-top, but he was well-meaning, and he was great with the kids. He had the patience of a saint. The one thing everyone could say about Thor Myers was that he could handle troubled teens without batting an eyelash.

"Have you had breakfast? I could make you something or take you somewhere."

She shook her head. "I'm okay for now."

"You need to eat and keep up your strength."

"I know," she said softly. She really didn't want to sit here and have any kind of conversation with Thor. "I have—"

"I'll just run up to the house and whip you up some eggs or French toast. My grandmother's recipe is amazing. Have you had your morning coffee? I know how much you like that."

She blew out a puff of air. She'd gotten in the habit of drinking coffee while at camp when she was about seventeen. It had taken her all summer to learn to like the bitter brew. But now, she truly enjoyed it. Still, she'd rather have cocoa on a morning like this.

"I'm not hungry right now," she said with a stern but hopefully friendly tone.

He gave a slight nod. "I'll be right back with your coffee."

Before she could say a single word, he raced up to

her house and disappeared through her sliding glass doors.

Wonderful.

Well, she could use a second cup of the leaded. She hadn't been sleeping well, and last night had been even worse. She leaned back in her chair and closed her eyes. The sun beat down on her face. She wished she could enjoy her first summer living on the lake. Of course, she'd be spending time up at camp, except for her days off. But she could sneak back here during hikes and other times if she really wanted to.

Yeah. It was time to make this her last summer being the girls' unit director. Time to pass the torch and start living her life.

An image of Cameron danced across her mind. He might only be a year older than her, but he had an old soul, and that was just one of the many things that had attracted her to him. She only wished she trusted that he wasn't like every other man on the planet.

The dock shook.

She inwardly groaned as she blinked open her eyes.

"Here you go." Thor handed her a mug and once again made himself comfortable. "When was the last time you spoke with Oliver?"

"I really don't want to talk about it." She lifted the mug to her lips and took a sip of the hot, bitter liquid.

"I know it's hard, and it hurts, but it will help you heal to remember him and share stories about him with those who knew him."

"I'm tired," she said behind a tight jaw.

"I'm sure you are," he replied. "How is your mother holding up?"

"About as well as can be expected." Maybe if she spent just a few more minutes with Thor, he'd say his piece and leave.

"I can't imagine what she's going through right now." Thor reached out and patted Vivian's knee.

She tried not to outwardly cringe at his touch.

"I saw on the news that no cause of death was given. Do you know what happened? I know your father died by suicide. Do you think Oliver did the same thing?"

She sucked in an audible breath. Her lungs burned. This was not how she'd wanted to start her day, but she knew it was on everyone's mind. It was what everyone was thinking and whispering about behind her back.

Curiosity was part of human nature, and why should Thor be any different? Only, he was the only one asking the questions out loud.

And she wasn't sure how to answer them. Cameron had told her to be vague if anyone asked, but not to speak to any reporters.

"Thor, I'm sorry. I really don't want to talk about this right now," she said softly, and that was true. Her emotions were raw, and she couldn't stop seeing her brother on the cold, hard metal table in the morgue. His body lifeless with no soul.

"That kind of legacy is a tough one," Thor said.

"I hope that if you ever feel blue like that, you know you can call me. Day or night."

Who the hell did Thor think he was, coming at her like this? She squeezed her hands into fists and then released them, wiggling her fingers. Thor was great with teenagers. However, he didn't always have those same social skills with his peers.

This was one of those times.

She needed to cut him a little slack, though. Thor was a lot of things, but he always showed up when she needed a friend.

"I appreciate the thought, but really, Thor, I'm fine. And I seriously need you to drop the subject."

"All right. But know I'm here for you," he said. "Tell me how I can help. Even if it's something as simple as mowing your lawn."

That was a weird offer. "There is nothing anyone can do right now but thank you." *Except maybe give me some space!* She knew Thor meant well. Everyone did. Hell, her phone had been blowing up all night and morning with well-meaning friends who only wanted to express their condolences and affection.

But at this very moment in time, Vivian wanted to be left alone.

"This is the time when you should be delegating things to your friends so you and your mom can grieve together. I can help do whatever you need. It's what friends are for."

"I appreciate the offer. I really do. But there's

nothing anyone can do right now. Now, if you don't mind, I need to head over to my mom's shortly."

"Would you like me to drive you? I worry about you being all alone in this house."

"She's not alone." Cameron's voice echoed across the lake. He strode across the dock with his head held high, and his chest puffed out. He wore his typical dark slacks, white shirt, sport coat, and dark tie.

He always wore a tie while working, which she found interesting because it wasn't always required, at least according to Jacob.

But damn, he looked hot.

Thor glanced between Vivian and Cameron. "Who are you?" Thor asked with his hand covering his eyes.

"The man she's not alone with. Who are you?" Cameron stood behind her with his hand on her shoulder. Normally, this kind of Neanderthal behavior would have had her shoving them both in the lake—and she would if they didn't settle down. But she'd struggled to put Thor in his place, and if Cameron could do that for her, then so be it.

"A friend," Thor said with a defensive tone.

"And does *a friend* have a name?" Cameron asked with a sweet-as-honey tone and smile.

"I don't like your attitude." Thor squinted.

"All right." Cameron stretched out his arm. "We can start over. I'm Agent Cameron Thatcher. I'm currently dating Vivian."

Vivian swallowed. That wasn't true, but it wasn't a

lie either since she'd agreed to go out with him the other day. "Cameron, this is a colleague of mine both at the high school and at Camp Lookout."

"Oh. We've met a couple of times." He shook Cameron's hand, but he didn't stand, which meant he didn't have a desire to leave.

Shit.

"Sorry. I don't remember." Cameron squeezed her shoulder. "I'm ready now," he said. "Shall we go to your mom's?"

"Yes." She was on her feet in less than a second. "Thor, thank you for stopping by."

"Please, call me if you need anything at all. I'll see you at school." Finally, Thor stood and breezed past her and Cameron. He glanced over his shoulder and waved when he reached the path toward the driveway.

"He was coming on a little strong," Cameron said.

"So did you." She arched a brow. "I agreed to go out on *a date* with you. That doesn't mean we're dating and please, you remember meeting him."

"Yeah. I remember the guy, but he didn't leave an impression. And I thought I was doing you a favor." He placed his hand on the small of her back and guided her toward the house. "I heard most of that conversation from my patio, and he wasn't going to leave until you let him do something for you. I think that's a little weird. Has he come on to you like that before?"

"He's asked me out. I said no. I've known the guy since I was ten. He's persistent but harmless."

"I apologize if I overstepped."

"No. It's fine." She paused at the back door and turned.

Cameron's eyes conveyed a soft place to land. They were inviting but not in a come-hither way. They were genuine and caring.

He looked at her the way Jackson had first looked at Shannon, and Vivian had to wonder if her eyes told a similar story, or if she simply gazed back with lust.

Her heart raced every single time she thought about Cameron. Butterflies formed in her gut when he entered a room. She would think of a million clever things to say, but the moment she opened her mouth, she had no intelligent words. Standing with him in this moment, she wanted to reach out and grab the connection forming between them and hold on to it.

Placing her hands on his shoulders, she leaned in. Her mind screamed at her how inappropriate it would be to kiss him. Her brother had just died, and he was the agent looking into his death.

And maybe she was just using Cameron to deal with the gut-wrenching emotions threatening to rip out her heart and squeeze until it stopped beating.

He wrapped his arms around her waist and pulled her close to his hard body. His warm lips gently pressed against hers, and heat radiated across her skin, running down her neck, all the way to her toes. It was a soft and slow kiss, and for the first time in her adult life, she felt like a desirable, whole woman.

She wanted to trust that it was real. That Cameron was more than a ship passing in the night. If she were going to trust her heart with any man, she wanted one who would be able to understand all of her.

And that was a big ask because she never expressed her true self. All her fears and insecurities were wrapped up in a secret bubble and buried deep within her soul.

Just like her father was buried in the ground with his dirty little skeletons.

Cameron palmed her cheek and broke off the kiss long before she was ready. He stared into her eyes, showing her a deep kindness that stole her breath. "I'm going to be busy for most of the day, dealing with things related to Oliver." Cameron ran his thumb across her cheek. "I'm going to have to go over some things with Stormi when she gets back here later, but I want to make sure I keep you in the loop."

"Thank you."

"While I didn't particularly care for Thor, I agree with him about you being alone, but for different reasons." He tucked a stray strand of hair behind her ear. He really did have an old soul that pulled her heart right to his, and there was nothing she could do to stop it. "The more I look over everything, the more

I'm convinced that your brother didn't take his own life."

"Should I be worried about my mom's and Larry's safety? Mine?"

"I don't think so, but still, you should be diligent, and I'd feel better if you let me take you to your mom's and I could pick you up later."

Vivian preferred to be in control, and while she planned on spending the entire day with her mother and Larry, not having her car to leave whenever she wanted, made her right eye twitch. "If I'm not in danger, I'd rather drive myself. That way, if I need to go anywhere, like if the police or the morgue need something, I can do it."

He nodded. "That makes sense. But will you promise me you'll keep me posted on where you're going? I'm not being an overbearing first-date, wanna-be boyfriend, I'm just being an FBI agent who happens to really like you."

She let out a slight laugh. "That's the most pathetic yet sweetest thing any man who's tried to date me has ever said."

"Is that a sideways compliment?"

"Pretty much." She patted his chest. "I'd better get going." A flash of her and her brother as children jumping off the sundeck into the cool lake below filled her mind. It had been one of Oliver's favorite things to do, and he would bribe her with half of his allowance because he wasn't allowed to swim alone. She blinked. A wave of guilt sloshed in her belly.

Oliver was gone.

Cameron took her chin between his thumb and forefinger.

"This case is my priority. My boss gave me the go-ahead to stay in Lake George and do whatever it takes."

"You mean if it turns out to be a murder. But what if Oliver really *did* take his own life? Because if the latter is true, there is nothing for you to look into now, is there?"

"The autopsy should be completed this afternoon. We'll know more then. For now, try not to think about this too much. I know it's hard. But focus on Oliver's celebration of life. It sounded like Larry and your mom really wanted to make that a special event."

"My father's funeral was so damn depressing. She doesn't want that, and neither do I."

Cameron kissed her temple. "I'll call you as soon as I know anything. I promise."

"Thanks." She leaned against the door and watched him stroll across the yard and disappear into the Heritage Inn property.

She knew she was young and inexperienced when it came to men and relationships. While many of her friends were getting married, she'd never been in love, and she'd never had a long-lasting relationship.

And that was by design.

She'd always feared that she'd end up with someone like her father. And because he'd been her hero until he wasn't, she didn't trust good men.

But she sure as hell didn't trust the bad boys, either.

So, what made Cameron different? Was it because he was a federal agent? No. Because she'd once dated a police officer and just couldn't get past the fact that he carried a gun wherever he went.

Cameron had had a gun strapped to his hip when they were in their lip-lock, and it hadn't fazed her in the least. Hell, she hadn't even noticed it until he walked away.

Maybe it was because he'd been the one man who hadn't come on strong but also didn't give up. He was always just…there on the sidelines, giving her space.

He was willing to be her friend.

Yet she was still afraid, and part of her wanted to tell him that she was sorry for leading him on with that kiss and that she shouldn't have used him like that to get rid of Thor. But the rest of her wanted to see where this might go.

Just a month ago, Oliver had told her that she was crazy not to go out with Cameron.

"Okay, Oliver. This one's for you."

6

Cameron stepped into the building where Doctor Shannon Armstrong's practice was located. He tucked his file folder under his arm and quickly glanced at his watch.

Ten minutes early.

He stood in front of the coffee maker and stuck one of the pod things into the machine. He pressed the button for the desired amount and waited.

Patience wasn't always his strong suit.

Snagging the paper cup in his hand, he stared at the images on the wall. They weren't of anything personal that he could tell. No pictures of her two beautiful children or her husband, Jackson.

But there was one of their personal sailboat, with a woman standing on the bow, back turned, arms stretched wide, and her long hair blowing in the wind.

He suspected it was Shannon, but whoever had taken the photograph had blurred out the person, keeping everything else in focus. It was a stunning picture.

The rattling of the door startled him, and he glanced over his shoulder.

A young woman quickly moved through the waiting room, not looking in his direction, and bolted out the door.

"Hi, Cameron," Shannon said. "It's good to see you again, though I'm sad for the reason. I can't believe Oliver is gone."

"I didn't know him too well, but he seemed like a good person."

"He was," Shannon said. "Let's take this in my office."

"Thanks so much for taking the time. I really appreciate it."

"Anything for a friend of Katie and Jacob's." She waved her hand toward the door that went into her office.

He crossed the threshold and found her space to be typical of every other therapist's office with its comfortable-looking sofa and chair on one side of the room and her desk on the other. Up against the wall was a built-in bookshelf and, of course, it was filled with books. He set his cup of coffee on the table in front of the couch, keeping his file on his lap, and made himself at home.

"So, what can I do for you?" Shannon sat in the chair and crossed her legs. She wore dark slacks and a yellow, short-sleeved top. She was an attractive woman, and she carried herself with style and grace.

He walked a fine line with how far he was pushing his investigation. His boss had given him a long leash when it came to Oliver's death, but that was only because Oliver had been tied to both murders from a year ago, and the two recent deaths by suicide. So, even if they didn't rule Oliver's death a murder, there was a strong connection that might help unravel some clues.

"I have two victims who were murdered on the dark web last year that were also involved in the same sex party. Fast forward to a couple of months ago and a death by suicide who was also involved in a sex party. We didn't connect it to the murders until we had another dead body, also involved in both a recent orgy and the one from last year. And now, I have a third death, but I don't know if it's murder or suicide."

"I've been following these cases closely."

"I believe it's all connected to the sex parties. I just don't understand why people are being murdered or killing themselves. I don't know the common denominator."

"Were any of them married? Could guilt be the reason for why they might have wanted to self-harm?"

"Yes."

"And the murder victims? Were they married?"

Cameron chuckled. Her mind worked much like an investigator. "One of the murder victims was married. Her husband was quickly ruled out as a suspect since he was out of the country when it happened." Cameron leaned forward and lifted his coffee mug. He didn't really want to drink it; he just needed something to fiddle with while his brain shifted all the information around so he could call up what he needed. Just because he had a photographic memory didn't mean things didn't get jumbled up sometimes. "However, the husband participated in the sex club, as well."

"It's a club?" Shannon uncrossed her legs and sat up a little taller. "An actual group that has a list of members? Rules? Meetings?"

"When we first investigated the second murder a year ago, yes. But the group as I knew it has since disbanded. However, it seems as if they reorganized. And now, no one is talking. Since I'm dealing with an apparent death by suicide, and the only thing that was loaded to the internet was the orgy, it's not really a case I can pursue." He lifted his index finger. "That is unless Oliver Rose's death is ruled a murder."

"I'm sure you know something about my past."

"I know some," he admitted. "It's part of the reason I'm here. I also wanted to show you some pictures. I know you can't break client confidentiality, but if any of these people are your patients by chance, you can ask them to speak to me."

"I can do that," she said. "But circling back to the organized sex clubs. There are a lot of different types. Some are benign and really just men and women needing an outlet for sexual energy they don't have any other place for."

"So, you believe orgies are acceptable?" Cameron wouldn't consider himself a prude but having sex with more than one person at a time wasn't something he would ever do.

Hell, he didn't even have the typical male fantasy of being with two women.

"I didn't say that, but I'm not in a position to judge. My job is to help people deal with their mental state and give them a safe space to deal with their emotions and uncovering why they do the things they do. That would include why they might have those sexual needs."

"So, why would someone be involved in a sex club?"

"First, sexual fetishes are not abnormal. If two people want to be swingers, that's not abnormal for them. You might think it's wrong, but that's only for you. It doesn't make them perverted or anything. The problem becomes when they try to convert someone who isn't into it. Or when their partner becomes uncomfortable. So, the vast majority of people get involved in sex clubs because they want to. However, their desire could be out of boredom, loneliness, or an addictive personality, and they are acting out already. They let their addictions or their sexual fetishes control their lives."

Cameron mentally pulled out the files of the two recent deaths by suicide.

Both female.

Which was interesting all by itself. But if Oliver was ruled the same way, that shattered the pattern.

One woman had been in her late forties. Married. Two kids.

The other one had been in her early thirties. Single. No kids.

Both had friends and family members who said they'd been acting strangely. Detached. That for a couple of months before they died, they avoided people and became secretive.

Kind of like Oliver.

"Do you find that there are a lot of predators in these groups?"

"I don't know that I'd say there are a lot, but the groups can sometimes be intense, and they can change people," Shannon said. "My father was part of one that was cult-like, and they were into young men and women—often their own children."

Cameron shifted uncomfortably in his seat. He'd seen a lot in his short time with the FBI, but crimes involving kids always made him nauseous.

"Mind you, that's extreme, and there is usually a leader who uses a lot of gaslighting techniques to get their victims—and they are victims—and make them stay. Often, the victims turn into perpetrators. It's a vicious cycle, and the guilt for those who aren't psychopaths is extreme. I saw that firsthand with some of the men my father recruited."

"I'm sorry for what you had to live through."

"Thank you," Shannon said.

Cameron opened the file and handed it to Shannon. "These are all the people that participated in the orgies. I know you can't tell me anything unless I have a search warrant—which at this point, I don't."

Shannon nodded as she glanced across the images on the page, expressionless.

He figured she'd been in this position before.

"The second page is a couple of emails that Oliver received from someone named Simon Says."

Shannon lifted her gaze with an arched brow.

"Do you know that name?"

"Everyone does. It's a child's game." She flipped the page and lowered her chin.

Cameron might not be a psychologist, but he understood psychology better than most, and he knew she'd heard that name before, at least in the context of an email. He rarely assumed anything, but he would, in this case, make an informed guess that she had a patient who had a connection to whoever this Simon Says person was. This might be the first break he got.

If Oliver's death was ruled a murder.

She closed the folder and handed it back.

"I didn't realize that Oliver was involved in a sex group. How did his family take that news?"

"I haven't told them yet." Cameron swallowed the bile that smacked his throat, only it didn't stay down in his gut. Instead, it lingered, making him want to vomit. He'd promised Vivian that he'd keep her in the loop, but why tell her something that might be considered distasteful if he didn't have to? "I will if this becomes a homicide. Because anyone in that video could be a suspect, and I'll need to know if they recognize anyone." He didn't know if he was making that justification for Shannon or for himself.

"That's reasonable," she said. "I'm going to make a bold suggestion."

"What's that?"

"If his case becomes a murder, get a warrant for his mental health records."

"His sister and mom did tell me he struggled in high school and contemplated self-harm. Were you his therapist?" Cameron wondered why Vivian hadn't told him that. Of course, therapy was a very private thing. He understood that, and most people didn't like to talk about it.

"I thought that was one of the reasons you stopped by," Shannon said.

Okay. Oliver had been under Shannon's care during his teen years. Had he gone back? And if he had, how did he really feel about what he had been doing. And was he the one who'd discussed Simon Says with Shannon?

Or was it a different patient?

Cameron's phone vibrated in his pocket. He glanced at his watch, which displayed his text and email messages.

It was from Stormi, informing him that the

medical examiner had completed the autopsy and wanted to speak to them.

In person.

"They didn't mention it." He stood. "I'm sorry, but I have to run. I just got a text from my partner. I have a feeling that I'll be asking a judge to request those records."

"If Oliver was murdered, it's a no-brainer, and I'm happy to help in any way I can." She rose, stretching out her hand. "Take care."

"You, too." Not that he wanted another murder, but this meant that his boss would give him all the resources he needed. He wouldn't be a one-man show anymore. He'd have the full backing of the FBI.

This was the kind of case that could make his career.

So why did he have a brick sitting in the middle of his gut?

Vivian couldn't believe that she was planning her baby brother's funeral. Her eyes burned, but not from tears. She'd cried so much, she didn't have any left, and no amount of artificial tears would lube her eyes enough to stop them from feeling as if they'd been assaulted by a sand storm.

She sat at her mother's kitchen table with her laptop open, staring at pictures of Oliver as she tried to make a special montage video. She'd sent a few messages to some of his friends, asking for their images, too, so she could really capture his life. She'd received a few, which made her realize there were things about Oliver she didn't know, and that crushed her heart.

She'd thought they'd been so close, and that he'd told her everything. When he was in his darkest hour, he'd called *her* in the middle of the night to talk him off the roof. When he couldn't decide what college to attend, he'd talked it through with her, not their mom.

Oliver even went to her for advice about women.

Or men, since he enjoyed being with both sexes—though he generally preferred women.

And then there was this Emma chick, whoever the fuck she was.

Vivian's heart rate sped up, and the heat in her body boiled.

She snagged her cell and stared at the screen, willing it to ring. She'd called Oliver's best friend Ray an hour ago. If anyone had information about Oliver's personal life, it would be Ray.

Nothing.

She let out a long sigh.

"Hi, baby."

She jumped, nearly knocking over her computer. "Shit, Mom. You scared the crap out of me."

"I'm sorry." Her mother bent over and kissed her temple before taking a seat at the head of the table. She reached into the popcorn bowl that Vivian had forgotten about. "Did you ever listen to that message from your Aunt Kiki?"

"No. And I'm not going to. I have nothing to say to her." Vivian glared at her mother. "You talked to her, didn't you?"

"Yes. I did. All she wants is to give you her condolences. And to maybe mend some fences. I know she hurt you. She hurt me, too, but maybe it's time to let this wound heal."

She wasn't going to have this conversation again. Her mother meant well, but it wasn't going to happen. "Kiki doesn't want a relationship with me, and you know it. She wants the ring you gave me that was Grammy's. That was always meant for me. And I'm not going to give it to her."

"If it makes you feel any better, Kiki didn't once bring it up."

"Of course, she didn't. Now, can we please drop this conversation?"

"Yes," her mother said. "How goes the video project?"

"It's a lot harder than I thought it would be."

"Would you like me to take over for a bit? I've done a full board of pictures from the photo albums." Her mother looked as though she'd aged ten years recently, and that broke Vivian's heart.

She reached across the table and took her mom's hand. "Maybe we both need a bit of a break." She glanced at the clock on the microwave. Four in the afternoon was a little early to start drinking, but sometimes life demanded a little alcohol. She stood and made her way to the wine cooler and pulled out her mother's favorite liquid gold. She chuckled. "Do you remember the first time Oliver tried wine?"

"Do I ever. The look on his face was about as funny as a baby eating a lemon."

"He never did acquire a taste for it, but he loved that tequila."

"I have to admit, that bothered me," her mother said.

Vivian pulled down two stemmed glasses and poured the wine nearly to the top of each. She handed one to her mom and motioned to the family room. "Why?"

"Your father enjoyed tequila way too much. He didn't drink it a lot in front of you kids, but when we went out or went to parties, that was his go-to." Her mother sat in her favorite chair, which was this oversized, fluffy thing that she'd had for as long as Vivian could remember.

"I didn't know that." Vivian tried not to think about her dad too often. It amazed her how one bad memory negated fourteen years of him being a good father.

And he really had been.

Until he chose to betray his wife and family.

That was something she couldn't forgive.

"Back then, we didn't want to drink much in front of you kids, so we reserved it for when you were in bed asleep or when we went out. I liked my wine."

She raised her glass. "And he liked his tequila on the rocks. So, when Oliver developed a taste for the same drink as your dad, it wigged me out."

"You never said anything to me." Vivian found a blanket and covered her feet as she sprawled out on the sofa.

"I didn't want to upset you. The fact that you've had to live with the knowledge of what your father did has eaten away at my soul. I've worried about you kids. Oliver with how he'd react to his father's death and our lies."

"He didn't know we lied."

"Not the point," her mother said. "And then there's you. I can see in your eyes the pain all of this has caused. You've never given any man a chance."

"Mom. I'm not going to have this conversation with you again." Vivian loved her mother. She also *liked* her mom, something that a lot of her friends couldn't say about theirs. They had a great relationship, and she enjoyed spending time shopping and having lunch, and doing girls' weekends. But this was the one topic that could make Vivian get up and walk out of any room.

"I can tell you like that FBI agent, but I can also see you pushing him away. And I fear it's all because of what you saw. I know trust isn't an easy thing after what happened. It took me a long time, too. But you deserve to be happy."

Vivian took a large gulp of her wine. This was not something she wanted to discuss, considering she'd barely processed her brother's death and had no idea why her mom insisted.

"I'm not pushing Cameron away."

"Have you gone out on a date with him?" Her mom waggled her finger, something Vivian always hated. "And I know he's asked you more than once. Jacob's mom tells me he's quite smitten with you."

"Smitten?" Vivian laughed. "That's an interesting word." She felt as if she had been transported back to the nineteen fifties. Maybe it wasn't such a bad idea to talk about her love life—or lack thereof—and her feelings for Cameron, which confused the hell out of her. She'd spent the winter successfully avoiding him, mostly because he lived in Albany, and she lived an hour away. They only saw each other at the occasional party.

But lately, they were running into each other more often, and she'd caved to his advances.

However, it wasn't because of his persistence. Because he hadn't been pushy. He'd been respectful, and she valued that. Mostly, he made her feel like she was the most important person in the room each time she saw him, and no one else, outside of her immediate family, had ever done that for her before.

"Do you know why I've thought lately that we should have told Oliver about what your father did?"

"Because of what he went through in high school when he was depressed and had thoughts of self-harm?" Vivian said matter-of-factly.

"No." Her mother took a slow sip of her drink,

swallowing a few times before setting her glass down on the end table. "He spent two years in therapy, and I went with him a few times. His depression didn't start over his fear of doing what your dad did. That was a byproduct."

"I know all this, Mom. And I know that it started when he struggled with his sexuality. All the more reason not to tell him."

"I believed that, too, back then. But as he got older and became more confident in who he was as a man, I wanted him to know that his dad had a much stronger reason for what he did, and that it had absolutely nothing to do with you kids."

Vivian scooted closer to her mom and curled her fingers around her wrist. "Telling him would have only shattered the love he had for Dad, making it worse for Oliver. Trust me. Living with that knowledge is just as hard as having a dad who took his life. I don't think that would have helped." Vivian leaned back. "Because you're right about me. I do push men away because of what Dad did. I can't trust that they won't do the same thing. And it's not just him. I see my friends deal with cheating boyfriends. Or look at what happened to Mrs. Hollenbeck. They were married for like thirty years when her husband ran off with a younger woman. And as much as I like Cameron and would love to date him, I'm afraid he'll be no different." Saying it out loud made her heart hurt. She could barely admit it to herself, and she never thought she'd voice it to her mother.

"Baby. You were so young, and your daddy was your hero. If I could go back in time and change that one part of your life, I would."

Vivian nodded. She wished she could, too. "But would you want to tell me later in life?"

"I guess you have a good point. I'm not sure that I would." Her mother raised her wine. "That damn double standard thing."

"No one needs to know that about their parent."

"Amen to that."

Vivian's phone dinged. She pulled it from her back pocket and gasped.

"What is it?"

"It's a text from Cameron. He can't talk right now, and he won't be back for a couple more hours and didn't want me to hear this from anyone else, especially on the news."

"That doesn't sound good."

"It depends on how you look at it." She blinked, staring at the text and the words: *Oliver's death was ruled a homicide.*

7

Cameron pinned the photographs of the two crimes scenes from a year ago onto the corkboard.

Melony Hati

Alana Richards

He rifled through all the papers and files on the table and tacked Oliver's images next to those. He took a step back and mentally compared every detail.

"Do you see anything?" he asked Stormi. Now that he'd been given the official lead on this case and both the suicides and the murders had been lumped together, he needed to find every connection he could.

And not just the sex club because he knew there was more to this than met the eye.

"It's six in the morning. I haven't had a full dose of caffeine. My brain isn't functioning yet." Stormi inched closer. "Both murders, the two suicides, and

Oliver were all killed with the same caliber weapon. That's interesting."

"I agree." Cameron found the few pictures that were taken of the two deaths by suicide and added them to the board, along with the suicide notes.

Edna Almond had left a note for her parents that simply said she was sorry for causing them any pain.

Tim Dorit had left a note for his wife that pretty much said the same thing that Oliver's note did.

"Look at how similar those are. Short and apologetic, but they don't say sorry for anything specific. I've seen suicide notes before. And while many are like that, I think it's strange that these were all from people that attended the same sex party."

"Are you thinking these two are murders now?"

"I am."

Having a body exhumed wasn't an easy task, and having a judge sign off on it could be nearly impossible. Not to mention, families usually didn't take too kindly to the idea.

Nor did the medical examiner who'd done the autopsies.

But Cameron had already spoken to Doctor Victor Hemmings, who'd just completed Oliver's. He'd also done one of the deaths by suicide, and he told Cameron that he had no problem having his findings come into question.

It took four days for him to complete that autopsy, and he nearly ruled it inconclusive.

The thing that pushed him over the edge was the

evidence the police found on Edna's computer where she talked about ending it all in great detail, and the fact that there was no other explanation.

Except Doctor Hemmings couldn't give any valid reason for the bruises on Edna's body. A few of Edna's friends from the sex club had come forward and suggested that maybe they had been from the last orgy. They mentioned that Edna tended to like things a little on the rough side.

That was a convenient solution.

"Victor's going through his autopsy findings for Edna, and we're going to re-examine the file in hopes of re-opening that case."

"What about Tim Dorit's case?"

"That one's going to be a little bit harder. The ME that did that autopsy is standing by his ruling, so we're having Hemmings go over the report. We have to start from the beginning with fresh eyes."

Stormi marched over to the coffee machine and put in one of the pods. "I was warned about working with you and how meticulous you can be."

He laughed. "I was like a deer in headlights when I first started working with Jacob."

"Yeah. I'd be terrified if I were a defense attorney and had to face him as a prosecutor."

"He's badass in the courtroom, that's for sure." Cameron continued pinning all the pertinent information he thought was necessary to his board. He had about an hour before the time he'd promised Vivian he'd be at her place, and then he had to head out for a full day of questioning people and hopefully getting Oliver's medical records. "Are you still good with divide and conquer this morning?"

"Absolutely. We can meet somewhere this afternoon." Stormi pointed to the door. "Are you good with talking to Vivian about what her brother was involved in?"

"Of course. It's my job."

"Look. I know it was late when we got back last night, and you didn't get to see her, and that bothered you because you care about her on a personal level—which will make this hard."

"I can compartmentalize." Cameron tried like hell not to wear his emotions on his sleeve at work. However, he and Stormi had been through a lot together, and this case could become all-consuming for both of them. Which meant, their lives would be entangled.

He'd learned from his time with Jacob that your partner was not just your work lifeline.

They became a part of the fabric of your very soul.

"Dude, you're falling so hard for that chick, it's almost painful to watch."

Cameron had thought he'd been in love before.

While he didn't date much, he'd been head over heels for a girl he'd gone through Quantico with. They'd had a passionate love affair, but that's all it was at the end of the day.

Great sex.

When they broke up, he'd realized that he hadn't really loved her like he was supposed to love a woman.

And she'd only enjoyed the time they shared between the sheets. Which was pretty much all they did. Looking back, there was no romance. There were no late-night walks through the park. No picnics with cold fried chicken and a bottle of cheap wine.

"She's pretty special, but my feelings for her won't affect my ability to perform my duties." He stared at the picture of Oliver and wondered how he'd gotten involved in the sex club. He didn't seem like the type. Though Cameron had learned that there wasn't really a specific type of person that was into that stuff. It was just that Oliver didn't have much game when it came to the ladies.

Cameron didn't, either. However, at Jacob and Katie's Christmas party, Cameron had seen how Oliver could barely go up to a girl he was obviously attracted to, no matter how much Vivian had encouraged him.

"You're missing my point about Vivian." Stormi leaned in and punched his shoulder. "Don't get so wrapped up in the case that you let her slip through your fingers."

He turned and stared at his partner. "Her brother was murdered. Right before I was to interview him. I tried to meet with him, but he didn't answer my calls, nor did he answer the door when I rang the bell."

"His death isn't your fault."

Intellectually, he knew that to be true. However,

he couldn't help but think that maybe Oliver would still be alive if Cameron had tried harder to find him.

Oliver hadn't done anything wrong—that they knew of anyway. All the FBI wanted was to talk to him about what he knew about the people who'd died—both the murders and the deaths by suicide.

And also his knowledge of how the sex club worked.

So far, no one in the group had been available to talk. Or they had magically disappeared. It was as if they were all hiding something.

Or protecting someone.

"Maybe not. But he was involved in a sex club that might also be some weird murder club." He lifted the last thing to pin on the board. "And this Simon Says email, I think, is the biggest clue we have. Yet I have no idea what it means except that more people are likely going to die if we don't figure this out."

Stormi filled his to-go coffee mug with a fresh blend. "Go say good morning to Vivian. Spend a little time with her because she needs that right now. She needs the people who care about her showing up, and that means you, too. And then go off and help me catch this asshole." She handed him the mug and the file on all the people involved in both the orgies. Names and profile pictures only.

Cameron chuckled. "Isn't it more like you helping me?"

"Get out of here." She shoved him gently toward

the door. "I've got my list of things to do. We'll touch base in a couple of hours and re-group."

"Thanks." Cameron stepped out onto the deck. The morning sun bouncing off the lake smacked his face. He pushed his shades over his eyes and strolled across the yard to Vivian's place.

His breath hitched.

She stood on the deck; her long, blond hair pulled tightly back in a ponytail at the nape of her neck. She wore a blue dress with long sleeves that hugged her body, showing off her womanly curves.

She turned and smiled. "Good morning," she said softly, her eyes glistening in the sun's rays.

He could tell she'd been crying.

Again.

That broke his heart.

"Did you sleep okay?" He made his way up the stairs. His pulse pounded in his throat.

She didn't make him nervous, but she did send his senses down paths he'd never been before. He desired her like no other, and yet, merely being in her presence was satisfying enough.

"To be totally honest, no. And I drank nearly an entire bottle of wine to try to help, and all that did was give me a slight headache this morning."

He wasn't sure if he should go in for the big kiss or simply press his lips to her cheek and give her a tender hug. Setting his file down on the table and his mug on top of that, he opted for the latter. It seemed more appropriate.

She rested her delicate hands on his shoulders and sighed.

"You can always call or text me, even in the middle of the night," he whispered. "I'll answer if I can."

"You've got to sleep sometime." She took a step back and leaned against the railing. "My mom wants to go pick out the urn today for my brother's ashes. I told her that they won't be releasing the body for a while and that we don't have to rush, but she wants everything taken care of."

"She needs to keep busy, and now that this case has shifted to a murder investigation, both you and your mom are going to be dealing with all the unknowns. That can take a toll."

"I can already see it with my mom," Vivian said. "Larry texted me at five this morning, asking me to call her as soon as I woke up. When we first got the news, it was almost a relief that Oliver hadn't harmed himself. But now, neither of us can understand why someone would want to kill him." She raised a finger to her cheek and swiped away a single tear. "I think my mom is going to go out of her mind."

All the more reason that Cameron needed to keep his focus on catching whoever did this. But if he was going to do that, he had to find out why, and that meant having a tough conversation with Vivian.

One he really didn't want to have.

"I need to ask you some questions related to your brother. Can we sit down and talk for a bit?"

"Of course." The way she walked across the deck was more like a dancer gliding across a stage to a slow waltz.

She had style and grace.

And an old soul.

He admired that about Vivian.

"You have one of the most amazing views of the lake." He adjusted himself in the chair.

Her home sat on top of a hill, overlooking the water. She had a massive front yard, with only a driveway in the back.

"The original house was right on the water. Doug Tanner and Jim Sutton bought this place when they first became business partners and tore down the old cottage to build this house. I couldn't believe my luck when they put it on the market. It's so pretty. Now, all I need is to pay off some debt so I can afford to buy a small boat."

"I've been looking to buy a house, but every time I find something perfect, I can't pull the trigger."

"Why is that, do you suppose?" She pulled her ponytail over her shoulder and twisted it with her fingers. The sun's rays caught her golden hair, and it shone like a jewel.

"If you ask my mother, it's because she doesn't believe a single man should be living in a big house alone."

Vivian laughed, and the sound was like warm honey on a thick piece of sourdough bread.

"If you were to ask my dad, he'd tell you it's

because I'm living in the wrong city, doing the wrong job."

Vivian tilted her head, and her jaw dropped open. "But you're really good at what you do. At least Jacob says you're the best agent the FBI has."

"Jacob is exaggerating. However, not to sound conceited, but I am excellent in my career. My father just believes that working for the government is stifling my abilities."

"What does he think you should be doing?"

"If not joining him in his bodyguard operation, then perhaps working as a private investigator. You see, my dad likes to bend the rules and do things his way, or so he says. But when push comes to shove, he works well with the police and other agencies."

"Have you ever considered working for your father?"

"Nope. He and I would kill each other." Cameron loved his dad, but they were like oil and water. His father was big and full of muscle. It wasn't that he was more brawn than brains, but he tended to use force before thought.

Cameron was more contemplative, and he and his father didn't often understand each other's methods.

"However, I have thought about working for Jackson and Katie."

"Really?" Vivian's lips turned into a seductive smile. "I know they've talked about hiring someone. Katie's got her hands full and tries not to work long hours, and Jackson wants to be home at a reasonable hour to spend time with his kids. But neither wants to give up their careers—which I don't blame them for. They've worked hard to make that business a success."

"It would be an honor to work alongside them."

"So, you've considered it? They've asked you?"

He hadn't expected to have this discussion with anyone. However, it was Vivian. His comfort level with her was like no other. He trusted her in ways he hadn't trusted even his family, and that was a weird feeling. "I am seriously thinking about it, but I won't until I've cleared this case off my desk." He tapped his finger on the file. "I have some things to ask you about your brother that might be a bit unsettling."

She leaned forward, resting her forearms on the table. "What do you mean?"

He flipped open the file and handed her a piece of paper. "Do you know any of these people?"

"Who are they, and how do they fit into this?" She glanced between him and the sheet in her hands.

"I'll explain in a minute. Just tell me if you know any of them." He leaned back and took a long sip of coffee. He had no idea if she knew about her brother's exploits or not. It wasn't something people usually discussed in casual conversation, and he passed no judgment.

Only now it was all in the middle of a murder investigation, and he needed to know the players.

"I know Annabel Edwards and Thomas

Redding." She handed back the first piece of paper from the orgy a year ago.

"How?"

"Annabel used to be our babysitter when we were kids, and Thomas is a bartender down at the brewery."

Interesting. "What about anyone on that piece of paper?"

She nodded. "George Wilkins and Heather Hay. They both went to school with Oliver and also attended Camp Lookout." Vivian set the paper on the table. "What do these people have to do with my brother's murder?"

"This might be difficult to hear," Cameron started, "but everyone on that second sheet was involved in a sex club that videoed their orgies and sexual exploits and loaded them onto a website."

"No. No way. Oliver wouldn't be involved in anything like that." Vivian shook her head wildly, her hands gripping the table. "You're lying." Her already porcelain skin turned even paler.

Cameron reached across the table to take her hand, but she yanked it away. "Two people from that second list that I showed you, Edna Almond and Tim Dorit took their lives, and I'm thinking that maybe they too were murdered."

She snapped her gaze to his and blinked. "How do you know that Oliver was involved in this orgy thing."

"I saw it." He swallowed the horrible taste that

smacked the back of this throat with such force that he thought it might come back up again. "I know this is hard to hear, and I'm sorry, but I'd rather you hear it from me."

"This can't be happening. History can't be repeating itself," she whispered.

"What are you talking about?" He scooted his chair closer. He wanted to touch her. To pull her into his arms and make all the pain go away. But he knew he couldn't.

"You don't understand, and I can't tell you." She pressed her hands firmly to the table and stood. "My mother cannot know of this," she said with a firm voice.

"Vivian. I know this is disturbing, but we must tell her. And whatever it is that you think you can't tell me is exactly what I need to know. You can't keep secrets from me if I'm going to find who killed your brother."

She brushed her hands down the front of her dress and inhaled sharply, lifting her chin. "I overreacted. I'm sorry."

He lifted himself from his chair and inched closer, not wanting to scare her away. "I can see the fear and pain in your eyes. Talk to me, Vivian. I'm on your side."

Her chest rose and fell. Suddenly, she turned and raced toward the railing. Gripping it, she leaned over, taking in deep breaths.

He came up behind her and gently placed his hand on her back. "Breathe slowly. In through your nose and out through your mouth." He'd been around enough people who had panic attacks to know one when he saw it. "Focus on your breathing and my voice. Nothing else."

She took in a slow, shallow breath and blew it out in a long puff.

"That's it. Keep it going."

She turned and glared.

That old saying *if looks could kill* filled his brain.

"What's going on, Vivian?" He hated pushing her, but whatever had sent her over the edge, he figured he needed to know. "The smallest of details might help me catch whoever did this."

"I don't want to believe this is related, and no one but my mother and I know." She let out a short, sarcastic laugh. "And all the people my father was fucking."

He jerked his head back. "Your dad died eleven years ago. He—"

"Took his life because I caught him loading a sex video of him and two women to some website."

Cameron's jaw dropped. Of all the things he could have imagined, that was not one of them. "And you're saying Oliver didn't know?"

"He believed our dad took his life because he'd ruined us financially. Which was true. He had. His sexual addiction got the best of him, and he did some crazy things, I guess."

"But your mom knows about the website and the sexual exploits?"

"She knows about some of it." Vivian wrapped her arms around her middle. "I didn't tell her about everything I found."

"What the hell did you find?"

"A couple of external hard drives with things no fourteen-year-old should ever see." She covered her mouth.

"Come here," he whispered, holding out his arms.

She shook her head. "When my dad saw me standing behind him in his office, he tried to explain it away. But what he was doing with those women was violent."

"He was hurting them?"

"That's the way it looked to me at the time, but the adult me knows there are fetishes and role-playing, so I don't know," she said with a tremble in her voice. "I told my mom, who confronted him, and we found other things on his computer. A day later, he was gone."

"I'm so sorry." Cameron inched closer.

She held up her hand, and he had to respect her wishes, so he hung back, even though all he wanted to do was comfort her and keep her safe.

"I found the drives and some other things when I was going through his stuff. I didn't want my mom to be curious, so I put it in my room. It took me years before I could plug those drives in and look, but when I did, I was mortified." She closed her eyes and exhaled. "I still have it."

"Jesus," he mumbled. "I'm going to need whatever you have."

She blinked. "I understand. But I don't see how this is related. Oliver couldn't have known. The only time he worried about being like our dad was when he thought about harming himself."

"Only, he was involved in this sex club, and if your father was involved with one, maybe someone from your father's past recruited him," Cameron said. "Does the name Simon ring a bell?"

"I don't think so, why?"

"Your brother got a strange email from someone with the screen name of Simon Says."

"That's weird." She took Cameron's hand. "I have the few things I kept of my father's in my closet. I'll get them for you. But could you please try to keep it from my mom for as long as possible?"

He nodded.

"Thank you."

He followed her into her kitchen, which was incredibly large. Off to the side was a small, winding staircase that led to the master bedroom, which took up the entire upstairs. It was impeccably decorated with a king-sized bed overlooking the lake and a large, plush sofa next to a sliding glass door.

She pulled open the door to a walk-in closet. "I honestly don't know why I kept this all these years. I've barely even looked at the files or the notebook. I was so disgusted and humiliated by my dad. But every time I went to destroy it or toss it, I worried that it would somehow come back and haunt me or something."

"I can understand that." Cameron stood awkwardly in the middle of her closet as she pulled open a drawer and rummaged around. She glanced over her shoulder with horror emanating from her ice-blue eyes.

"What's wrong?"

"The box. It's not here. Everything of my father's is gone."

8

Cameron couldn't let Vivian rifle through her brother's things for a box filled with their dad's belongings, considering Oliver's place was still a crime scene. But he could certainly do it for her. However, that meant leaving her alone, and he hated that just as much.

She wasn't a fragile young woman. Far from it. But what she was going through wasn't easy and finding out that her brother might have headed down the very path she'd tried to protect him from had to be eating at her conscience.

"Yo. Agent Thatcher. Agent Swanson. There's a Katie Donovan here to see you," the uniformed officer said.

"It's okay. You can let her in." Cameron avoided his partner's glare. Katie wasn't a cop and letting a civilian cross the crime scene line was always a risk. But Katie wasn't just any civilian. She was a licensed private investigator that many local law enforcement agencies utilized. "Just keep looking," Cameron said to Stormi. "Vivian said the notebook had her father's business logo sticker on it, and the external hard drives were cobalt blue. When we searched the place the first time, I only had them take his computer, phone, and tablet. So, if he had them, they have to be here somewhere."

"We still need to find out who this Emma chick is," Stormi said.

"That's where I come in." Katie stepped into the small apartment with her red hair tucked under her New York Jets cap. "I've been following some social media postings about Oliver's death, and I came across this one person who posted a few times." Katie held up a portable tablet. "The screen name they came up with is what struck me." She tapped the screen. "EM_MA123."

"That's interesting. What does she say?"

"Just that he will be missed and what a sweet man he was, and that she was sorry. But here's where it gets odd. I had an IT buddy of mine do some digging, and it appears that all the postings came from this building."

"You've got to be fucking kidding me," Cameron said. "This girl has been right under our noses?"

"Maybe." Katie tucked her tablet back into her purse. "I haven't gone knocking on any doors yet. I wasn't sure if you wanted me to, or if you wanted to do the honors."

"How about we do it together?" He glanced over his shoulder.

Stormi stood in the middle of the kitchen with her hands on her hips. "Seriously? You're going to leave me to do your dirty work?" She smiled. "The things I do for this man."

"Thanks." He stepped out into the hallway. "There are eight apartments in the building."

Katie handed him a piece of paper. "I got the list of tenants. There isn't one listed with an Emma on the directory, but there *is* one with an EM Mendola."

"That's interesting. Where is her statement from the day Oliver died?" He'd had all the tenants' statements sent over to his office the moment this became a murder. Tristan had already checked on their alibis, and nothing stood out as suspicious.

"According to the landlord and Tristan, she wasn't here," Katie said. "She's been at her parents' house for the last two weeks. Her father recently had a heart attack, and she went home to help out."

"Where do her parents live?"

"Syracuse," Katie said. "I had Jackson check, and she was there."

"Okay. Where's her apartment?"

"One floor up. Shall we take the stairs?" Katie waved her hand toward the exit sign. "How is Vivian holding up?"

"She's doing okay, I think." Cameron's heart dropped to the pit of his stomach. When he left Vivian earlier, she'd been talking with her mother and making more plans for Oliver's celebration of life. But he'd heard the tension and strain in her voice. Her eyes pleaded with him to do his best to make sure that her mother never had to hear about the ugly mess Oliver had gotten himself into.

He had to agree that, right now, Eva Ludwig didn't need any more stress in her life. But he couldn't control the media, and as the investigation continued, the news of the sex club—and Oliver's role in it—would come out. He'd warned her that she should tell her mother sooner rather than later.

"I remember when her father died. Everyone was shocked."

Cameron paused at the top of the stairs. "If we find her father's hard drives and notebook in Oliver's apartment, she's going to blame herself."

"She already does," Katie said. "It's going to take time for her to come to terms with the fact that none of this is her fault. That she couldn't have prevented it if she tried. Which she did."

"It's not easy to see that when you're smack dab in the middle of it." Cameron pulled open the door and headed for the apartment in question. "What else do we know about this EM Mendola?"

"Her name is Emma Marie and she's lived here for a year. I didn't do any more digging since I found out you were in the building."

"Her name is what?" He let out a long breath. "I don't need you to repeat it. I heard you the first time." Well, it looked like Cameron might have found the girlfriend. He raised his hand and pounded on the door.

It rattled, and the doorknob twisted.

"May I help you?" a young woman with short brown hair asked. She rested her cheek on the door, leaving it open only about eight inches. Her eyes were bloodshot, and her clothes disheveled.

"I'm Agent Cameron Thatcher, and this is my associate, Katie Donovan. We'd like to speak with you for a moment."

"What about?"

"Did you know Oliver Rose?" Cameron asked, playing it cool.

"Of course, I did. He was my neighbor." She narrowed her stare. "The state police already questioned me the other day, asking me if I'd heard anything the day he…he… Is it true that he was murdered?"

"That's what we're trying to figure out," Cameron said. "The name on the mailbox downstairs is EM. Does the E stand for Emma?"

"My name is Emma Marie. Why?"

"May we come in for a few minutes?" Katie asked.

"Sure." Emma Marie pulled open the door. She wore a pair of sweatpants, rolled down low on her hips, and a cropped tank top that barely came to her belly button, which was pierced.

She had a couple of different tattoos, mostly of dancing girls and trees. Her apartment was scantily decorated with furniture that looked as if it'd come from discount stores. The space had a dorm-like feel to it, and Emma Marie couldn't be more than twenty-one at most.

"Can I get you some water or something?" Emma Marie stood in the middle of her tiny kitchen and waved her hand to her small table with two chairs.

"We're good. We don't want to take up too much of your time," Katie said.

"How well did you know Oliver?" Cameron asked as he scanned the small space. The setup was different from Oliver's place—much more compact. And as Cameron peered into the other room, he realized that her living room was also her bedroom.

"We dated for a little bit," she admitted. "But that ended about two months ago."

"Do you mind me asking why?" Cameron asked.

Emma Marie lowered her head and sniffled. "He cheated on me."

"I'm sorry," Katie said. "That's the worst feeling in the world, and I hate to make it worse by asking with whom, but it might help us find out who killed him."

Emma Marie lifted her gaze. "I don't really know the woman. He was sexting with her, and I saw the messages. My dad was a cheater, and it's not something I'll tolerate." She swiped at her eyes.

"Weren't you just visiting your father?" Cameron asked.

"Just because he cheated on my mom doesn't

mean I'm not willing to go to his bedside when he's down," Emma Marie said. "Besides, I went for my mom. She decided to take him back. Why? I have no idea. I think she's crazy. But I love and support her, so I guess I have to suck it up," she said, real bitterness and rage lacing her words.

"When did you return?" Cameron asked.

"The day Oliver died. I couldn't get into my apartment because the police were here." She shook her head and sniffled. "I thought it was my fault that he harmed himself. We'd had words right before I left for my parents'. I told him I could never forgive him. But then I found out he might have been murdered. Who would do such a thing to him?"

"That's why we're here," Cameron said softly. Textbook training told him that she was the best thing they had to a suspect. "I have to ask. Was anyone with you during your travels?"

She nodded. "A friend of mine went with me. Tina Profit. She works at the Heritage Inn as a hostess in the restaurant."

"We'll need to talk to her," Cameron said.

"She's working tonight. We both are."

"You work there, too?" Cameron arched a brow.

"Tina helped me get the job. Tonight will be my first shift."

Cameron trusted his instincts, and they told him that Emma Marie had nothing to do with what happened to Oliver.

Katie inched closer and set her hand on Emma

Marie's shoulder. "We know this is hard, but can you tell us anything about who Oliver was sexting with?"

"Her name was Annabel. I think they had a history. That's all I know."

The babysitter.

Fucking wonderful.

"I'm sorry to have to do this, but I'm going to need an official statement from you."

Emma Marie nodded.

"Is there anything else you can think of that we should know?" Cameron asked.

"I don't know if this means anything, but he recently begged me to pretend to be his girlfriend at some family event. He said he needed me to do this one favor to get his family off his back. I refused. After that, other than the few times we ran into each other in the halls of this building, he ghosted me. And to be honest, I was fine with that. He'd changed."

"Changed how?" Katie asked.

"When we first started hanging out, he was kind of awkward and sweet. He didn't have much game, you know?"

Cameron laughed. "I can understand that."

Emma Marie looked him up and down and smiled. "When I first moved in here, he would always help me with my groceries and be all shy and shit. It was cute. It took him forever to ask me out. I thought he was the one, but when he didn't want to introduce me to his family right away, I should have seen that as a warning sign."

"What was the reason he gave for that?" Cameron asked.

"He said his sister was overprotective and would ask me a million questions and make it awkward and uncomfortable, and that his mother and stepfather wouldn't be much different. Considering the way his father died, I gave him the benefit of the doubt. Besides, I enjoyed our relationship. But then he got secretive, and I got suspicious, and…I've told you the rest."

"Unfortunately, I'm going to have to make you do it all again, plus look at some pictures for me," Cameron said.

"I'm happy to help."

"My partner is downstairs. I'll send her up in a little while to take your official statement and have you look over some things. If there is anything you think of that might be helpful, please don't hesitate to call me, okay?" He handed her his business card. "I really appreciate your help."

Emma Marie nodded.

Cameron turned on his heels and headed toward the hall. He closed the door behind Katie. "My gut tells me she's being completely honest. What do you think?"

"I agree," Katie said. "But I'll do some checking into her life and see what I can come up with."

"Do you know Annabel Edwards?"

Katie narrowed her stare. "I knew a girl by that name in high school. Well, I knew her brother, who was in my grade. She's a few years younger. Are we talking about the same Annabel that Emma Marie was talking about?"

"I think so." Cameron didn't like where this was going one bit. Sex clubs. Orgies. Deaths by suicide that might be murders. All connected and circling back to Oliver. "Vivian confirmed one of the names on the orgy list as Annabel Edwards, who was one of her babysitters."

"Jesus," Katie mumbled. "That's fucked up."

"Yeah. It is." Cameron ran a hand across the top of his head. "She also confirmed two others on the list. George Wilkins and Heather Hay. They both went to school and camp with Oliver."

"I know the Wilkins family, but I don't think I've ever heard of Heather Hay."

"I spoke with Shannon. She told me that if it turned out to be a murder investigation, I should ask for a warrant for Oliver's mental health records. I have a feeling she knows something she can't tell me."

"That's possible," Katie said. "But Shannon knows how to play the system. If she believes any of her patients are in danger, she'll break patient confidentiality, no problem. She's done it before."

"She's required to by law in those cases."

"But if she didn't know at the time that these were connected, she had nothing to say. We need to help her connect the dots."

Cameron understood where Katie was going with this, and it made sense. Doctors had to protect their patient's privacy, both those living and dead. There were clear-cut laws for when they could break them, and then there were ways to bend them.

"I should have a warrant for those records by lunchtime." He glanced at his watch. "I better go help Stormi. Thanks for your help with this."

"Anytime." Katie turned and headed down the stairs.

Cameron went back to Oliver's apartment and nearly collided with Stormi as she bolted through the front door. "Hey, watch where you're going."

"I was coming to get you," she said, slightly out of breath. "I found the hard drive."

"Shit," he mumbled. He'd been hoping that wouldn't be the case.

"And that's not all." Stormi held up a tablet. "This was in a box in his closet, under a butt load of stuff."

"Didn't the state police search?" Cameron asked.

"They did, and I'm as surprised as you are. Tristan is very thorough."

Cameron scanned the room and glanced over his shoulder toward the hallway. No way did Tristan miss that tablet. "I want to look at the log of everyone who has entered this crime scene."

"You think it was planted?"

"I don't know, but my gut says something is off."

"But that means someone else knew about it, and Vivian swears she never told anyone."

"She didn't have to. There are other people in those videos. They knew."

"Good point," Stormi said.

"Did you turn it on?"

"It's password-protected. We're going to have to get an IT guy up here to check it out. I've already called."

"I want Kidd. He's the best."

"I know. I made the request, and Townsend agreed. Kidd is on his way, and he's bringing all the stuff we seized earlier."

"We need a bigger place. That cabin is only a two-bedroom."

"Townsend is going to call Reese and see if he can do anything for us. You know the Heritage Inn always has an open cottage for the state troopers. I bet we can use that for the IT guys."

"I hope so. I want to stay close to Vivian," Cameron said. "Anything else?"

"Yeah," Stormi said. "I also found a burner phone, and it only has one number on it."

"That's interesting. Did you call it?"

Stormi tilted her head. "Now you're just being funny." She flipped open the cell. "The name associated with the number is Simon."

"Well, I'll be damned."

Vivian stared at the hard drives, the tablet, and a cell phone, mocking her from the table inside a cabin at the Heritage Inn. The air in her lungs suddenly escaped, leaving her gasping for breath. Her chest tightened, making it hard for her heart to pump the necessary blood through her body. Her throat went dry, and she couldn't form words. It was as if she'd been catapulted back to the day when her innocence had been stripped. All her well-crafted defenses had been shaken to the core, and she'd been forced to face everything she'd spent a lifetime keeping locked in a safe that she believed no one had the key to.

"I know this is an awkward question, but did you recognize anyone in those videos when you saw them?" Cameron asked.

She closed her eyes and inhaled sharply. The memory of her father touching himself as he watched himself with two woman was something she'd tried to forget. Yet it played in her brain like a horror show, and she couldn't stop it if she tried. She blinked. "No. I'm sorry," she whispered.

Oliver knew her father's dirty past. She'd failed to protect her baby brother from her family's secret legacy.

And now, he was gone, too.

But why? Who would want to kill him?

It made no sense.

"Are you sure this Emma Marie doesn't have something to do with Oliver's murder?" she asked, suddenly aware that she was in a room filled with federal agents. She hugged herself.

"She wasn't in the area at the time of the murder.

We have no reason to suspect her at this time," Cameron said in his most professional voice, which right now, grated on her last nerve.

She understood that he couldn't wrap his strong arms around her body, kiss her temple, and ease some of the pain that tortured her soul while around his colleagues. But what she couldn't comprehend was why she needed him so badly. It wasn't like her to want help from any man. She'd always been fiercely independent, never wanting to rely on a male for anything.

Ever.

"How do you know she's not involved in this sex club thing?" Vivian asked.

"We don't know that for sure." Cameron held up a piece of paper. "But she wasn't at either of these two parties, and other than being in your brother's contacts, we don't see any mention of her in reference to the orgies, and no one we've interviewed knows her."

"How many have you interviewed?" she asked.

"Not enough," Cameron admitted.

Vivian wrapped her arms around herself tighter and shivered.

Cameron inched closer and pressed his hand to the small of her back, his thumb rubbing gently. It was the human contact she needed.

She closed her eyes for a long moment and breathed deeply.

"I'm going to catch the person who killed your

brother. But in order to do it, we need to investigate what Oliver was doing, and that might not be pretty," Cameron said. "Do you have any idea what he might have used as a password on this tablet?"

"You have his regular computer. I bet he has a password spreadsheet on it somewhere. He was always doing stuff like that." Vivian's throat felt like someone had rubbed sandpaper across it. "He was organized that way."

"We've searched all his documents for something like that and haven't found it," a man by the name of Kidd said.

She suspected that it was either a nickname or his last name, and considering that he had gray hair and deep wrinkles around his eyes and lips, she figured it was the latter.

"You can try *Matilda*," she said. "He loved that movie when we were little. Or maybe *Mulan*."

Kidd tapped at the keyboard. He glanced up and shook his head.

"Why not *Simon Says*?" Stormi planted her hands on her hips.

"Try it." Cameron nodded.

Vivian held her breath. She still hadn't processed half of what Cameron had told her when he returned much earlier than expected.

"I'm in," Kidd said.

Vivian turned.

"You don't need to be here." Cameron took her

by the biceps. “I’ll walk you home. Or maybe drive you to your mother’s house? Or Lilly’s?”

“No. I need to know what my brother was doing and why.” She knew why. Her brother had wanted to understand his father. He’d been so close to him when they were growing up and losing their dad at such a young age had done a number on him in ways that Vivian hadn’t comprehended until it was too late.

And how could she have known? She’d only been fourteen herself. When her mother told her not to tell anyone about what she’d seen her father do, she had no problem agreeing to that request. So, when she found the hard drive, it’d made sense for her to bury it.

Only, she hadn’t been able to bring herself to destroy it.

That decision had led her brother into the very fire she’d been trying to save him from.

“It’s a journal,” Kidd said. “It goes back about eight months, and it’s written in French.”

“Do you know French? Because I don’t,” Cameron said, letting out a long breath.

Vivian turned and leaned over Kidd’s shoulder. She’d never been much interested in learning a second language in high school, but her brother relished it. Something she thought strange, considering he was a techno-geek and preferred his gadgets to people.

But since he could speak tech talk, it shouldn’t

have surprised her that he'd picked up a foreign language so easily.

"I don't," Kidd said. "But I know someone in our office who does. I'll send the files to them. It's going to take a while to translate everything. Anything specific you want me to have them do a quick search for?"

"Yeah." Cameron strolled to the other side of the room and rummaged through some files on the table. He handed over a couple of sheets of paper. "These names and terms. I want them flagged in the translation regardless."

"Is there anything else on this tablet?" Stormi asked.

"Not that I can tell," Kidd said. "But I'll poke around while I work on recovering those deleted files and emails."

"Thanks. I appreciate it." Cameron looped his arm around her waist. "Let me walk you home."

"That's it? That's all you needed me for?" Her eyes filled with tears. "Let me stay. I can help."

"There's nothing here for you to do," Kidd said. "If there's something we don't understand and think you might, we'll call you."

"He's right." Cameron nudged her closer to the door. "Let him do his thing." He opened the door, and the warm summer air coated her skin like a thick, heavy downpour. "I bet you haven't had anything to eat since breakfast, and it's pushing five in the evening. Why don't you let me order us some dinner?"

"Are you going to stay? Or do you have to run out

again?" She hadn't meant to sound so clingy. The last thing she wanted was to keep him from doing his job. She didn't need a babysitter. She needed him out there looking for whoever had ended her brother's life.

More importantly, she needed to know why.

"I'm sorry," she said softly as she walked across the yard toward her home. "I didn't mean to imply that you owed me anything."

"No. It's okay. This is a difficult time for you and your family right now, and I know you're trying to take the brunt of it for your mom. I commend that, but these investigations take time, and this one has a lot of moving parts."

Vivian could only imagine; however, it didn't make her feel any better. She wanted answers, and she wanted them now. She felt helpless and out of control.

"I want to help."

"You are." Cameron hopped in front of her and pulled open the gate to her property. "Just by being open and honest about everything. That and your willingness to answer our questions whenever we have them. You'd be surprised how many family members we have to chase down in cases like these."

"I want you to catch this bastard." She unlocked the deck door and immediately went for the wine cooler. She held up a bottle.

He glanced at his watch. "I'll have a glass."

"Are you calling it a day?" She blew out a puff of air. "Shit. I sound like a bitch."

He took the wine from her hand and set it on the counter. "No. You don't."

"I tell you I want you to go out there and do something, yet I want you to stay here with me at the same time. It's not fair."

He took her chin between his thumb and forefinger, tilting her head slightly. "Nothing about this is fair, and I want you to know that I'm here for you, one hundred percent."

"You can't be in two places at once."

"I have a team, and my boss has allowed me to move all the resources we need to this location. I'm going to need you to answer questions as they arise. And while I want to solve this, I can't go twenty-four-seven. I must eat, and I have to sleep. So, right now, I say we order some food and talk through some things that pertain to the case. Then, I will go chat with my team and see what else needs to be done before I catch an hour or two."

She palmed his cheek. "You need more than a couple of hours of sleep."

"I'm good if I get three or four." He took her hand and kissed the backside of it. "Now, how about we order a couple of fish fries from the Boardwalk and enjoy a glass of wine out on the deck while we watch the sunset?"

She laughed. "We face the east. Not the west."

"My bad." He pulled down two glasses and poured the wine. "Come on. Let's do our best to at least enjoy the nice weather."

"Will you tell me about Emma Marie?" She took the stemless glass and made her way out to the deck. She sat in one of the chairs facing the lake.

Cameron fiddled with his phone. "I placed our order. It will be here in thirty." He set his cell on the table before taking her feet and lifting them to his lap. He removed her shoes and began rubbing her feet.

She'd momentarily died and gone to heaven.

Of course, she should tell him to stop. This was highly inappropriate. But hell. She didn't give a shit. Not anymore.

"What do you want to know?"

"Was she nice? Did she seem like she cared about my brother?" Vivian swallowed. For the longest time, she'd resented this Emma Marie girl. Mostly because she thought Oliver's girlfriend either didn't want to meet the family, or Oliver didn't want to bring her around. Both equally disturbing for different reasons. Vivian couldn't respect any woman who wouldn't want to meet Oliver's family. And she sure as shit couldn't comprehend why Oliver wouldn't want to keep any girlfriend he cared about from meeting his sister, who was his biggest fan.

"She was pretty shaken up and genuinely upset by what had happened, but she's being very cooperative with us."

"Do you believe everything she said?"

"I do." Cameron reached for his wine and brought the glass to his lips.

She glanced out over the water. Living on the lake

had been a dream come true for Vivian. Never in a million years had she thought she'd be able to afford a house on the water. But thanks to doing some serious saving and the fact that no one wanted to live next to the Heritage Inn, her fantasy had come true. "You know, Annabel lives in Bolton Landing with her husband and one-year-old."

"That's all sorts of fucked up."

"She was always prim and proper. She still comes off that way. I can't believe she'd be sexting with Oliver, much less involved in any sex club."

"If her husband isn't aware of what she's doing, then I'm sure she puts on a good face."

"My father certainly knew how to do that." She stared at a fishing boat floating close to her dock. The man in the boat worked with a young boy, teaching him how to cast. She shifted her gaze to the swimming area of the Heritage Inn. Young children were playing Marco Polo in the roped-off area while a couple of teenagers back-flipped off the float as the parents enjoyed an evening cocktail on the Adirondack chairs.

This was one of the reasons she'd been able to afford this house. No one wanted to live next to a hotel.

Of course, she wouldn't be around much this summer, spending most of her days and nights at the camp. Her heart tightened, remembering all her days off last year and how she'd spent them with Oliver.

"Vivian? Are you home?" a familiar male voice startled her, and she sloshed her wine into her lap.

"Shit," she mumbled, swiping at the wetness seeping into her dress.

Cameron reached over and did the same thing.

She dropped her hand to the side. "Who's there?" she called.

"It's Thor. I've been trying to reach you all day." He stepped onto the deck and leaned against the side of the house. "Oh. I see you have company."

Cameron pushed back his chair and stretched out his arm. "Hello, Thor. Not to be rude, but do you always show up places unannounced?" He shrugged off his sport coat, exposing his weapon. Carefully, he folded his jacket and placed it on the back of the chair.

Vivian pulled a piece of hair from her ponytail and twisted it between her fingers. Not only would she have to tell Thor to stop coming over without permission, but she needed to have a long chat with Cameron about behaving like a macho man. It drove her crazy. Although, she hated to admit it, Thor probably needed more of a push than she could muster up.

"I get you two are a thing," Thor said with some sass to his tone. "But Vivian and I have been friends for a long time. And I was friendly with her brother. I'm only trying to be neighborly and offer my support."

Not really, but Thor *was* harmless, and he did have a big heart. Sort of.

Thor had the nerve to step around Cameron, and then pressed his hand on her shoulder and squeezed. "I couldn't believe it when I heard the news. A murder? Who would want to harm Oliver? And what are the police doing about it?" He glanced over his shoulder. "Shouldn't you be out there looking for the killer? Aren't you a federal agent?" he asked with a heavy dose of sarcasm.

Cameron smiled. It looked like a genuine one. As if he'd taken that as a compliment.

God. Men sometimes.

Cameron tugged at his pant legs and then sat back down in the chair. He leaned back as if he didn't have a care in the world. "We are doing everything we can to find out who killed Oliver."

"Right now, it looks like you're enjoying a glass of wine and a beautiful view," Thor said with his hand still on her body.

She should shrug it off. But she seemed frozen in some weird vat of manly testosterone and she couldn't shake it. She rolled her tongue around in her mouth, hoping to rid herself of the raw dryness that tasted like sand so she could speak and stop this madness.

"Actually, Thor, I'm not. I don't owe you an explanation, but I can tell by the look on Vivian's face that she's not happy with either of us right now. So, I'm going to try to dial this down."

"What the hell does that mean?" Thor asked.

"There is nothing enjoyable about the conversation I was having just now, which had to do with Oliver and the case. I'm constantly working, and after I eat my dinner, which I'm allowed to do, I will be out there, searching for answers." Cameron lifted his cell. "If you will excuse me, I need to take this call. It happens to be about the case." He stood and stormed off into her kitchen.

"He's a moody one." Thor adjusted the chair and planted his butt in it. He leaned forward and took her hands.

She glanced down at their entangled fingers. She cleared her throat as she pulled away.

"How are you holding up?" Thor asked.

That was the worst question on the planet, and she had no answer for it.

"You can't keep showing up here," she said under her breath. "You need to call me first and give me a chance to respond."

"I'm worried about you. I tried calling and texting, but you didn't answer."

"I'm not answering anyone right now. Not unless it has to do with the celebration of life or finding out who did this. I'm sorry, but I just don't have the energy for visitors." She wanted to push her chair back farther. Thor wasn't a bad guy, and even after that awkward kiss, he hadn't come on this strong before. Of course, she'd never known Thor liked her that much because he'd acted as if her rejection wasn't that big of a deal.

So, what the hell was going on now?

"You need to rely on your friends right now. And you shouldn't be in this house all alone. I'm sure that's what's happening when he's not here."

"I'm with my mom and Larry most of the daytime hours." Why the hell was she explaining herself to Thor?

"Let me help with the planning of the celebration of life. I have pictures from when Oliver was my camper. I can help coordinate and do the things that you and your mom don't want to do. Please. I know what a big undertaking this is and how painful it can be, especially when you don't have closure."

She had a horrible feeling that if she didn't let Thor do something, he'd never go away. But she didn't want him at her house or at her mom's. "Maybe you could get everyone who knew Oliver from camp to pool all their pictures and short videos together and make a camp video to honor him. I know my mom would like that."

"I'd be honored. I'll send out an email, and when I'm done, I'll bring it by," Thor said.

She shook her head. "Just email it. My mom really isn't up for any visitors, and I don't think it's a good idea for you to come here unannounced."

"I'll call first. That way, you and that jealous, hotheaded boyfriend of yours will know I'm coming." Thor stood. "I'll be in touch."

She opened her mouth, but before she could

respond, Thor had disappeared around the side of the house. She reached for her wine and gulped.

Men.

And their chest-pounding.

The sliding glass door opened.

"Where'd Thor go?" Cameron asked.

"I gave him a project so he'd leave me alone," she admitted.

"I'm not sure I like the sound of that. He really likes you." Cameron curled his fingers around the back of his chair. "I'm sure he'd like it if I were to get shot in the line of duty."

"Don't even joke about something like that." She narrowed her stare. "It's not funny."

"Sorry," he said. "I won't do it again."

"Good. Now, tell me why you look like you've got some bad news and don't want to tell me."

"You're a smart woman." He waggled his finger. "I have to go, so when our dinner comes, can you put mine in the fridge? I'll come collect it and heat it up later."

"Sure, but what's going on?"

"Kidd and Stormi found a list of people on your brother's main computer that they believe are involved in this sex club. I'm going to go interview a couple of them."

"Who?"

He smoothed down his tie. "I can't get into that right now." He lifted his sport coat off the back of the chair. "Are you going to be okay?"

"I was thinking I could do some searches on the computer."

Cameron leaned closer. "What kind of searches?"

"My brother's social media. He was really into posting, but I noticed some changes in the last couple of months, and I thought it odd that he never posted pictures of him and Emma Marie. I find it even odder that he only called her Emma."

"Stay away from the internet," Cameron said. "It's a dark and dangerous place, especially if you're going to go hunting for things your brother ended up in."

"But maybe I can find something. I knew my brother better than anyone."

Cameron arched a brow. "Actually, you didn't. Because you didn't know what he was doing."

She tapped the center of her chest. "Ouch, that hurt."

"That wasn't my intent. I just don't want you poking around and landing yourself in some twisted world. I have a team of people doing just that. If they need intel from you, they will either call, text, or walk across the yard, okay?"

"Fine," she mumbled. "But I feel so helpless and out of control. I need to do something."

"Why don't you call a friend or something?"

"Yeah. Lilly texted me a little bit ago. Maybe she can come over."

"That's a good idea. I shouldn't be too long. I'll stay in touch." He leaned over and pressed his lips firmly against hers in a promissory kiss. His fingers curled around the back of her neck, and he massaged gently. "Don't hesitate to call me if you need to. I'll do my best to get back to you as soon as I can."

"Thanks." She fiddled with her phone as she watched him jog down the steps and stroll through the gate toward the Heritage Inn. Tapping the screen, she cringed at all the texts and voice messages from Thor.

Five texts and two messages, to be exact.

That was certainly excessive.

She read the texts, which were kind, simply asking if she was okay or if she needed anything and saying that she could call him day or night.

She opted not to listen to the voice messages, assuming it would be more of the same.

"Hey, Siri, call Lilly."

"Calling Lilly, home."

Vivian laughed. She'd never changed it to mobile, and no one had landlines anymore.

"Hey, girl. What's up? Are you okay?"

"No. I'm not. And I'm not sure I'll be okay again," she said between sniffles. If there was anyone she could be real with, it was Lilly.

"Aw. Sweetie. Do the cops have any new leads?"

"Cameron just left to go interview some people that might have been involved in this sex ring. I can't believe this." Part of Vivian wanted to break down and tell Lilly. Not because it was possible that it would get out about her father. But because the only people she had to talk to about it right now were her mother and Cameron.

Her mom didn't know everything, and that made it difficult. And while Cameron knew everything, and she felt amazingly close to him, a part of her still held back.

"I know. It's crazy. I don't understand how Oliver got involved with something like that. No offense, but I find it so gross."

Vivian shivered. She'd been physically sick when she saw what her father had been doing with those two women. Of course, she'd only been a child at the time, and it was her dad. The man she looked up to and admired most. And she barely even knew what sex was, so to see that had been insanely traumatizing.

"Oh, God. Vivian. I'm sorry. I know that's your baby brother we're talking about," Lilly said.

"No. Don't worry about it. I don't understand it either," Vivian said. "Hey. Can you come over for a little while? I know it's dinnertime, and Ethan loves to have his time with you, but—"

"Ethan's working late on some project. Give me ten minutes to freshen up, and I'll head right over."

"Perfect. I'll see you then." Thank God Lilly didn't expect Vivian to rush over to her big house they'd just recently remodeled over on Assembly Point. The last thing Vivian wanted to hear about was all the horrible things Lilly had to put up with, like when they had to wait an extra two weeks for their custom cabinets to be done. Or the fact that the couch she really wanted didn't come in the leather she wanted and she had to buy a different one that cost five thousand dollars more.

Vivian's entire family room and bedroom sets didn't come to that much combined.

She loved Lilly, but since she married Mr. Moneybags, she's started taking after him with his privileged attitude.

Not that Vivian ever wanted for anything. Even after her father's death, her mother always managed to provide her with more than she needed.

She collected the glasses and the wine and headed inside. Pausing by the sink, she set everything down and gasped as she stared at Ethan's car pulling into the Heritage Inn.

No. It can't be.

She blinked. Twice. And by the time she opened her eyes, the car was hidden behind the trees.

Lots of people drove Range Rovers. She'd seen two of them the other day in the hotel's main parking lot.

Her cell buzzed. She pulled it from her dress pocket and smiled.

Cameron: *Do you have an air fryer?*

Vivian: *Yes. Why?*

Cameron: *I was going to buy one if you didn't because my fish and fries would taste like shit if I had to microwave them. I'll see you in a couple of hours.*

Visions of seeing all of him danced in her head. Her heart nearly jumped right out of her chest. She should not be having thoughts of him naked between her sheets. She feared she'd only be using him and that wouldn't be fair. Her fingers hovered over the screen as her pulse beat wildly.

Vivian: *I don't want to be alone tonight.*

She couldn't believe she hit send. She stared at the screen for what seemed like an entirety.

No response.

No bubbles.

Fuck.

She shouldn't have said anything.

It buzzed.

She dropped it to the floor. "Shit." She bent over and lifted it into her trembling hand and gasped.

Cameron: *You won't be. I'll be with you.*

9

Cameron didn't like interviewing Ethan at the Heritage Inn. Not only did he worry that Vivian would see him, but he had no idea if Lilly knew what her husband had been up to.

Thankfully, Reese had a second cabin that Cameron and his team could use. That way, he had all his research, his board, and Kidd and the rest of the tech team could work without interruption.

"Relax," Stormi said as she pressed her hand on his shoulder. "I've never seen you so nervous before."

"I'm not nervous."

"Then why the hell are you pacing?"

Cameron had met Ethan a few times. He was a snot-nosed, spoiled, rich man used to getting his way, but he wasn't a bad guy. At least, from what Cameron had seen. "This list that Kidd pulled off Oliver's computer. It was in a file titled: *Chat.* Nothing about sex clubs."

"The name *Simon Says* was on that list, as well as two people who were in the orgy from a year ago, and one from the orgy that Oliver participated in. Kidd also found some videos on the website with others on the list." Stormi held up the list, which had forty-two names. Some were screen names, and some of those names were matched to actual ones. "You're really stuck on this Simon guy. Why?"

"It was the tone of the email he sent to Oliver. And the idea that it was some kind of game with consequences. And now Oliver is dead."

"I know, but we haven't been able to find more emails or any other connection." Stormi took three strides to the table. She lifted a folder. "Right now, we have at least a dozen suspects, but not one single motive."

Cameron let out an exasperated sigh. So far, they'd interviewed two people from the sex parties, and they both liked Oliver. Neither seemed to hold a grudge or had a bad thing to say about Vivian's brother or knew of any disagreements or arguments he'd had with anyone else in the groups.

However, they were also close-lipped about how the group worked, basically saying that that it wasn't a club. That they didn't meet regularly, and that they had no idea that anyone had posted a video to a website.

Cameron found that hard to believe.

"Oliver didn't owe money to anyone. It doesn't appear he had any enemies," Stormi said.

"That we know of." Cameron took the list and scanned the names. He knew a few of the people and was shocked they had participated. He didn't judge, he was simply surprised. "There has to be a reason he wrote the journal in French."

"Agreed." Stormi pointed to the door. "He's here."

Cameron glanced at the big picture window just as a black Range Rover rolled to a stop in front of the cabin. He admired Ethan's taste in vehicles. Hell, he admired Ethan's taste in most things. The man had a thirst for the finer things in life, and he could afford them.

Good for him.

Cameron just didn't like how he made decisions for those around him as if he knew what everyone wanted or desired. He pulled open the door before Ethan had a chance to knock. "Thanks for coming."

"You really didn't give me much choice." Ethan crossed the threshold. Before closing the door, he stuck his head out and glanced around. Probably making sure Vivian wasn't lurking in the shadows. "I don't understand how I can help you."

"Why don't you take a seat?" Stormi waved to the sofa in the main room.

"Why do I get the feeling I'm about to be interrogated?" Ethan sat on the edge of the couch.

Stormi perched on the other side, and Cameron chose the chair across from them.

"Should I be calling my lawyer?" Ethan asked.

"This is an informal interview," Cameron said. "We're trying to gather information on a sex club that Oliver was involved in."

"And what makes you think I know anything about it?" Ethan always had a coolness to his tone, but right now, there was a slight tremble in his voice that told Cameron the man was frightened.

Cameron pushed a piece of paper across the coffee table. "Your name is on this list."

Ethan picked up the paper, and his eyes went wide. "What is this?"

"You tell us," Stormi said.

"I have no idea." Ethan set the sheet down. "I'm not sure I like what you're implying."

"We don't care what you're into," Cameron said, tapping his finger on the paper. "We know some of the people on this list were involved in the orgies with Oliver. Now, what we don't know is who all the players are because some appear to be just screen names."

"Do you all meet in some kind of chat room before you hook up? Is that how this sex club works?" Stormi asked. "And what do you know about a guy who calls himself Simon Says?"

"I really have no idea what you're talking about." Ethan uncrossed and recrossed his legs.

"Your screen name isn't *TheWineGuy*?" Cameron asked. "Kind of fitting since you love wine."

"If I were to give myself any kind of nickname anywhere, it'd have to do with cars." Ethan folded his arms across his chest and glared. "That's not me. Where did you get that list, and why would someone think that's me?"

Cameron opened his mouth, but Kidd busted through the door. "I've got something," Kidd said.

"I'll be right back." Cameron stood and quickly made his way outside. "What's going on?"

"The translator is still working on the journal, which is incredibly long, but we have something interesting from it." Kidd swayed back and forth like he had ants in his pants.

"Well, go on. Don't make me extract it from you like you're a witness or something."

Kidd laughed. "So, Oliver wrote in his journal that he was going to put a stop to things and that Simon and his Simon Says game could go fuck himself."

"That's interesting."

"Oh. It gets better," Kidd said.

"He purposely let his girlfriend catch him sexting because he didn't want her to be caught up while he set a trap for this Simon guy."

"What was the trap?"

"To lure him out of hiding. To make him show his true identity by not breaking the rules of the game. But Oliver doesn't go into detail about what the game was or any of the rules. However, he did mention the two people who died by suicide."

"Jesus. What did he say about them?"

"That Simon made them do it."

Cameron's breath caught in his throat. "We need to find out who this Simon character is and what control he has over these people. Does Oliver mention his own screen name? Or any of the chat sites?"

"We believe Oliver's name is *Olidude*, but he doesn't mention the adult sites. However, we're searching them now. It shouldn't be too hard to find."

"One more thing," Cameron said. "Does he mention anything about TheWineGuy?"

"Yeah. But he mentions a few on that list that he knows personally and how he wants to protect them. Not just from Simon Says but from themselves."

"He used the word *protect*?"

Kidd nodded.

"Does he mention his father anywhere in the journals?"

"Not that we've found."

"Do a search for that," Cameron said. "I'd better get back in there." He turned on his heels and waltzed back into the cabin. "All right," he started. "I'm done beating around the bush. We know that Oliver knew that you were TheWineGuy in these chat rooms. I need you to give me the URLs to any sites you used. I need you to give me the real names of any of the screen names that I don't already have. I also need to know who's involved in the sex club. The rules. Where you meet, and how often. And, finally, I need to know who the hell this Simon Says guy is, and I'm not going to listen to you sit here and lie to me. Oliver was murdered. And we have reason to believe that two other people are dead because of someone in this group."

Ethan lowered his gaze and clasped his hands. He cracked his knuckles one by one. "I've never been to an orgy or had sex outside of my marriage." His words were slow and deliberate, and he didn't sound like the self-absorbed, confident man that Cameron had come to know. "I will admit to logging into some adult websites. Watching porn and chatting with some people. But I've never met any of these people in person."

"But you know some of them?" Cameron pushed the paper in front of Ethan.

"I avoided anyone I believed was from the area or that I thought I knew—for obvious reasons. When I chatted with someone, I always told them I was from somewhere else, changed my age, my background, my history."

"I don't give a shit about that." Cameron sat on the edge of the seat and leaned forward, tapping his finger on the paper again. "Tell me what you know about Oliver and Simon Says."

"I know very little." Ethan squeezed his eyes closed. A tear managed to escape from under his lashes before he blinked. He stood, turning his back. "I started in these chat rooms when I was sixteen. Out of boredom. I've had various screen names over the years. I've tried to stop, and there have been times where I have. Actually, last year, when Melony Hati's murder was loaded to the dark web, I swore I'd never go back."

"And did you stay away?" Stormi asked.

Ethan turned; his face contorted with shame. "Lilly went away on a girls' weekend about two months later. I told myself it would be just one night. I tried to convince myself that I only wanted to see what people were saying about Melony's death."

"Did you chat with Melony?"

Ethan nodded. "Her screen name was Audi. I liked it because of the car. And, back then, my screen name was TheRover."

Cameron snatched up the list and, sure enough, there was someone named TheRover, but no name next to it.

"She lied to me about who she was, and I did the same to her, but then we did a crazy thing and exchanged pictures. Real ones. We were both freaked out, but then we thought it was kind of cool because we knew we'd never hurt each other."

"She lived in the area," Cameron said. "And you never hooked up?"

"No. We talked about it, but then she started to get weird. She started daring me to do things. Things I wasn't comfortable doing. That's when this Simon Says guy reached out to me and told me that I'd better play along. Or else."

"He used those words?" Cameron asked.

Ethan nodded.

"What did you do?"

"I stopped going to the chat room. A month later, Melony was dead." Ethan ran a hand over his freshly shaven face. "It's not my fault she was murdered. I didn't do anything wrong."

Cameron could agree that he wasn't the reason Melony had been killed, and he shouldn't judge, but it was hard not to when his wife was next door with Vivian. "But you went back to the chat room."

"Yes. I did. And for a while, it was cathartic."

"What is that supposed to mean?" Stormi asked.

Ethan strolled to the picture window, which had the curtains drawn. He lifted the fabric slightly. "I grieved with others that knew her. Of course, this was under a new screen name. They told me about a second woman who had been murdered. One that I didn't know. There was no sex talk this time until I met someone by the name of *SweetGirlJane*. I'm ashamed to admit it, but I really cared about her. We would talk for hours, and not just dirty talk about things my wife would never do, but real things. I could tell her anything, and there was no judgment."

"How long did you talk to her for?" Cameron asked as he scanned the sheet for that name but never found it.

"Maybe three months."

"What happened."

"She told me she'd met someone else. Someone more exciting. Someone willing to play the kinds of games I didn't want to."

"Had she asked you to do things you weren't comfortable with?" Stormi asked.

"Not at first," Ethan said. "But I'd been doing the chat room sexting thing for a while, and that's how it goes. It's one of the reasons I made myself stop."

"What do you mean?" Cameron asked.

"The more you do it, the more you push your boundaries. The more exciting it becomes, the more willing you are to do those things you swore you wouldn't do. Like sending pictures, or meeting in person. She started pushing me to do videos and to meet. I wasn't willing to do those things. So, she would get mad and disappear. I knew it was time, but it's so hard. It's addicting."

"How did you and Oliver know about each other?"

"We were both talking to *SweetGirlJane*," Ethan said. "She mentioned that someone by the name of Olidude was willing to play the games that I wasn't. I didn't know it was Oliver at first."

"How'd you make the connection?" Cameron asked.

"I logged on one night and started a conversation with him. I figured it out after a couple of weeks."

"You talked to him for that long?" Cameron's stomach soured. He didn't want to think about what those two were chatting about.

"I was worried about my friend and what she might have gotten herself into, and as it turned out, so was Oliver. One night, while we were all over at

Vivian's, he said something that made me wonder if Oli was him. So, I said something that only he would catch. I logged on that night, and he brought it up. He told me he didn't want to talk about it in the chat room. I logged off, and he called me. Told me he wanted to meet me the next day to talk about it. He said he was worried for the girl's safety—and, frankly, mine. I thought he was over-the-top. The next day, he was dead."

"Jesus, and you didn't think to come to me?" Cameron bolted to a standing position. He raced across the room and got right in Ethan's face. "Your wife's best friend's little brother was murdered, and you didn't think this was important enough to bring to my attention?"

Ethan let out a dry laugh that sounded more like a dying pig. "And you don't think I hate myself right now? If Lilly were to ever find out, she'd leave me. And, frankly, I wouldn't blame her."

"You should be more concerned about being arrested for obstruction of justice," Cameron mumbled. "I'm going to need an official statement, and I'm going to need you to look over names, images, dates."

Ethan swiped at his eyes. "I'll do whatever you need. But I need you to let me be the one to tell my wife."

"She's at Vivian's right now. No time like the present." Cameron rubbed the back of his neck. "Before we wrap this up, do you have theories about who this Simon Says guy is or what his game is all about?"

"I have no idea who he is, but he's all about pushing boundaries and daring people to do things. It's almost like a game of tag mixed with Simon Says. He's a master manipulator and predator, which… there are a lot of in those chat rooms. Like I said, it's addicting, and you don't even realize how bad it's become until it's too late. Simon's the kind of guy that preys on your weaknesses. He will be your best friend. Your confidant. He will act as though he'll go to the ends of the Earth for you, and then he'll turn on you. For him, it's not about having a little fun and getting your rocks off."

"Is that what it was—never mind," Cameron mumbled. He really didn't want to know. "Stormi can take your statement. I'd prefer that we do this now rather than later."

"I'd appreciate it if you didn't say anything to Vivian and let me deal with my wife."

"I won't say anything to Lilly because I have no reason to, but I can't make that same promise when it comes to Vivian. This is an active case, and your involvement and knowledge could be helpful in more ways than one." Cameron stood by the front door, turning his attention to Stormi. "I'm going to see if Kidd and his team were able to come up with anything else. Call me when you're done with his statement." He stepped outside and pulled out his cell, bringing up Jacob's contact information. Cameron couldn't believe the recent turn of events.

Or how it had brought up so many different, seemingly unrelated case files.

Jacob answered on the third ring.

"Hey. What's up?" Jacob asked.

"I've got some information that you might be interested in."

"What's that?"

"Those two deaths by suicide that I was looking at as possible homicides because of Oliver? Well, there's been an interesting twist, and we might have some twisted bastard talking people into taking their lives on the internet. Does that sound familiar to you?"

"No fucking way," Jacob mumbled. "What was that woman's name? She was absolutely positive that someone had told her sister to take her own life, but the only evidence she had was her sister's journal, and we could never prove anything or make any kind of connection. It was ruled death by suicide. Our hands were tied, no matter how much we thought it was a bit fishy."

"Her name was Babs Dillard. That was literally my first week on the job, and we turned her away."

"We had no choice. There was no case," Jacob said. "There wasn't even a crime—that we knew of."

"My gut said otherwise."

"So did mine," Jacob said. "All my notes on her interview should be in the archives. You should have no problem accessing them."

"Looks like I need to go find her and have a little chat." This case was getting weirder and weirder. But, finally, Cameron had some leads. Now, all he had to do was pull it all together.

Before someone else died.

10

Vivian wasn't much for hard liquor, but sometimes life required a little buzz, and tonight was one of those nights. She lifted the shot glass to her lips and downed the harsh liquid. She swallowed, trying not to gag. "I don't know how you drink this shit all the time." She coughed. "I don't know how my baby brother made this his drink of choice."

Lilly laughed. "I don't know how you don't." She raised the bottle of tequila.

"One more." But this time, Vivian would sip, or she'd never make it up the yard and into her house. She set the glass on the table and stared at the moonlight dancing across the lake. A boat hummed along the shoreline, sending its waves crashing into the breakwall. The entire evening had been all about Vivian and Oliver and the murder.

However, Vivian could tell that something was

eating at her best friend and had been for the last few weeks. Every single time they'd gotten together, Lilly had put on her best smile and kept all topics of conversation away from anything having to do with her life—unless it was superficial, like what color to paint the living room, or if she should buy a new car, even though hers was only two years old.

Vivian hadn't pushed because either Ethan was always around, or she'd been hyper-focused on Oliver.

But now that they both had a few drinks under their belts, it was time to find out what the hell was going on with Lilly.

Vivian adjusted her chair so she could see her best friend's eyes. "I sense some sadness with you. What's going on?"

"I've just been so worried about you, and now that Oliver's death was—"

"No. You've canceled a dozen times on our lunches or girls' night in the last six months. The only time I see you is if it's with Ethan. And if I do see you alone by chance, we never talk about anything real unless it has to do with me." She lifted her glass and took a tiny sip. "I'm not going to let you leave here tonight until you tell me what's going on with you."

Lilly tossed her head back, downing a shot. She poured a second one and did the same thing. "You're going to have to schedule me an Uber, or I'm sleeping here."

"Either can be arranged," Vivian said. "But you've got to stop stalling."

Lilly blew out a puff of air. "I haven't voiced this out loud to anyone. I've barely allowed myself to even think it. But I can't ignore it anymore."

"Ignore what?"

"I think Ethan is cheating on me."

"Excuse me?" Vivian bolted upright in her seat. She gripped the sides and leaned forward. "Why do you think that?" Ethan was a lot of things, but he'd always been such an attentive boyfriend and husband. Whenever Lilly needed him, he was there. Or at least that's how it looked.

"It's not the first time I've wondered if he's seeing someone." Lilly dropped her head back and gazed into the sky. "It's been on and off for our entire relationship."

"What?" Vivian's stomach turned over as if it had filled with sour milk. She glanced over her shoulder, wondering if that Range Rover was still in the Heritage Inn parking lot, and if Ethan would have been so bold as to meet someone there, knowing that Vivian was right next door. "I'm sorry, but I find it hard to believe that Ethan's the type of guy who'd cheat."

"I know. He's so good to me. He's kind. Considerate. He treats me like a princess, but there are periods of time where he becomes secretive and withdrawn. I wake up in the middle of the night, and he's not there."

"Where is he?"

"In his office, but the door's shut, which is so unlike him."

"Did you go in to see what he was doing?" Vivian asked.

"No. I was too frightened. But one night, I woke up and texted him, asking him where he was. He responded immediately and said he couldn't sleep and didn't want to wake me, so he was in his office watching television."

"That makes sense."

"Except, other nights when that's happened, I've found him in the guest room." Lilly turned her head. "There are times he doesn't care if I have his cell phone and then months when he gets weird about it."

"Have you confronted him?"

"No," Lilly admitted. "As soon as I get up the nerve, he does something to make me feel so special that I think I'm crazy. He's a good man, and he provides a great life for us, and we're trying to have a baby." Lilly let out a long breath. "Saying this to another person, I realize I'm being an idiot. I think I'm just bored and looking for trouble. My mom told me that quitting my job would be hard. She suggested I wait until I was either pregnant or even until a baby was born, but I didn't listen."

Vivian scooted her chair closer and took her friend's hand. "Look at me, sweetie." She couldn't picture Ethan being a cheater. Then again, she'd never imagined her father, her hero, betraying his family either. Nor would she have ever expected her baby brother to be involved in an orgy. She couldn't even begin to understand her father or his actions, especially when she was a child. And now, her brother had made similar choices. However, as an adult, she had to come to terms with the fact that she loved her brother unconditionally. And that maybe, just maybe, there were some things she couldn't comprehend. That didn't mean she would excuse the behavior; it just meant she wanted answers. "You need to talk to Ethan. Tell him what you're thinking and feeling."

"Do you really think that's a good idea?"

"If you don't, you're going to make yourself crazy. And, eventually, it'll cause a rift between the two of you."

"I suppose you're right," Lilly said.

The sound of something rustling behind Vivian caught her attention. She snapped her gaze toward the house. A tall silhouette approached them from the side of the property. "Who goes there?" she called.

"It's Ethan."

"Shit, you scared us," Vivian said.

"Sorry," Ethan said. "I saw my wife's car in the driveway and thought I'd see if she was too tipsy to drive home."

"You know us too well." Vivian lifted her shot glass and downed the rest of it.

"What are you doing on this side of the lake? It's not on the way home from work," Lilly said with a terse tone.

"No. It's not," Ethan admitted. "Cameron asked

me to come to the Heritage Inn. He needed to talk to me about something related to Oliver's case."

Vivian coughed.

"What about?" Lilly asked.

"We'll talk about that on the way home." Ethan stretched out his arm and helped his wife to a standing position. "Thanks for keeping Lilly company tonight. I'm sure we'll see you soon."

"Drive safely."

"We'll get her car tomorrow." Ethan nodded. "Cameron said he'd be over in a few minutes."

Something was way off with Ethan. It wasn't just his tone but also the way he carried himself. It was as if he'd been deflated or something. Even the way he walked was different; wasn't with the usual spring in his step.

Vivian closed her eyes and rested her head on the back of the chair. She stretched out her legs, crossing her ankles, and clasped her fingers together. Focusing on the sounds of summer, like the crickets making their sweet music, or the few boats zipping across the lake, or the laughter coming from a campfire at the Heritage Inn, she sucked in a deep breath and let it out slowly. Her mind had filled with a bit of an alcoholic fog. It wasn't too bad, but just enough to take the edge off.

Someone cleared their throat in the background.

"Cameron?"

"In the flesh."

She didn't bother to open her eyes. "I saved you a seat."

"Where's Lilly? Her car's still here."

"She had too much to drink. Ethan took her home." She blinked open her eyes. "Why did you need to speak with Ethan tonight?"

Cameron sank into the Adirondack chair and lifted the tequila bottle. "May I?"

"Of course."

He took a shot. And then another one.

"Bad night?"

"Kind of," he said. "I don't know how to tell you this delicately, so I'm just going to blurt it out. Ethan's been playing around in those adult chat rooms."

"You've got to be fucking kidding me," she mumbled.

"I wish I were. And he knew Oliver was playing around in there, as well."

"Give me that bottle." She leaned forward and curled her fingers around the tequila. She brought the bottle to her lips and gulped.

Twice.

She coughed. "Lilly just confided in me that she's been worried Ethan's been cheating on her."

"Well, her worst fears are about to come true because he's going to tell her. Though he's never actually been with another woman in the physical sense of cheating. It's all been chatting on those websites and sending the occasional naked picture. Although, he has rules about that."

"Right, because rules will make Lilly feel so much better about this situation."

"Of course, not."

She narrowed her stare, noticing that he wasn't wearing a suit and that he'd changed into a pair of jeans and a T-shirt.

He also looked everywhere but at her.

"What else did you uncover tonight that you're avoiding telling me about?"

He let out a dry laugh. "Perhaps you should quit your job as an English teacher and join the FBI."

"No, thank you. Now, spill." She had no patience left. She and Cameron had been through too much in a short period of time for him to play games with her now.

"I don't think your brother had any knowledge of your father's exploits."

"But the hard drives? And all the stuff I kept of my dad's. How did that get into Oliver's apartment if he didn't take it?"

"I'm not exactly sure. But we're nearly done with the journal, and there isn't a single mention of your dad. I would think if Oliver had found out, he would have written about it. I mean, if that's what sent him into that world, he would have mentioned it."

"I wish I knew when that stuff went missing." She hugged herself. "But if he didn't take it, and the last time I saw it was when I moved, which was in February, that means someone was in my house. That scares me."

"It frightens me, too. Which is why I'm going to ask if it's okay if I stay here with you at night until this is over and hire you a bodyguard when I can't be with you."

She didn't like the idea of having someone with her all the time, but she wasn't about to say no. Not with a killer on the loose. "I'll agree to that."

"Thank you for not making me beg or pull out all my tricks," he said. "However, there's more."

"Of course, there is." She dared to take another sip of the nasty liquid, only this time she didn't feel the burn as it went down her throat.

That couldn't be a good sign.

"I believe, based on your brother's journal, that he got involved in the chat rooms because of Annabel and a friend of hers who got tangled up with this Simon Says guy and ended up nearly dying of a drug overdose a year ago."

"But he was sexting with Annabel. Isn't that why his girlfriend broke up with him?" None of this made any sense.

"That's what we thought, but it turns out he was pretending. All of this might have been a ruse to draw out this Simon guy. And it looks like he was successful, only it cost him his life."

A guttural sob escaped her mouth. She pushed down another and drowned more with a few more gulps of tequila.

So much for having a headache-free morning.

"Vivian, you don't want to drink any more of that."

She bolted to an upright position. "Don't you dare tell me what I don't want to do." Her legs felt wobbly, and she swayed back and forth. Her stomach sloshed about. "I make all my own decisions." Her tongue felt heavy and stuck to the roof of her mouth. She tried to swirl it around, but she was afraid she might swallow it.

He stood, taking her by the biceps to hold her steady. "You've had too much."

"More like not nearly enough." She raised the bottle and stumbled.

"I'll take that." He snatched the bottle right from her hands.

What a jerk. "I have more in the house." She turned on her heels and took two steps, but unfortunately, the ground reached up and smacked her in the face.

Stupid fucking grass.

"Come on." He wrapped his hands around her midsection and hoisted her off the ground as if she were light as a feather. "Let's get you inside."

She hiccupped. She struggled to recall how she'd ended up on the ground, though she knew it had something to do with the current rage that ran through her veins. She shrugged off the hands currently on her body, even though she knew she liked them.

A lot. "Leave me alone." She gave up and leaned

into Cameron's strong body as her legs completely gave out.

"I guess we're going to do this the hard way." He lifted her into his arms.

She dropped her head to his shoulder. "I'm going to regret this in the morning."

"Probably."

She closed her eyes and pressed her lips against Cameron's neck. "I'd let you take advantage of me."

"I'd never take advantage of you. Besides, when we're together, I'd kind of like you to remember it."

"Yeah. Me, too."

Cameron blinked open his eyes and shifted on the sofa. Stretching out his arm, he grabbed his cell off the coffee table.

Three in the morning.

So, he'd slept for two hours.

Better than some nights while working a complicated case.

He quickly checked his emails, texts, and voicemail, but everything was quiet. He wasn't sure if that was a good thing, or a bad thing.

The sound of footsteps upstairs followed by running water filled his ears.

Vivian was awake. He suspected she might not be feeling too well right about now, considering how much booze she'd drunk in a short period of time.

The stairs made a squeaking noise. He lifted his head, and his jaw went slack. He did not expect to see her slinking down the stairs wearing a see-through nighty.

With only a tiny pair of boy shorts underneath.

That was not what he'd put her to bed in.

He cleared his throat, hoping she didn't do anything to cover herself, and then mentally slapped himself for having such a horrible thought.

"Oh. Hi," she managed. "You could have slept in the guest room."

"I was working on the case and basically just passed out." He pushed himself to an upright position. "How are you feeling?"

"Like I drank the worm at the bottom of a tequila bottle."

He laughed. "Sorry. I know that's not funny."

"I came down to get some water. I feel so dehydrated."

"That will help with the hangover, that's for sure." She watched as she padded into the kitchen and opened the fridge.

That didn't help as the light literally shone right through the flimsy fabric, showing off her feminine body.

He dropped his feet to the floor, pooling the blanket around his middle. He'd slipped from his clothes and wore only his boxers, figuring he'd be up long before she came downstairs.

Now, he wished he'd slept in at least his jeans.

"I checked my cell. I thought Lilly would have called or texted me, but she hasn't." Vivian took out two bottled waters and brought one to him before plopping onto the sofa.

Right next to him.

She dared to tuck her feet under her butt, letting her knee fall dangerously close to his thigh. "Maybe he decided not to tell her?"

"I doubt it. Only because I told him that there was no way I was keeping this information from you."

"I appreciate you keeping me in the loop."

"I made you a promise. I intend to keep it." Too many people in Vivian's life had betrayed her trust. First, her father by cheating his family. Then her brother by not being telling her what they'd been up to. Cameron knew that she'd been devastated when she found out that her brother had entered the world of adult chat rooms and sexting for the purpose of helping a friend. And that he hadn't confided in her.

Vivian valued honesty above all else. Even when it hurt.

He valued *that*.

And while he knew he'd been the one to deliver the devastating blow, he'd never be the one to hurt her with betrayal or lies. He'd tell her the truth, even if it meant taking the brunt of her anger.

"I don't understand why anyone would break into my house, steal the crap I kept of my father's, and put it in my brother's house." She fiddled with her water bottle. "I know some people knew about my dad and the things he did. But no one knew *I* had any idea."

He placed his arm over the back of the sofa. "It's the middle of the night. We can talk about this after we've both had a few more hours of sleep."

"I've already got a splitting headache. I don't think I'll be able to sleep."

"Come on. I've got a remedy for that, and it will also help you sleep." He stood, letting the blanket drop to the floor. He took her hand and tugged her off the sofa.

She looked him up and down as she bit her lower lip. "I did not have you pegged for a boxer-brief man." She wiggled her finger. "Much less ones so colorful."

He glanced down and groaned. "Guys can have fancy underwear, too." He tugged her toward the stairs.

"I do recall mentioning something about being taken advantage of."

"I'm not suggesting we have sex to cure your hangover or help us sleep—though that isn't a bad idea." He laughed. "However, I was going to rub your temples, scalp, and neck until you drift off."

"And how do you know that works?"

"When I was a kid, I used to get anxiety and stress headaches. My sister Erica would do this for me, and it always helped."

"Well, I *do* like a good head massage."

"So do I."

"I can't believe you just said that."

"Yeah. That was in poor taste." He released her hand and sat on the edge of her bed, covering her sexy body with the light blanket. "You have an amazing view." He needed to get his mind out of the gutter and focus on helping her rest.

Lord knew she needed it.

"I know." She let out a long sigh, resting her cheek on her hands. She blinked; her long lashes fluttering over her sweet eyes.

He brushed her blond hair from her shoulders, letting his fingertips glide gently over her skin. He pinched the back of her neck, increasing the pressure with his thumb and forefinger. He moved his hand up the back of her head and then lowered it to her neck again.

She moaned.

That didn't help with the growing sexual tension filling his body, mind, and soul.

"That feels so good."

"Close your eyes and relax. Clear your mind of anything negative. Only think about the things that make you happy. The sounds. The scents. The places."

She tilted her head, lifting it slightly off the bed. "I like the way your voice tickles my ears. And you always smell like morning dew." She rolled to her side. "Do you always take this much interest in the people involved in your cases?"

"No," he admitted. "If this weren't you, I'd be

sitting in my car outside, and other agents and I would be taking turns keeping an eye on you." He let out a slight chuckle. "Actually, since no one has threatened you, we probably wouldn't be here at all."

"So, why are you?"

He tucked her hair behind her ears and stared into her soft blue eyes. "You really have to ask that question?"

She reached up and palmed his cheek. "I'm sorry I got drunk early."

"Don't be. It's understandable."

"Perhaps. But I texted you earlier to say that I didn't want to be alone tonight, and I meant it."

"And you're not. I'm here, and I'm not going anywhere. I'll be downstairs on—"

"I want you to stay here." She curled her fingers around his neck and pulled him close until their lips were less than an inch apart. "In this bed. With me."

He kissed her, soft and sweet. He wanted nothing more than to spend the night with her and feel her naked body next to his in the throes of passion. But he worried that she only wanted him out of fear.

Or out of the kind of need that went away once the raw emotions she was dealing with settled.

She jerked her head. "You don't want me," she said with such hurt in her eyes.

He cupped her face. "I want you in the worst way."

"It doesn't feel like you do."

He dropped his forehead to hers and breathed

deeply. Giving himself to her would be easy. Losing his heart to her…he'd probably already done that, and he knew he'd never be able to get over her if things didn't work out.

"I want things to be perfect. I want to take you out to a nice, romantic dinner. Bring you flowers. Sweep you off your feet and make it the most special night ever."

She pulled her lips into her mouth and coughed.

No. She was muffling a giggle.

"What's so funny?" he asked.

She rested her head on his shoulder and busted out laughing.

"I'm so glad I can amuse you."

"I'm sorry. What you said was very sweet." She lifted her gaze. "You really are a romantic at heart. And an old soul."

"That's what my mother tells me."

She kissed him tenderly. It wasn't the kind of kiss that generally led to heavy petting, but it certainly turned up the volume.

"You're not making it easy for me to walk out of this bedroom."

"If I told you there was box of condoms in the nightstand, would that make it even harder?" She ran a hand down his chest, letting a finger graze his nipple.

He hissed.

"Interesting choice of words." He squeezed her thigh, inching higher and higher, his hand toying with the hem of her nighty, contemplating raising it over her head.

"I invited you over earlier, and you accepted."

"I was going to stay with you, but I was also going to resist being with you. I don't want to be that guy who takes advantage, and I certainly don't want you to regret being with me."

"Anyone ever tell you that you overanalyze everything." She got on her knees and lifted her nighty, tossing it across the room.

The moonlight danced across her porcelain skin.

The air in his lungs flew out like the wind in a hurricane, and he couldn't suck in oxygen quick enough.

"It's actually a really good trait to have in my line of work." He traced a path with his index finger down the center of her chest to her belly button and back up. "Tell me this is what you want."

"How about if I show you?" Her mouth came down on his, hard and relentless. It was sloppy and wet and filled with wild promise.

They groped each other as if they were each other's last meal. It was urgent and messy.

He yanked her panties to her ankles and nearly pulled her right off the bed. "Shit, I'm sorry," he mumbled.

"Payback's a bitch." She smiled. "Stand up and take those bright things off."

"I think I'm scared." He stood at the end of the

bed, staring at her as she licked her lips and curled her fingers in the elastic of his underwear.

Carefully, she rolled them down over his hips.

"You're dangerous," he whispered and then gasped when she took him into her hands, stroking gently, all the while staring up at him.

It was the most erotic thing he'd ever seen.

Or done.

His sex life hadn't been very extensive. Granted, he was young, but not *that* young. However, he'd been an awkward geek growing up, and the youngest in all his classes since he graduated early from high school and did college in three years.

He'd been everyone's kid brother.

Her hot lips pressed against him, and he thought his heart might stop beating at any moment.

Either that or it would pound right out of his chest.

"Two can play this game." He gave her a little shove, pushing her back onto the bed. He grabbed her ankles and lifted them over his shoulders.

She smiled at him with seductive anticipation in her eyes. It humbled him in unexpected ways. He wanted to satisfy her like no other had. And like no one ever would again.

He'd never felt so protective of another human before, and it was uncharted waters. He knew he cared for her more than he'd ever cared for another woman. He'd come to accept that.

He just hadn't realized how much.

Oh, and she tasted like champagne and strawberries.

He desperately wanted to feel her pleasure wrapped around him, tightening against him, torturing him in ways he could only imagine.

Without thinking about anything but the heat and growing pleasure between them, he settled between her legs, following the rhythm she commanded.

He let her hips guide their lovemaking.

Whatever she needed, he would provide.

Whatever made her feel the most, he'd give.

Whatever she wanted, he'd make sure she had.

He was under her spell, and that was where he planned to remain.

Her nails dug into his back as she ground herself on him. "Yes," she said with a throaty moan. Her body quivered right before her heels slammed into the back of his thighs, and she arched, groaning in delight.

His climax tore through him like a stampede. His toes curled as he slammed into her, holding his breath for a long moment.

She ran her hands up and down his back, tickling him with her fingernails.

It took a good ten minutes before either of them could breathe normally again.

He rolled to the side, pulling the covers over their bodies and tucking her head to his chest. Running his fingers through her long, blond hair, he stared at the ceiling as she drifted quickly off to sleep. He doubted she remembered that neither of them had reached for the condoms.

Maybe she used another form of birth control.

He kissed her forehead and pushed that thought from his mind. There was nothing he could do about it now. Closing his eyes, he allowed himself to drift into a semi-dream state where being with Vivian was his only thought.

11

"Thanks for meeting with me again." Cameron stepped into Shannon Armstrong's office. This time, he brought Stormi with him. "This is my partner, Stormi Swanson."

"It's nice to meet you," Shannon said. "Not to be all weird about this, but I need the warrants."

"Not a problem." Cameron handed all the appropriate paperwork over to Shannon. "That's for all of Oliver's records, and this one is a blanket, covering anything you can tell us about our case without breaking client confidentiality."

"As you'll see by Oliver's records, he struggled with what he was doing in the name of helping his friend. It created real darkness in him that he wasn't sure what to do with, and he was afraid it would take him to that dark place where he wanted to self-harm again."

"And did it?" Stormi asked as she sat on the edge of the sofa.

"I thought maybe it had when I heard about his death because he'd skipped his last few sessions with me. But once I learned that he'd been murdered, and you brought this Simon Says to my attention, I knew I had to do something." Shannon took her regular seat and crossed her legs.

"Did Oliver talk about this Simon guy often?" Cameron asked, taking a seat next to his partner.

"No. Not once. He never mentioned him to me."

Cameron stole a glance at Stormi. "Then how do you know about him?"

"From three other patients," Shannon said. "One of which passed away about fifteen months ago. I can't tell you their names, but I have suggested to one that they should come forward. When I see the other one, I will do the same.

"And they are being bullied by this man online. He wants them to do things that make them uncomfortable," Shannon said. "It started out as a fun, sexual game. And they were enjoying it. They didn't realize they were being gaslighted. Controlled. Or that this man was a predator."

"I need the names. For their protection," Cameron said.

"I'll call the judge." Stormi stood and stepped out into the waiting area.

"You do understand that all I want to do is protect my patients. They have a right to confidentiality."

"I believe this person may have killed Oliver. Along with two other people last year. And he could have pushed two others to take their own lives."

"That does change things." Shannon stood and walked to her filing cabinet.

"I wonder why Oliver never mentioned Simon," Cameron said.

"We didn't talk about what he was doing so much as how it made him feel. I don't judge people. I'm here to listen and help them process their emotions. He didn't want to end up where he'd been in high school. He was just trying to help a friend find some answers."

"Did you ask about what those answers were all about?"

Shannon glanced over her shoulder with a disparaging look. "Of course, I did. And Oliver refused to tell me."

"Fair enough," Cameron said.

Stormi re-entered the office. "The judge sent over the warrant." She held up her phone. "Shannon, it should be in your in-box right now."

She nodded. "Here they are. Janet Yuri and Andrea Michael are both current clients and dealing with this right now. Sally Ludwig is the past patient. She died while dealing with this."

Ludwig. As in Larry Ludwig's first wife?

No. It couldn't be.

"What did she die of?"

"Accidental drug overdose," Shannon said. "She

was an alcoholic and mixed pills with a little too much booze one night. It proved fatal."

"Was she married to a Larry Ludwig?"

"I'd have to look at her records." Shannon thumbed through a file. "Holy shit. Yes. Isn't that Vivian's mother's new husband?"

Things just got a whole lot more interesting.

"Cameron, you should know one more thing about Sally Ludwig."

"What's that?"

"She was having a physical affair with someone she met in that chat room. And, oddly enough, it was a man who worked with her husband. It wigged her out so bad, it was one of the reasons she fell off the wagon."

All Vivian wanted to do was go search the internet. Instead, she was sitting on her front patio with Thor, of all people, Larry, and her mother, discussing Oliver's celebration of life ceremony, wondering what the hell was up with Larry, who had ants in his pants, and worried sick about Lilly, who hadn't called, texted, or said one single thing about Ethan.

"Oh. That's a great picture of Oliver," Thor said, tapping an image.

Vivian's mother nodded and then glanced in

Vivian's direction with an arched brow and a look on her face that said: *Get rid of this guy.*

"Thor, I really appreciate you stopping by and showing us what you've done so far, but we have some things to deal with that are just about family."

"Oh. I see." Thor leaned back in his chair. "Are you sure there isn't anything else I can do?"

"No. But if I think of anything, I'll call. I promise." Vivian knew she shouldn't toss the man a bone, but she figured that might be the only way to get rid of him without completely offending him and creating a different set of problems.

Ugh. She was way too freaking nice.

Thor stood, cleaning his plate and glass. "I'll just go put this in the dishwasher and be on my way."

"You don't have to do that," Vivian said.

"I don't mind. Can I get anyone anything while I'm inside?" Thor asked.

"I'll take a beer," Larry said.

Vivian's mother lifted her arm and glanced at her watch. "Honey, it's not even four in the afternoon."

"Fine. I'll take a soda." Larry ran a hand across the top of his head.

"I'll be right back." Thor disappeared inside.

"That boy has it bad for you," Larry said. "But he's so wrong for you in so many ways."

"Tell me about it," Vivian said under her breath. "But he means well."

"I don't know about that." Her mother lifted her tea mug to her lips and sipped. "I get you've known him since you were a kid, but the older he gets, the weirder and more possessive he seems to become. I don't appreciate anyone who stops by unannounced."

Vivian let out a dry laugh. "Cameron does it all the time these days, and you think it's adorable."

"That's different. He's doing his job." Her mother smiled. "Besides, he's better suited for my little girl."

"We're not having this conversation," Vivian mumbled, but she knew her mother would keep coming at her when it came to Cameron.

Thor stepped through the sliding glass door and walked over to hand Larry his soda. "Well, I'll be on my way. Please, let me know how I can help."

"I will. Thanks for stopping by." Vivian waved. She didn't want to get up and give him a hug, and she hoped he got the hint. "Drive safe." She smiled weakly.

He stood awkwardly at the top of the stairs as if waiting for her to give him a proper goodbye. Only this was about as proper as it would ever get between the two of them from now on, especially since she'd slept with Cameron.

Oh, boy.

She'd gone to bed with Cameron.

She swallowed, wondering if the heat that had filled her cheeks made them red or not.

"Okay. See you later." Thor turned and slowly made his way down the stairs, glancing over his shoulder at least four times before disappearing around the side of the house and heading toward the main road.

"Damn, I thought that young man would never leave." Larry said, letting out a long breath. "Does he not understand body language? And you're not firm enough. You need to stop being so kind and just tell him you're not interested."

"He knows that," Vivian said. "I've turned down his advances and told him we're friends."

"Maybe you should stop being his friend." Larry leaned against the railing. "He's waiting around for you to change your mind."

"That's not going to happen." Vivian turned her attention to the project on the table, though her mind kept going back to Cameron.

And last night.

It had been magical.

Special.

In her twenty-five years on this planet, she'd never experienced anything like it before. He'd made her the center of his world in a way that no one outside of her family had ever done.

"Cameron has been waiting around for you to get that he's right for you, and now you're finally considering it." Her mother arched a brow. "Thor's doing the same thing. The only difference is, you've been giving Cameron all the right signals. Where you're pretty closed-off when it comes to Thor."

She knew her mother was right and that she'd eventually have to set Thor straight. Shit, Cameron kind of had when he'd told him that they were dating. That should have made Thor stand down.

Larry tapped his knuckles on the wood railing.

"Honey, could you stop that, please?" her mother said.

Larry nodded. "Do you still want to swap out your closet shelving from that wire stuff to actual wooden shelves?" Larry asked.

"I do." Vivian glanced up from the list of music she'd been putting together while her mother went over food choices. Of course, they still hadn't decided when they were going to have this little party. They weren't sure if it made sense to do it now.

Or wait until Cameron solved the murder.

Vivian wanted to believe that Cameron would be able to do that within a few days.

However, realistically, she knew that was a ridiculous notion.

"But I'm not in any hurry. Why are you bringing it up now?"

"I need something to do. All this sitting around and waiting for the police to find out who killed Oliver is making me feel helpless." Larry was retired. He had a good fifteen years on Vivian's mom. They had met two years ago on, of all things, a dating app.

Which now made Vivian cringe, though it hadn't been her idea. She'd never liked those stupid apps. But her brother had thought it would be great and had talked their mother into it, and she'd met Larry on the first match.

He was a widower with three adult kids and two grandkids.

All of whom lived a few hours away. Vivian had gotten to know one of his daughters—the one with the kids. He was the closest to her. Nice family.

The other two kids struggled with their father marrying so quickly after their mother's death and didn't come around that often.

Vivian could understand that.

"He's been calling his kids and grandkids nonstop, too," her mother said. "I told you, dear, you should go see them. Try to mend fences again."

"Bo's talking to me. We actually had a nice chat today." Larry nodded. "He's working on his other sister. We're making progress, but I'm not leaving you right now, Eva. Not until this is over."

"I can stay here with Vivian. Or she can stay with me," Vivian's mother said.

Vivian felt her cheeks heat. She wouldn't deny her mother if Larry left, but that meant no fun between the sheets with Cameron.

Of course, they needed to talk about the fact that they hadn't used protection last night. He'd gotten out of bed before her, and by the time she'd come down the stairs, he'd had to leave. And that wasn't something you discussed via a text message.

And that was at six this morning. She'd heard from him a few times throughout the day, but nothing substantial.

She lifted her cell.

No recent texts. No calls.

"I'm not leaving you, dear." Larry pushed from the railing and made his way across the deck. He stood behind his wife and rested his hands on her shoulders and squeezed. "But I'm not very good at this celebration-of-life-planning stuff. So, put me to work doing something else. Or I'm going to go crazy."

"If you want to go measure, feel free." Who was Vivian to deny the man an outlet for his energy? Her mother was constantly complaining that he needed a few new hobbies anyway. "But I'll worn you, it's a mess up there."

"I doubt that." Larry laughed. "Your idea of a mess is when a throw pillow isn't turned in the right direction." He leaned over and kissed her mother on the temple. "You girls holler if you need me."

"Will do," her mother said with a bright smile.

Considering everything, her mom was handling things quite well. But what were they going to do? Her mother had decided that she wouldn't let whoever had killed her son know they had broken her, even though her heart would never heal, and her soul would never be complete again.

Her words.

"So, how's that sexy FBI agent?"

Vivian tried not to revert back to being a teenager, which was hard to do when her mother got all weird about her dating life.

"Who? Are you talking about Cameron?"

Her mother picked up one of the cookies from the

plate of food and broke off a chunk. "Don't you be coy with me. Your face lights up like a Christmas tree every time he calls or texts or you talk about him. What's going on?"

"I don't know." Vivian let out a long breath. She turned her gaze toward the lake and her empty dock. God, she wanted a boat. Just a small one. It didn't have to be extravagant. Maybe a little twenty-foot Boston Whaler or something. "I like him, and I'm pretty sure he likes me, but he's trying to solve who murdered Oliver. The timing isn't right."

"If we sat around and waited for the perfect time for anything, we'd be waiting our entire lives for shit to happen. If you want to be with him, you've got to make it happen."

The corners of Vivian's mouth tugged into an unwanted smile.

"Vivian Ann. What aren't you telling your mother?"

"Shit I *never* tell my mom," she mumbled. "It was rare that she kept a secret from her mother. Though she didn't often tell her about her sexual exploits, she also didn't refrain from sharing her feelings about men. "He kissed me."

"By the look on your face, I'd say it was more than a kiss."

"I'm not having this conversation with you," Vivian said under her breath. "But I don't want to distract him from what's important."

Her mother leaned across the table and took her

by the chin. "Your happiness is just as important as finding out who killed Oliver." A single tear rolled down her mom's cheek. "Cameron seems like a good man. And he's out there doing his job, so I'd say he's taking that seriously."

"He is, Mom." Vivian leaned forward. "Please, be quiet. He's coming."

Her mother winked.

Shit. Her mom sometimes didn't have a filter.

"Hello, ladies." Cameron jogged up the steps to the deck, wearing a black suit and a dark tie.

Very *Men in Black.*

"Hello yourself, young man," her mom said. "Do you have any news for us?"

"Actually, I have questions. Where's Larry?" Cameron held a folder under his arm.

"He's upstairs, measuring my closet for new shelves." Vivian tilted her head. She tried to get a good read on Cameron, but he often kept his poker face, and today was no different.

"Shall I go get him?" her mom asked.

"Would you mind?" Cameron rested his hand on Vivian's shoulder.

"Not at all." Her mom stood and made her way into the house.

Cameron leaned over and kissed her lips. It was a quick but powerful kiss, and she was glad that her mom wasn't there to see it. He pulled out a chair and sat. "How's your day going?"

"It's been uneventful," she said. "But it concerns

me when you come here wanting to ask me, my mom, and Larry questions."

"I need you to trust me," he said.

She rubbed her hands over her thighs. "Why?"

"I'll tell you when we're alone."

Larry and her mother reappeared and took their seats around the table.

Cameron set the folder on the table and flipped it open. "Larry, you used to work for Jenkins and Associates, right?"

"I did. For thirty-five years. Why?"

"Did you know a Peter Kilper?"

"I did. He was part of my sales team, though I haven't seen him since I retired shortly after my wife passed," Larry said with a puzzled expression. "What does he have to do with Oliver's murder?"

"I don't know that he does, except he had a screen name of DirtyDozen on many of the adult sites that Oliver played on. And we know that Oliver chatted with him."

"What?" Eva's voice screeched. "He chatted with men?"

Vivian reached across the table and took her mother's hand. She glanced at Cameron, unsure of what she was allowed to tell, and what she should keep to herself.

"Oliver was trying to help a friend," Cameron said matter-of-factly. "At least, that's what we've found out so far."

"I don't understand," Eva said.

"Nor do I," Larry added.

"Long story short, Oliver was trying to find a man who went by the name of Simon Says. He plays this game on the internet where he dares people to things."

"What kinds of things?" her mother asked. "Sexual things?"

"And other things. It's not a good game, to say the least." Cameron nodded. "Did Peter ever say anything to you about these adult websites? Did he ever mention a Simon to you that you can remember?"

"No. He never told me he did anything like that, and I wouldn't have asked," Larry said. "I'm not into stuff like that."

"I know this will sound like a really strange question, but I have to cover all my bases. What about your late wife? Did she know Peter?"

Larry glared at Cameron. "They knew each other. Why?"

"How well? Would you say they were acquaintances? Close friends?"

Vivian didn't like how Cameron leaned forward with his forearms on the table. It felt like an aggressive move. But what disturbed Vivian even more was the way Larry responded by folding his arms across his chest and retreating as if he had something to hide. "Peter and I worked together. They saw each other at company parties. He and his wife were at my house a couple of times. Other than that, they barely knew each other."

"That's not the picture that Peter paints."

"Excuse me?" Larry cocked his head. "What are you getting at, son?"

Cameron lifted his hands in the air as if someone were holding a gun to his head. "I'm trying to find out what happened to Oliver, and a man in your employ was talking to him. That same man told me that he'd spoken to your late wife on the same adult chat room that he spoke to Oliver on."

"I don't know what Peter is trying to do. Or why he would disparage my late wife's good name, but that's not true," Larry said from behind a tight jaw.

Vivian glanced at her mother, who sat in her chair, gripping the arms. Cameron shouldn't be doing this in front of her mom. She'd been through enough, and this was the last thing she needed.

"I don't know," Cameron said. "But I need honest answers, no matter how painful."

"Peter's fucking lying." Larry pounded his fist on the table. "My Sally wouldn't have ever done such a thing. And how dare you come here and say something so vile in front of my new bride and her daughter after they just lost Oliver? You should have come to me in private."

Vivian stared at her mother, who stared at her husband with her jaw gaping open.

"Why would Peter lie?" Vivian's mother asked in a hushed voice. "What motive does he have?"

Vivian was shocked that her mom asked those questions, as if she didn't believe her husband.

"Because he had a thing for Sally. I had to put him in his place more than once." Larry let out a puff of air. "I had no idea that he was into that kind of shit, though." He reached out and took his wife's hand. "I'm sorry I snapped. I have issues with Peter. He used to say horrible, disgusting things to Sally. I loved her, and he would call her…" Larry shook his head. "How did all this even come up?" He turned his attention back to Cameron.

Yeah. That was something Vivian wanted to know, too.

She closed her mouth, tight. She thought the way Cameron handled the situation was poor. He could have spoken to Larry alone. In private. Spared her mother the humiliation.

"I can't get into the details of how I found all this out. Not yet anyway," Cameron said. "And I want to apologize for railroading you like that. I just needed to make sure that what I believed in my gut was true."

"And what's that?" Larry asked.

"That you didn't know anything, and that Peter was lying." Cameron closed the folder.

But now, Vivian didn't believe a word Cameron said. She knew him and knew by the look in his eye and how he tilted his head that he didn't actually believe Larry.

He believed that Larry knew what his wife was up to.

Fuck.

This was going to break her mother's heart.

"Well, thank you for that." Larry stood. "Eva, I think we should go. I want to stop at the hardware store and pick up some things for Vivian's closet."

"Okay, dear." Her mother stood, obviously still shaken by the conversation.

Cameron made his way across the deck. He took her mother by the forearms. "I'm truly sorry that I put you through that. But I believe in being honest and putting all the cards on the table, and I promised Vivian that I would always keep her in the loop. With everything. I want to do that with you, as well."

"Thank you," her mother said with a tremble in her voice. "I appreciate that."

Vivian couldn't stay mad at him when he did shit like that, but she would try. She hugged her mother and Larry goodbye and waited about five minutes before pulling her anger to the tip of her tongue.

"That was really fucking uncool." She puffed out her chest, holding her ground, even though she wanted to march herself across the deck and get right in his face.

"Maybe," Cameron said. "Do you know how Larry's wife died?"

"Yeah. She was an addict and died of an accidental overdose."

"Did you know he had met with a lawyer about getting a divorce a few weeks before she died?"

Vivian opened her mouth, but all that came out

was a noise that sounded like an engine that wouldn't turn over. She snapped her jaw shut and tried again. "What does this have to do with Oliver? And why would you do this in front of my mother? That was cruel."

"Look. I don't know if Larry was involved in those chat rooms or not yet—"

"Wait. You told Larry you believed Peter was lying. I'm so confused." She rubbed her temples. Her mind raced with so many ugly possibilities.

"Larry knew about his wife and those adult chat rooms. He knew Sally was having an affair. I've spoken to two of his kids. One of them stated they don't speak to him because—"

"He married my mom so quickly after their mother died."

"That's part of it." Cameron inched closer, reaching for her, but she jerked away. He took a step back, giving her the space she needed.

That pissed her off even more.

"But Larry didn't even go to his late wife's funeral. He's never once gone to her gravesite, according to his son, Vance. While he might act like the grieving husband with you and your mom, with his kids, he doesn't shed a tear."

Vivian had noticed that he never liked to talk about Sally the few times they'd been around his kids. Larry had gone as far as to ask that they not bring her up, saying it was too painful for the family.

That was something she could understand.

"I told you I'd be honest with you through this investigation. I'm not going to start sugarcoating things now." Cameron closed the gap.

She glanced over her shoulder. Only one step before she'd be pushed up against the railing. "I suppose I should thank you for that, but your delivery sucked in front of my mom."

"I owe your mother the same honesty. Maybe more since she's Oliver's mom."

"But you just played both her and Larry for a fool."

"No. I didn't." Cameron placed tender hands on her biceps and squeezed.

She nearly melted at his touch. He had a way of making her feel as though she could handle anything when she was in his arms. "You hurt her feelings, and I'm certain you started an argument."

"I really hope Larry hasn't been messing around on the websites. But the only way your mom's marriage will survive is if Larry is honest. This is his chance."

"What gives you the right to play marriage counselor?"

He laughed. "I'm not. I'm playing FBI agent." He reached into his back pocket and pulled out his cell. "I'm hoping that, in the next hour, I'll get a call from Larry, wanting to talk about what he knows or what he doesn't know."

"You didn't have to do that in front of my mom."

Cameron turned and strolled toward the table. He

took a cookie from the tray and nibbled on it. "No. I did. If I'd done it in private, he would have lied, and there would have been no incentive. And do you really want your mom to go through a second marriage that's filled with lies? At least this way, if all he did was hide his shame, they have a chance of moving forward. Because your mother hid hers. They have common ground, even though they never knew it. This has the potential to bring them closer together."

"Why do you have to be like this?"

He removed his sport coat and folded it over the chair. He did that exactly the same way every time. "Like what?"

"Fucking right all the time? Ridiculously smart. You don't have the best game in town, yet you've swept me off my feet. So much that I can't even be mad at you for being a total asshole." She waved her finger under his nose. "Which is what you were."

"Being an FBI agent sometimes requires me to be a dick. I get it. I've been called worse, by the way."

"Trust me. My mind is saying all sorts of foul things." She pointed to the kitchen. "Do you want something a little more substantial than a cookie?"

"Actually, I would. I haven't eaten since breakfast," he said. "And I need to ask you something else."

"I don't like the sound of that." She tugged at his arm. "Come on. I'll make you a meatball sub."

"Sounds amazing. But you should know, I don't

have much time, and I feel a little awkward asking you this."

She laughed. "Seriously? I find that hard to believe after what you just did out there with my mom and Larry."

"I can do anything when it's work-related. This is personal."

She glanced over her shoulder and arched a brow. "You've got my attention."

"We didn't use a condom last night. Do we need to be concerned about you getting pregnant?"

"Oh, that." She stepped behind the counter and twisted her blond hair with her fingers. "Well, yeah. That could be an issue."

"From now on, we use them," he said. "I want to have children someday, but not just yet."

"Agreed."

"Please tell me as soon as you know. And for the record, I'm not going anywhere, regardless."

"Good to know," she said. "But there isn't anything we can do but wait for my period to show up. Or not. So, let's talk about something else. What are you going to do after you leave here?"

"I have a few more interviews this evening, and Kidd has been able to pull some emails from your brother's computer that we thought were lost. I need to read those and have a meeting with my team." He had to admire her poise in how she handled the potential issue they faced.

But the real scary part was that he wasn't scared.

Not one bit.

She moved about the kitchen, finding the Italian bread, meatballs, and sauce, along with the cheese. "Do you have any real leads?"

"Everything points to this Simon guy. Everyone who was at those orgies spoke to him."

Vivian shuttered. "I can't believe Oliver actually went to one just to help a friend. It seems extreme."

Cameron didn't like that his mind had been assaulted by all those images that he'd never be able to get rid of. However, because of his photographic memory, he could call up all the snippets of Oliver. "I'm not sure if this will help you, and I honestly don't like talking to you about it because it's weird, but Oliver didn't seem to be enjoying himself like the others, and he constantly left the inner circle."

"Yeah. Okay. I don't want to know the details," she said. "But I appreciate what you're saying."

"I'm meeting with Annabel in forty minutes," Cameron admitted. "She's been difficult to get ahold of. She's scared and afraid this Simon guy will come after her."

"Can you protect her?"

"We're putting her in a safe house with an agent on her twenty-four-seven." He lifted the sandwich she pushed in front of him and took a large bite. Half a meatball spilled out and landed, thankfully, on the plate. "Oh, my, this is good."

"Thanks. I made it from scratch."

"Jackson and Katie have a buddy of theirs posted at your driveway, and I put a camera lakeside that— "

"You did what? I don't want anyone spying on me."

"No one is *spying* on you," he said. "You can download the app and check it. It will also give you notifications if there is movement. However, for the time being, I'd like to have my people with access to it because I won't always be able to have eyes on both sides of the house, and someone could come at you from the lake."

"You're asking for permission?"

"Sort of," he said with a slight smile. "I still don't believe you're any kind of target, but I'd never forgive myself if anything happened to you."

"All right. You can have access, but when this is over, I'm changing the passwords and all that shit."

"I wouldn't have it any other way." He wiped his fingers on a napkin. "Can I be so bold as to recommend getting a security system?"

"I've said I should get one for a while now. That and a dog."

"I've wanted to get a dog. I keep looking at rescues. I swear if the right one comes up, I'm getting it."

"Me, too." She rested her elbows on the counter. "How late do you think you're going to be tonight?"

"I'm thinking maybe nine." He smiled. "Is that an invitation for the sofa, or the master?"

"I haven't decided yet."

"That's fair." He stared deep into her eyes, reaching into her soul. "Just know that I'm doing everything I can to find your brother's killer, and I'm not going to stop until I do."

Even if she didn't like his tactics at the moment, she believed without a doubt that Cameron would go to the ends of the Earth to find her brother's killer. But she wasn't one hundred percent sure if he was doing it for her or because he was so driven by his job.

It shouldn't matter.

But for some reason, it did.

12

"That was a shit thing to do, young man." Larry slammed the cabin door, rattling the picture hanging on the wall by the window.

Stormi glanced up from behind her computer with an arched brow.

"I have half a mind to go talk to your superiors about the stunt you pulled," Larry said.

"Go right ahead," Cameron challenged. The pounding between his ears had steadily grown since leaving Vivian's two hours ago. "They are all well aware of what I did."

"You put me in a very bad situation with my wife."

"And you put me in a crappy place with this investigation by not coming forward with what you knew." Cameron turned and held out his hand. "Where's that file with the emails from Peter?"

"Right here." Stormi handed him a folder.

"A month before Sally died, she and Peter were talking about this Simon guy, and she told Peter that she was going to go to you about him. Said she was scared that Simon was actually going to hurt her." Cameron handed Larry a piece of paper. "In another email, she informed Peter that she told you and that it didn't go well. That you were going to divorce her."

"I was." Larry sat on the sofa in front of the picture window. He tossed the paper onto the coffee table and cradled his face in his hands. "I met with an attorney, and I had every intention of leaving her. I'd had enough of her cheating and her lies." He glanced up with tears in his eyes. "I loved her with everything that I was. I stayed with her for a long time, but she always went back to those damn websites. It was an addiction, and she couldn't stop. And *I* couldn't live like that anymore." He waved his finger at Cameron. "You had no right to push me in front of Eva."

It wasn't Cameron's place to tell Larry about his wife's secret, though it surprised him that it hadn't come out yet. However, he had a killer to catch, and he couldn't concern himself with these things. He took out a third piece of paper. "We found an email exchange between you and Oliver. You knew what he was doing. You knew he was talking to Simon, and you even suspected this Simon guy had something to do with why your wife started drinking again."

"I didn't know about what Oliver was doing until two weeks before he died, and I begged him to stop. I told him that I didn't care that he was helping an old friend. If he didn't get the hell out of that world, it would destroy him and his mother."

Cameron double-checked the email, and it was dated ten days before Oliver's death. There had been no other correspondence.

That they had found anyway.

"What did he say?"

"He told me he had to see it through." Larry let out a dry laugh. "Said people had died, and he wasn't going to let that happen to his friend. He told me that he was in therapy, and he'd be okay. I told him I didn't care. That I saw firsthand what this world could do to people, and he had one week to bring it to the authorities, or I would do it for him. But he'd learned some things about Simon, and to be honest, I wanted that fucker six feet under. Still do."

Cameron tugged at his slacks and took a seat across from Larry. "What did Oliver find out?"

"He wouldn't tell me much. He didn't want me or his family involved. But he told me that he knew Simon was a local person. That he never attended any of the sex parties that others did but that he liked watching. That was his thing. He wanted people to video things so he could watch, live. He made a game of it, and if you didn't follow through, bad things happened. He'd tell your family. Or things that you did for him would show up on the internet. According to Oliver, this Simon guy is twisted, but Oliver had become one of his disciples."

"Jesus. What the fuck does that mean?"

"Someone who got people to do things for him, as well. And Oliver said that earned him a seat at the table, meaning he would get to meet Simon. That's when he planned on outing him, once and for all, but that never happened."

"And you kept that knowledge to yourself." Cameron rolled his neck. "That's obstruction of justice. I should arrest you."

"From the tone in your voice, I take it you have other plans for me."

Cameron nodded. "This might be none of my business, and my parents would probably give me a good lecture about respecting my elders, but I care a great deal about Vivian. I'd appreciate it if you told your wife and Vivian everything."

"I already told Eva most of it, though I skimmed over a lot of the details about Oliver. I think I might need a hotel room tonight."

"I'm sorry."

Larry waved his hand. "It's honestly not your fault. I should have come clean with all of this from the start."

"I'm probably going to end up sleeping in the doghouse tonight for saying this, but Eva isn't just upset about you keeping secrets about your late wife. It struck a chord with her because of her late husband."

"I learned that a little bit ago," Larry said. "Sexual addiction isn't easy to understand."

"I'm sure it's not."

"So, what is it that you need from me?" Larry leaned back on the sofa and let out a long breath.

"Information. Details. Anything you can remember. Or if you have access to your late wife's social media accounts. Messenger. Email."

"I gave her computer to Oliver." Larry sat up taller. "You don't have it? I mean, isn't that how you figured all this out?"

Cameron glanced over his shoulder and looked at Stormi.

"We had a different source," Cameron said.

"Why would you give Sally's computer to Oliver?" Stormi asked.

"He thought it might have something he could use when it came to dealing with Simon." Larry's eyes grew wide. "Where's the computer?"

"Probably with whoever killed Oliver." Cameron didn't like where his mind was going because it meant he had another murder on his hands. "You mentioned you thought Simon pushed your wife over the edge when it came to her drinking."

Larry nodded. "I caught her talking to him once in a messaging app. He told her she wasn't any fun when she was sober, and if she didn't start acting like her old self, she knew what would happen to the other players. I didn't know what that meant until Oliver told me he thought it could mean something as bad as death." Tears rolled down Larry's cheeks. "Do you think Sally was murdered like Oliver was?"

"It's possible."

"Oh. No. What have I done?"

Cameron handed Annabel a glass of water. Her hand shook as she raised it to her lips. In the background, her one-year-old fussed while her husband tried to keep her calm.

This was a shitty situation all around.

Cameron took a seat and kept his demeanor open and approachable. "I appreciate you coming forward."

"After Oliver died, I didn't feel like I had a choice." She glanced over her shoulder. "My husband wants to leave me. I can't say I blame him. The only reason he's here now is because Simon Says threatened our daughter."

"We're not going to let anything happen to her."

"You can't make that promise," Annabel said. "But I know you will do your best to keep us all safe and catch this asshole."

Cameron had to appreciate her bluntness. "I know it's late, and you must be tired, so let's get started."

She nodded.

"How did you meet this Simon Says guy? Did you approach him?"

"No. And if you do ping him first in a chat room, he often blocks you. He's paranoid that people are coming after him, so he's always the one to start the conversation. He also sometimes doesn't start off as Simon. He uses other screen names, gains your trust, and then comes back as Simon, using the information he's gathered on you to gaslight you." She pointed to the massive folder on the table. "I compiled a list of names I know he's used."

The file that Annabel had was impressive. And should be quite helpful. Cameron wished he had gotten it sooner, but he understood fear, and Annabel had it coming at her from all sides.

"Tell me about his game."

Annabel took another few sips of water. It was obvious that she didn't want to talk about any of this with her husband so close. But Cameron needed as much information as possible.

Cameron gave a little head nod to Stormi, who tried to shuffle the husband and daughter into the other room.

"I know this is hard. Uncomfortable. Embarrassing, even. You won't get any judgment from me. I'm not here for that. Anything you did is your personal business, and I'm sorry I have to invade your privacy. I wish I didn't. But I believe this man killed Oliver. And he may have killed others."

"I know he has. Or he's made them do it." She lowered her head. A few gulping sobs echoed in the room. "I'm sorry. I should have come forward a long time ago, but he knows where I live. He knows who my husband is. My daughter. He has pictures, and he's sent me back pictures that he's taken of my family. He's followed them, and I know he'll kill them. I was just trying to protect them."

Cameron leaned forward, rested his hand on her forearm, and squeezed. "I know that, and I'm sorry to put you through this, but you have the power to stop this man. Please. Tell me what you know."

She stiffened her spine and nodded. "Those chat rooms are addicting, and he sucks you in. The game is silly, and it starts off with stupid things like sending a picture of yourself naked in the tub. Or naked with your spouse."

Cameron did his best to keep everything about his body language and facial expressions neutral. He wasn't there to make her feel bad about her poor decisions. "Does he do anything in return?"

"That's the weird part about this. We get involved in his game because we find it exciting. It's hard to explain."

"Would you mind trying?"

She glanced over her shoulder again. "When I got laid off from my job and then found out I was pregnant, my husband took it as a sign that I should stay home. We never saw eye to eye on that. And, frankly, I got bored. You probably don't need to hear this, but during my pregnancy, Nico thought he'd hurt me or the baby, so we barely had sex. And then after watching the birth, he just had issues. He's old school. And, well, I sought pleasure through porn and stumbled across these adult sites. That's where I met Simon. He made me laugh, and he made me feel sexy.

It got to the point where I'd do almost anything for him. That's how addicted to him I was."

"What other kinds of things did you do, besides taking naked selfies?"

"I masturbated for him. Videoed myself having sex with other men. An orgy. But you already know about that."

Cameron nodded. "You said you know he's killed. How?"

She pointed to her backpack. "Oliver gave me a computer for safekeeping."

"Whose is it?"

"His stepfather's. Well, not his, but his late wife's."

Well, fuck.

"He wasn't positive, and neither am I because there's no video of her death, but both Oliver and I believe that Simon Says, as part of his sick and twisted game, told Sally to kill herself and video it for his viewing pleasure."

Cameron's jaw dropped open. He'd heard of—and seen—a lot of fucked-up things in his life, but that one went right to the front of the line to get on the crazy train.

"Have you heard of other deaths like this?" he asked.

"I've seen them," Annabel said. "He shows them to people when they try to stop playing his game." She swiped at her cheeks, wiping away the tears. "And he's showed his followers killing other followers when they don't do what he says."

"Have you ever heard of a woman by the name of Babs Dillard? I don't know what her screen name would be, but her sister may have been involved with Simon, and she died by suicide." Cameron swallowed the bile that lurched to the back of this throat, but it didn't do any good. It just kept coming back up.

"There was a girl who went by the name of Dolly-Dill on the boards. She died a few years ago. Maybe that's her."

Shit. "I think you might be right about that," Cameron said. "Do you have any of these videos that Simon asked people to make?"

She shook her head. "He shows us through the chat sites via video streaming. He doesn't show them to us more than once or twice. The only reason he let Oliver take over for me in the game was that Oliver promised he'd do both. Kill for him and take his life, all while letting Simon watch."

13

Vivian's fingers hovered over the keyboard. She wasn't sure what to search for, so she went for the obvious.

Adult chat rooms.

She jerked her head back, staring at the long list of choices.

Shit.

Be careful what you do web searches for.

Glancing over her shoulder, she made sure the guest room door was closed. Her poor mother.

She picked up her cell. There were eight unread messages from Cameron in response to her nasty note after her mother showed up a few hours ago, sobbing over what Larry had told her about his past.

And about Oliver.

Only the difference between Larry and Vivian's father was that Larry hadn't been being doing anything wrong—unlike Vivian's father. Larry lied because he genuinely cared and was trying to protect those he loved. However, it might take some time for Vivian and her mother to forgive him. If they ever did.

Otherwise, deep down, Vivian knew that Larry was a good, decent man, who felt the same shame that she and her mother had the moment they found out what Lukas Rose had been doing behind closed doors. Part of Vivian wondered if this Simon guy went back eleven years and if he could have been talking with her father.

She tapped the screen and pulled up Cameron's messages.

Cameron: *I know you're mad. I'm sorry.*

Cameron: *I know you think I betrayed you and kept something from you, but I told you that I would do my best to tell you as much as I could. I couldn't tell you everything that I knew until Larry came to me or until I had more information.*

Cameron: *Please just let me know you're OK.*

Cameron: *I'm between interviews. Just text me back.*

Cameron: *I'm not above begging.*

Cameron: *Call me.*

Cameron: *Okay. Since you're not going to respond, I'll do this in text. I'm about to interview Annabel. It turns out she has Larry's late wife's computer. That's a long story. I know you and your mom are hurting and I'm sorry for my part in that. What Larry did regarding Oliver, I struggle to defend him, but I will when it comes to his wife. It's the same reason you and your mom don't talk about your dad.*

Cameron: *Oh. And Larry has agreed to allow me to have his wife's body exhumed. I think she was murdered.*

Vivian covered her mouth and gasped. Once again, she looked toward the guest room. Larry should have come to them when he knew that Oliver was in trouble. But he didn't know about their secret legacy.

He didn't know they had a bond.

Nor did her mom, and that might have changed the course of everything.

Secrets didn't help anyone. They only served to destroy everything.

She blew out a puff of air and hit the call-back icon.

It went right to voicemail, but a few seconds later, another text came through.

Cameron: *Sorry. In the middle of an interview. Will call as soon as I'm done. Promise. Thank you for calling.*

Vivian: *I'll be waiting up.*

She'd let him figure out if she meant he could come over or just call, because she wasn't sure what she wanted from him at this point.

She turned her attention back to the computer screen. She wished she knew which sites were the ones that everyone used. She clicked on the top one since it'd come up first. It asked for a screen name. She glanced at the ceiling and tried to think of a name that wouldn't give her away. God forbid someone knew it was her. And if she'd learned anything from the last few days, it was that more and more people were doing this kind of thing.

She typed in: *LadyLuck* and hit the enter key. It was the only thing she could think of that seemed benign.

Immediately, she got eight private chat messages.

She opened one.

"Ew. Gross." She closed the image of some guys large, hard cock. Quickly, she opened all the messages, blocking those who sent pictures. She didn't want to start that way.

Shit. *Start?*

All she wanted to do was see what the draw was and maybe find some information.

Her heart raced as she read a message from someone by the name of *FriendlyFire.* It said he was male, in upstate New York, looking to chat with a woman for the night. Any kind of chatting would be acceptable.

She could handle that.

Maybe.

Blowing out a puff of air, she typed in her response.

LadyLuck: *Hi. How are you tonight?*

FriendlyFire: *Good. Just hanging out having a beer and watching TV. You?*

LadyLuck: *Drinking wine and doing the same*

FriendlyFire: *What are you watching?*

LadyLuck: *You'll laugh. I'm catching up on* Real Housewives.

So far, this seemed like it wasn't a big deal. But then she realized this was how people got sucked in.

FriendlyFire: *My wife watches that stuff all the time. I'm not a fan, but she has gotten me hooked on* Below Deck.

LadyLuck: *You're married? How long?*

She shouldn't be surprised, and she sure as hell shouldn't be upset. She wasn't doing this because she was looking for anything but answers.

Maybe she should go looking for Simon. But what would she do if she found him?

FriendlyFire: *I am. Ten years. Does that bother you?"*

She needed to play the game if she was going to gain his trust so she could poke around for information on Simon.

LadyLuck: *No. Not at all. I take it that you're not all that happy?*

FriendlyFire: *It's not that. She's a good person. Really. The best. I love her. But, and I'm a real jerk for saying this, we're just not always compatible in the bedroom. Especially since she had our second child.*

Shit. She didn't expect him to be so honest.

Or was he? Was this how people got others to do weird shit? Or was he just lonely and needed someone to talk to.

FriendlyFire: *Are you married? Or in a relationship?*

LadyLuck: *I'm married. Though I don't always tell people that.*

Wow. That lie came out quickly.

FriendlyFire: *That's the one thing I never lie about. I* *want women to know that so they don't think I'm looking for something beyond chatting.*

That gave her an idea.

LadyLuck: *I'm pretty sure we've never chatted before, but I should tell you I've recently had to change my screen name because of a weirdo that got a little too close to my home life.*

Jesus. Who the hell was she and what the hell did she think she was doing?

FriendlyFire: *You've got to be careful on sites like these. I've been lucky that I've never had to do that. But I also lie all the time. Sorry. I never give my real name, where I'm from, or show faces and I'd never ask you to. I just like to chat, maybe do a little sexy talk, get off. So, if that's not cool with you, I understand.*

LadyLuck: *No. It's okay. I lie about shit too, but I also try to be real about some things. I do like to get to know people, but most here go right for the naked dick pick.*

FriendlyFire: *You won't get that from me. Not unless you ask, then I might be inclined to share if the chat is going particularly good. But like you, I kind of like to know a little bit about who I'm fucking, even if it's pretend.*

FriendlyFire: *If you don't mind me asking, who was harassing you? We try to protect each other here, but it is an adult sex website, and there are a lot of crazy motherfuckers here.*

LadyLuck: *I'd feel weird saying. I think I've handled him.*

FriendlyFire: *Well, I'm going to toss this out there. Stay the hell away from a guy with the screen name* Simon Says. *He's bad news. No one has seen him on this site for a* *couple of months since we all complained, but he's not about having a good time. He's twisted.*

Her heart lurched to the back of her throat, and it became impossible to swallow. Did some stranger just warn her about Simon? Could that have randomly happened? Her entire body shook.

LadyLuck: *How do you know about him?*

FriendlyFire: *He messed with a friend of mine here, and her husband got wind of it. It was a clusterfuck. I haven't seen her since it happened, and I'll be honest, I've been worried about her. I don't ever exchange emails or cell numbers, so I have no way of knowing how she is. But she seemed like a nice lady. I know that sounds weird. I might be a dog and a cheater, but I'm not a total douchebag.*

That was certainly an oxymoron.

LadyLuck: *That doesn't sound good. And yes, I've come across that asshole before.*

FriendlyFire: *Shit. I'm sorry. My wife texted. She's coming home early. I've got to log off. Maybe we can chat again sometime.*

LadyLuck: *I'd like that.*

She took screen shots so she could show Cameron.

Who would be livid with her. But at this point, she didn't fucking care. She had a lead. Could Cameron say that?

Maybe she could get more.

She scanned the main room for a name that might mean something or that jumped out at her, but none of them sent a shiver down her spine. She logged out and found another chat room, and the first name she saw was Simon Says.

Holy shit.

She leaned back on the sofa, adjusting the computer on her lap. Her heart beat in her throat. She clicked on the name and requested a private chat.

Nothing.

She waited a couple of minutes, and Simon Says still didn't respond, so she pinged him again.

Simon Says: *Aren't you an impatient little girl?*

What the fuck did she do now that she had his attention?

LadyLuck: *I don't like being kept waiting.*

Had she lost her ever-loving mind? This was not her, and she currently wanted to take a wool scrubby to her body. But even that wouldn't take off all the filth she'd allowed to seep into her pores by even entertaining these assholes.

Simon Says: *I don't even know you, so excuse me while I go back to my other chat.*

He logged out of the private chat and blocked her from creating a new one.

Shit. Well, that didn't go too well.

She took a screen shot of the chat and slammed the computer closed. Cameron would be beyond angry. He would likely be downright pissed. She could keep this to herself, but she knew that more secrets would lead to more devastation, and she couldn't allow in her world.

Not anymore.

Not when it came to Cameron.

Cameron folded his arms and took a step back. He needed to look at the deaths by suicide and the murders one more time before heading over to Vivian's.

"It's after eleven. Shouldn't you be next door?" Kidd said from behind his perch at the table.

Cameron swore the man never left that spot. Never slept. And the only time he ate or drank was when someone put something in front of him.

"If the two deaths by suicide were videoed, where's the camera? Where'd the feed go? There'd have to be a computer. A tablet. A cell. Something. But there was nothing at either scene."

"Are you saying Annabel's lying?"

"No. I believe every word she said." Cameron ran a hand across the top of his head. "Simon Says gets to know these people. Their lives. He studies them. But it's more than that. He must be close. He only targets people who are nearby." Cameron inched closer to his board. He tapped a couple of the images. "The farthest one away was eighty miles, but they had ties to the area."

"So, Simon Says is a member of this community."

"I was beginning to think it could be Larry."

"I've checked all his electronics. His whereabouts when our murders happened. It's impossible."

"I know," Cameron said. Besides that, his gut told him that Larry wasn't his man. But whoever it was, Cameron knew he was right under his nose, and that pissed him off. He might not have ever met the person, but Simon knew who Cameron was, and he was watching. "Simon must have snuck in or had one of his followers come in to take whatever was streaming to Simon."

"Nothing was missing from any of those scenes."

"Then Simon put it away." Cameron took the two murders and the two deaths by suicide and pinned them side by side. Then he took Oliver's crime scene photo and pinned it just below. "Look at this."

Kidd got up from behind his screens and stood next to Cameron.

"What do you see?" Cameron just couldn't believe he hadn't seen it before. It was subtle, but still, it was there.

"I'm sorry. I have no idea what I'm supposed to be looking at here."

"Do you remember a vintage electronic game called Simon?"

"You mean the one where you had to follow the colors?"

"That's the one." Cameron pointed to one picture. "These earrings look exactly like that game. And in this one, it's the necklace." He moved to one of the males. "This one is obvious; the guy has a mouse pad with the game on it. I don't see anything at the other murder scene, but I suspect we'll find something."

"Oliver's wearing all the colors," Kidd said. "I never would have put all that together."

Cameron had enough of this asshole and his sick, twisted, childish games. "Simon's not going to have anything more to say when I'm done with him."

14

Vivian lay in her bed, staring at the ceiling. It was almost midnight, and still no Cameron. She rolled to her side, took in the moonlight glistening on the lake.

Her cell vibrated on the nightstand.

Cameron.

Finally.

She contemplated if she should go let him in. His text indicated that he could go and sleep in the cabin over at the Heritage Inn if it was too late.

No. She wanted to see him.

She slipped from the bed and pulled her robe sash tight around her body as she made her way down the stairs and opened the door. "You're late," she said.

"I'm sorry. I don't have to stay here if you don't—"

"Come in but be quiet. My mom is sleeping." She grabbed a bottle of wine, two glasses, and a bag of

Oreos. "I'm hungry, so if you say a word about my food choice, I'll hurt you."

"Processed snacks and alcohol. My favorite." He tossed his backpack over his shoulder.

She paused, glaring. "You came planning on spending the night?"

"A man can hope that the original invitation still stands, but I'm happy to sleep outside, or on the sofa, or leave altogether. Whatever makes you the most comfortable, but only if I get to take some of those double-stuffed cookies with me."

She laughed, shaking her head. "Don't expect to share the bed."

"I would never be so presumptuous." He tossed his bag onto the chair in the corner of her room and loosened his tie before taking off his coat.

"Good." She reached out and tugged his tie the rest of the way and unfastened the first two buttons on his shirt. "You look tired."

"It's been a really long fucking day, and the last thing I want to do is fight with you. But I do know that you're mad at me, and you have every right to be."

She handed him a glass of wine, and he gladly took a hardy gulp.

"However, I stand by what I did with your mom and Larry. If you and I weren't dating, I would have tossed him completely under the bus with everything."

"I know," she said. "And now it's your turn to be pissed at me." She took her laptop off her bed and flipped it open. She'd thought long and hard about how she planned to tell him what she'd done and decided it was best just to show him. "Before you freak out, read the screenshots, take a deep breath, and then talk to me."

He sat on the edge of the bed and stared at the screen. He blinked. Blinked again and then glanced up at her with a scowl. "You went on this adult website? You chatted with this guy?"

"Only for a few minutes. But did you see what he said about Simon?"

"Yeah. I can read." He set the computer aside and took another sip of wine. "I have a team of people searching those websites for Simon, and I have Annabel now, too. Why the hell would you do that, Vivian? Those places are dangerous."

"I'm trying to help find out why my brother had to die, and I know I probably shouldn't have." She picked up the electronic device and pushed it back under his nose. "Keep reading."

He glanced between her and the screen. "Are you fucking kidding me? You spoke to Simon Says and you didn't call me immediately?"

"He hung up on me, so to speak. In seconds. And I did text you, asking when you were coming home, and said that I needed to talk to you."

"You shouldn't have done that. We believe this guy is a murderer."

"He doesn't know who I am. I barely even spoke to him, and now you know where he's playing."

"We already knew that. You've got to trust that I know what I'm doing." He stretched out his arm and took her hand. "I understand that you have questions, and I know this investigation has taken more weird twists and turns, but I want you to promise me you won't go back there. I've got someone posing as Annabel now, and we've got a handle on Simon. As of tonight, and thanks to Larry and Annabel, I have some real leads. I don't need to worry about you getting messed up in this shit and getting tangled up with that sick son of a bitch."

She stood in front of him, taking his wine glass and setting it on the nightstand. "Everyone I love seems to be tied up with this Simon guy, including Larry. And that broke my mom's heart." She straddled him, even though she knew she shouldn't. She should be mad as hell, and she wanted to stay angry, but she couldn't. She wanted to feel Cameron's arms around her body, holding her close, keeping her safe.

He rested his hands on her hips. "I know I railroaded Larry into being honest with you and your mom, but I do believe he thought he was doing the right thing when it came to Oliver. Larry knew Oliver only wanted to help his friend. Larry had his own guilt over his late wife, whom he loved—and felt betrayed by, something I think your mom can understand. But, ultimately, Larry wanted to help Oliver's friend escape this crazy world. He just didn't go about it the right way."

"Mom can understand Larry's intentions. And so can I. But she doesn't trust herself anymore. Not to mention, it will be hard for her to forgive Larry for making a decision about her son." Vivian's heart wrestled with her mind. She knew that Cameron had to put the case first. Finding the killer was more important than his promise to her, and she accepted that. "I'm not sure she'll be able to come back from that, and I resent you for pushing that on her."

"But aren't you glad she found out now, rather than years from now?"

Vivian agreed that she was glad her mother knew the truth about Larry. But not all the family's secrets had been put on the table, and she had no idea how her mom would take it when she told her about what she'd done. "I'm scared for my mom because I need to tell her about the hard drive."

"I still don't know how that stuff got from your house to your brother's if he didn't take it. Which is still a possibility. Just because he doesn't say anything about his father in the journal, doesn't mean he didn't know."

"I've thought about that," Vivian said. "He would have talked to his therapist about it, and that didn't happen."

"Annabel didn't know anything about it, and neither did Larry. Not that this case makes any sense, but that's the one thing that sticks out like a sore thumb. You are only connected because you're related to Oliver, not because you've ever been involved in these websites or with Simon Says." He squeezed her hips. "You logging onto those chat rooms brings you closer, and that scares me. I don't want anything to happen to you. Promise me you won't ever go poking around the internet again."

She let out a slow breath and nodded. She knew he was right, and it didn't matter that she'd managed to come across Simon Says right away. Understanding him, the game, and fleshing him out wasn't her area of expertise, and she'd probably manage to screw it up. "I won't. But I'm tired of sitting around and waiting. It's been days, and I feel like we're no closer to finding out who killed Oliver."

"I know it seems like that, and I'm doing the best I can to keep you informed, but there are some things I can't tell you. Please, trust that I'm good at my job."

She cupped his face and pressed her lips over his mouth. However, she couldn't bring herself to deepen the kiss. It wasn't that she didn't want to be with him, because she did, but guilt swallowed her heart.

She'd enjoyed the attention that a stranger had given her behind a computer screen, and she didn't understand why. She wasn't turned on by it, but she saw how easily people could fall down that rabbit hole. And that terrified her for so many reasons.

Cameron pulled back. "As much as I'd like to climb into this bed with you right now, I need you to look at a few pictures first." He took her chin between his thumb and forefinger. "And something is really bothering you, so we need to talk about that, too." Lifting her from his lap, he stood and strolled across the room. He took out a folder and opened it. "Do you recognize any of these people?"

She took the papers, one by one, studying them carefully.

The first three, she'd never seen before. But the fourth one made her heart stop.

"That was an old neighbor of ours growing up."

"He was on one of your father's hard drives, but he's also on Oliver's list. And he's been talking with Simon Says." Cameron took the picture and set it aside.

Vivian swallowed. She continued flipping the pages. Six more that she didn't recognize, but the seventh stunned her. "No," she whispered. "This can't be happening."

"Who is that person to you?"

"That's my Aunt Kiki. How is she connected?"

"By a screen name on one of the chat rooms. We don't have any video of her anywhere."

"That would be gross if she and Oliver connected."

"They must have on some level since she was in his contact list on those sites."

She shivered. "We barely speak. She's been trying to get ahold of me since Oliver died, but I haven't taken her calls. She wants the ring my father left me when he died. It was always intended for me, but she somehow feels it should be hers and has made that clear."

"Where's the ring?"

Vivian made her way to the walk-in closet. "After my father's hard drives disappeared, I double-checked to make sure the ring was still here. It was Dad's mother's engagement ring. I never wear it. I figure I'll make a necklace out of it or something someday."

"How often does your aunt reach out to you?"

"A couple times a month. Pretty consistently over the last two or three years."

"And before that?" Cameron asked.

"Holidays and birthdays." She pulled open her jewelry drawer and the small, velvet pouch that held the ring. She had no emotional attachment to anything that had once belonged to her father.

But this had been her Grammy's. And she loved her grandmother with all she had. The feeling had been mutual.

She dumped the diamond ring into the palm of her hand. It sparkled under the bright light hanging from the ceiling.

"It's beautiful. and I'm glad it's not missing."

"Me, too." She tucked it back into the pouch. "I can't believe my aunt is involved in this and knew Oliver was, too."

"I'm not sure she knew she was talking with Oliver. It seems your brother was playing detective and wasn't all that horrible at it," Cameron said. "We've been able to uncover a lot of things from his computer and from that journal. He made a list of screen names and matched them to users. She was one of them. He only started hooking up with people when he was finally invited into the game with Simon."

"I have to ask something that you've never come out and said." She tucked the ring back into the drawer and held onto the sides of the dresser. "What exactly was Oliver trying to help Annabel with?"

"He was trying to get her out of the game."

"I'm not following."

"If he took over Annabel's role in Simon's game, then she'd be free to leave. Simon agreed. While Oliver played, he tried to find out who Simon was so he could expose him to the world. We believe he found out who he was and that's why he's dead."

Cameron curled his fingers over her hand. "I'm going to find him, and he will pay."

She lowered her gaze. Heat radiated from her cheeks to the bottom of her feet. Whenever he touched her, it was as if fireworks were being set off under her skin. Even when it wasn't sexual, it was still the most powerful connection she'd ever had with another human.

Out of the corner of her eye, she noticed an envelope with her name on it. "Cameron," she whispered.

"What is it?"

She swallowed, pointing. "That wasn't there this morning."

"Are you sure?"

She nodded. "This is my only jewelry drawer. I open it every day. But as you can see,"—she pointed to her neck—"I haven't taken anything off yet."

"Don't touch that note," Cameron said. He raced out of the room, muttering a few obscenities.

She froze, gripping the drawer, her gaze locked on the envelope. She heard Cameron talking to someone in the other room. She figured it was Stormi or someone else from the FBI.

Great. She would have to wake up her mother. That was the last thing she wanted to do. And then there was the question of who could keep an eye on her mom, because Vivian didn't think it was a good idea for her to stay at the house anymore.

Cameron returned, holding a pair of tweezers. He lifted the envelope and carefully ripped it open, letting a small piece of paper—her personal stationery—tumble out onto the dresser.

"I can't read it," she whispered.

"I'll do it." Cameron cleared his throat.

Vivian,

This is not what I wanted. When you find this note, it will be your turn to come and play. Meet me in this room. Log on as TheLastOne. I'll come find you.

If you don't do as you're told. Your little boyfriend will die. And don't think for one second I can't do it, because I can. I got into your house right under his nose.

See you soon.

Simon Says.

15

"The house is clean, and Larry's handwriting and fingerprints don't match."

"I didn't think they would." That knowledge didn't make Cameron feel any better. "I'm sure Eva will be glad to know her husband didn't have anything to do with this." Cameron stared at his two lists of names. The people who knew Oliver and Vivian, and the people who came to know Oliver through the chat rooms.

Interesting cast of characters, and there were too many that overlapped.

But if Oliver had figured out who Simon was, why hadn't he written that in his journal, which he kept in French for a reason?

Or put it in one of his folders that he purposely hid on his computer in an encrypted file that had taken Cameron's team a while to find?

"Where are Vivian and her mom?" Stormi asked.

"In the other cabin, resting," he said. "Tristan loaned us a couple of troopers. They are standing guard. I'll go get them shortly."

"Here." Stormi shoved a mug of coffee under his nose. "Did you get any sleep last night?"

"No," he admitted. "We found that note before I was able to even put my head on a pillow."

"That sucks." Stormi sat on the edge of the sofa and turned her attention toward Kidd, who had his screens and computer set up on a small table. He wore large headphones over his ears and was so hyper-focused on his task that Cameron had to wonder if he even knew Stormi had entered the room. "Has he even come up for air in the last hour?"

"No. I kind of told him I didn't want to hear his voice until he had Simon Says on the line. I've even got him using the screen name that Vivian came up with last night to try to hook that fucking asshole." Cameron rolled his neck. He hated feeling like a damned sitting duck. Knowing that dick was out there, waiting, watching, turned his blood ice-cold.

The very fact that Simon had set his sights on Vivian left more than a vile taste in Cameron's mouth. Jacob had told him last year that when Katie's murdering father had been hunting her for shits and giggles, Jacob had wanted to squeeze the life out of the man. That every sense of goodness had left his body for a moment, and it had terrified him because he knew that every good man could do bad things if pushed over the line.

This was Cameron's line.

"Has he logged in as Vivian?"

"Not yet," Cameron admitted. "I need her here to do that. I'm afraid he might know things about her that we don't or use things about Oliver. I don't want to tip him off."

Stormi chuckled. "He knows you're going to be right next to her the entire time. I'm pretty sure that's what he wants."

"Perhaps," Cameron said. "But I wanted to give her a chance to get an hour or two of rest before we put her in that position."

"Sounds like a plan," Stormi said.

Just then, Vivian came barreling through the door of the cabin, breathless.

Cameron jumped to his feet. His heart dropped to the pit of his stomach. "What's wrong?"

"I can't believe I didn't think of this before." She leaned forward, placing her hands on her knees.

He raced to her side and put his hand on her back, rubbing gently. "Breathe, Vivian."

"Thor was at my house yesterday." She stiffened her spine. "He showed up unannounced again. I would have sent him away, but he put together this nice video of Oliver from his days at camp. I thought it was sweet, and so did my mom. I couldn't turn him away. But he was inside my house. Without either myself or my mom."

"For the record, it couldn't have been Larry," Cameron said, pulling her into his arms. He didn't care that Stormi was there, or that Kidd was staring at him from his perch at the table. "I know your mom is still really upset, but the man made a mistake. He really loves your mom and he'd never cheat on her."

"I know that. My mom knows that. But are you hearing me right now? Thor was in my house. He could have put that note in my jewelry drawer."

"He's a teacher. His prints would have to be on file," Stormi said.

"I know he's liked me for a while, but he wasn't that aggressive about it until Oliver died. Isn't that weird?" Vivian's lashes blinked wildly over her questioning eyes. "Maybe he kept coming around because he wanted to know what you all were up to."

Fuck. Right under his goddamned nose. And he'd missed it. How could he have been so stupid? He wasn't so arrogant to believe that he could crack every case in a matter of minutes. It took a lot of work. Tons of brainpower. And a bit of luck.

But if Thor was his killer, and he hadn't seen a single sign?

Shit. Well, then Thor was one hell of a smart man. And ballsy, too.

Cameron snapped his fingers, waving his hand in front of Kidd, who pulled down his headphones. "Get ready to log on with *TheLastOne*."

"You got it." Kidd set his listening device on the table and tapped away on the keyboard.

"It's showtime." Cameron had to set aside his frustrations with himself. While it mattered, it wasn't what was important in the moment. Right now, he needed to focus on the script, setting the trap, and catching a killer. He pushed a chair next to Kidd. "I'm going to be right here with you the entire time, helping you with what to say. Kidd will work on figuring out where this asshole is hiding out. There's nothing for you to be afraid of."

"Oh. I'm not fearful. I just want to nail this asshole, and if it's Thor, I know where he lives," Vivian said. "If he's not there, he's up at his cabin at Camp Lookout. He likes to go there early, and the camp lets him."

"Good to know," Cameron said. "Stormi, take Tristan and go check it out. But don't spook the man. We don't have a warrant yet."

"On it," Stormi said. "Text me when I can slap the cuffs on this jerkoff." She smiled. "Unless you're going to make me wait."

Cameron groaned. "I'd like nothing more than to be the one to do it. But I wouldn't want to risk him getting away."

"Stay in touch." Stormi strapped on her weapon and headed out the door.

"Are you ready?" Cameron took Vivian by the biceps.

"Damn fucking right, I'm ready."

"That's my girl."

Vivian sucked in a deep breath and let it out slowly. She was painfully aware that five different dick pics came across a very large computer screen while Kidd was sitting next to her, and the man she was sleeping with stood right behind her, breathing down her neck.

"Where is he?" She tapped her foot nervously on the floor.

"No idea, but the last time Stormi checked in, she said he's not at the cabin at Camp Lookout. His car is at his house, but there's no movement. Stormi can't tell if he's inside or not." Cameron rubbed her shoulders.

It was supposed to ease the tension that had built in her muscles, but it honestly didn't help. That said, she wasn't about to ask him to stop. It might not make the stress go away, but it did feel really good.

"That was an hour ago," she said. "How long are we supposed to wait?"

"For as long as it takes."

Vivian didn't like that answer, but what choice did she have? She scanned the scrolling list of new names entering the main chat room.

No Simon Says.

"Stormi's calling," Cameron said. "I'll put it on speaker." He set his cell on the table. "What's up?"

"Thor's not at his house," Stormi said.

"What? When did he leave?" Cameron asked.

"I'm not sure. His cleaning lady showed up, and

we paid her a nice little tip to give us intel," Stormi said. "We have no idea why his car is still here, and I checked with the DMV. He doesn't have any other vehicles registered in his name."

"He could have a camp vehicle," Vivian interjected. "He often does a lot of work for them, spring cleaning and the like, and the camp director often lends him one of the vans."

"What would he be doing with it?" Cameron asked.

"The cabins often need repairs. Buying lumber? Or plumbing supplies? Even stocking up on bulk candy items for the trading post. Any number of things." She let out a sigh and leaned back in the chair. "But usually, that means his car would be at camp, so that doesn't necessarily make sense. Unless he's making runs with someone else."

"Or he borrowed a family member's car." Cameron didn't like how this day was shaping up one bit.

"I do have some good news," Stormi said. "Townsend got us a search warrant for Thor's house. Shall I execute it?"

"I'll be there in fifteen minutes," Cameron said.

Vivian turned her head and stared. She tried to stop the fear currently gripping her gut from reaching her eyes. "You're leaving me?"

"You need to sit here with Kidd and wait to see if Thor—Simon Says—shows up. If he does, Kidd knows the script." Cameron tucked her blond hair behind her ears.

"I can't do this without you."

He pulled her from the chair and wrapped his strong arms around her body. "You're in good hands with Kidd. I promise. I need to go search Thor's house. It's something I need to do." He pressed his warm, sweet lips over her mouth and let them linger for a long, passionate moment.

Too long, because Kidd had to clear his throat.

"I'll be in touch," Cameron said. "If anything happens, and Thor shows up in that chat room, I want to know, got it?"

Vivian nodded.

"This will be over soon." He holstered his weapon and slipped his arms through his sport coat before heading out the door.

Vivian fell back into the chair. She blinked, staring at the screen. "Is this what your job is with the FBI? Sitting in front of a computer all day?"

"Yup," Kidd said. "I'm actually on loan to this team. I work with the cybercrimes unit, specifically. My specialty is IT, so all I do is crack anything technology-related. Trust me when I say I'm a good shot, but you'd rather have me sitting here, rather than being out there dealing with people. Cameron's the guy you want doing that. He's one of the best. Actually, he's probably the best I've ever worked with."

"That's what I've heard Jacob say."

"Ah. I miss that man." Kidd folded his arms

across his chest. "However, he recently called me as an excerpt witness in a case of his. Man, he's really good in a courtroom. I can't say I was surprised when he left the FBI."

"Neither was his wife," Vivian said. "They have bets on how long it will take for Cameron to leave and join Katie and her business partner, Jackson, in their private investigation business." She cringed. She shouldn't have said that to one of his colleagues. Stirring up rumors at the water cooler wasn't being a supportive girlfriend.

Girlfriend?

Could she honestly consider herself that after one night?

And did she want to?

Part of her worried that she'd jumped into bed with him so quickly because of the pain she felt in her heart over losing her brother. It hurt so badly, she didn't know how to compartmentalize all the raging emotions that tried to suffocate her soul. She'd been attracted to Cameron, and even liked him before her brother's murder. However, the hunt for his killer had intensified her feelings for him.

"I miss Jacob, and I'll miss Cameron when he leaves. He's the best. But, honestly, better suited for something a little less rigid."

She leaned back in her chair and let her hands fall to her lap. If Thor really was Simon Says and was currently driving around in a camp van somewhere, he wouldn't be playing in some adult chat room, and she didn't need to be ready to try to catch him at his own game. "What do you mean by that?"

Kidd glanced in her direction. He was an older man with kind eyes that allowed the world to see deep inside his warm heart. Kidd was the quiet type. Introverted. He could be in a room and you wouldn't even know it.

Until you did.

Then…watch out.

Because this was the kind of man who, when on your side, would fight for you until the bitter end, no questions asked.

"I'm sure you know that Cameron is a genius."

She nodded. "I suspect his IQ is about as high as they come."

Kidd nodded. "He graduated from high school when he was sixteen and, sadly, even though he was athletic and played sports, was a total nerd. Like the kind of kid that no one wants to be friends with."

"I can't imagine that." She knew those kinds of kids. She taught them. And Cameron was far from socially awkward.

"Well. He was. He went to college and did it in less than three years."

"How the hell did he do that?"

"Summer school and by taking the maximum credits allowed. He had a love-hate relationship with school. He loved learning, but it came too easy to him. And he hated being at school. He was so much younger than everyone else, and he didn't fit in."

"I had no idea."

"He has a great support system with his family, and the teachers all loved him. And like I said, he played sports. That helped him get by." Kidd shook his head, laughing. "I do guest lectures at Quantico on cybercrimes. He was in one of my lectures, and the kid ate everything up. He's like a damned sponge. When his name appeared on my boss's possible-hire list, I was like, 'Take that kid.' He was only twenty-three years old, and he'd done more than some seasoned agents."

"He was a trooper before he became a fed. That blows me away because he's so young."

"You and me both. But you must remember, he graduated college when he was nineteen. Became a NY state trooper when he graduated, and while doing that for a few years, he got his master's degree in criminal justice and then went to Quantico. The boy has an amazing mind and mad skills, but he's so restricted working for the FBI. Or any law enforcement agency, really. It was Jacob's problem, too. Their hands are tied so often, and it forces them to sit back and wait, and that makes them crazy."

"I'm still not sure I understand."

"You're friends with Katie and Jacob, right?"

She nodded.

"Do you remember when Katie's father showed up and tried to hunt her like an animal?"

"I do." Vivian shivered.

"Jacob had to sit back and do things mostly by the

book. But his wife didn't. She was a private investigator, and while breaking or bending the law isn't necessarily a good idea and could get her into trouble, it's not the same kind of trouble. If Jacob had done some of the same things she had, he would have jeopardized the case. Cameron has tried to use Katie and Jackson as much as he can in this case, but the cyber division has been dealing with this asshole, Simon Says, for a while now. It's too intertwined with your brother's murder, and Cameron feels helpless. No amount of brainpower can change a sense of powerlessness. If he were in the private sector, he could be doing other things. Taking different risks. And knowing Cameron, he would."

"I'm not sure I like the sound of that any better than watching him strap on a gun and then put on a sport coat like he's off to shoot some alien. Have you ever noticed how he takes that thing on and off? It's the same way every time."

"He is a little weird about his clothes." Kidd laughed. "The really scary thing about Cameron is that he's the best damn shot in our office. If he were to join the military, he could have his pick of careers, including as a sniper."

"No one is that good at everything."

"The only thing Cameron's not good at is giving himself a break."

Now that she believed.

"So, what do we do now?"

"We do the worst part of this job. We wait."

16

"Thor Myers. Open up. It's Agent Cameron Thatcher with the FBI." Cameron held his gun at the ready.

Stormi, one step behind him, covered his back.

SWAT had the house surrounded, while the search team waited in a van across the street.

"Thor. We have a warrant to search the premises. You have exactly three minutes to open this door, or we come in with force." Cameron held up his watch. He would give the man the exact amount of time, just to be fair.

"Seriously?" Stormi whispered. "You're going to give this fucker time?"

"Patience, grasshopper."

"Oh, screw you," Stormi muttered.

This would be the longest few minutes of Cameron's life.

One minute ticked by while Stormi breathed

heavily in his ear. Probably on purpose to annoy him so he'd break down and open the door earlier than promised.

He glanced over his shoulder. "Did anyone ever tell you that patience is a virtue?"

"Have you met me? Because no one has ever used the word *virtuous* to describe me. Now, let SWAT open the fucking door."

One more minute ticked by.

He took in a slow breath. In through the nose. Out through the mouth. He did this until the third minute registered on his watch.

"Thor, we're coming in."

This could very well be a trap, and he had to be prepared for that. He tapped the center of his bulletproof vest. A stupid ritual he'd gotten in the habit of doing when he was a state trooper. He took a single step back, letting a SWAT team member maneuver in front of him and use the back of his large machine gun to bust through the front door.

The rest of the SWAT team members raced into the house.

Cameron followed.

Each room was secured.

Thor was nowhere to be found.

His house was extraordinarily neat. Like white-glove clean.

Cameron took a stroll through the kitchen, opening all the cabinets. "Stormi, take a look at this."

"Why? It's just canned goods."

"But what do you notice about them?"

"That he likes clam chowder from a can, which is kind of gross," Stormi said.

"There's that, but all the labels are perfectly lined up and facing outward. This guy has some OCD." Cameron pointed to the towels on the stove. "The lines on the bottom match exactly. I bet the corners on his bed are made like a hospital bed."

"Being OCD doesn't mean anything."

"I know, but he likes things a certain way. He gets upset when the universe is out of whack. If someone were to come into his house and say…do this—" Cameron adjusted the towels so they weren't matching and then went to the cabinet and arranged the cans and turned them so they weren't lined up neatly. "He'd get angry and possibly violent. He has to be in control at all times. When things get out of control, he doesn't know how to respond, and he lashes out. This isn't your typical OCD. I have that problem. I mean, have you ever seen the way I hang up my coat? It's a struggle for me every day. But this is extreme."

"What are you getting at?"

"Oliver changed his game, and now he's scrambling to adjust the rules. I'm sure he's done that before. It's getting out of hand, and he's losing control. He's losing people. His followers are no longer playing *his* game. Annabel told me that they've been warning people about him, and Simon's been more aggressive than usual. More threatening. She's worried he's going to do something crazy."

"Agent Thatcher," one of the other agents on the search team called. "You're going to want to see this."

Cameron made his way through the family room and into the den where Thor had set up a master room of manipulation.

Inside were a couple of computers. A dozen screens. Five corkboards. On the top of each one was the word: *Players.* Pinned to them were at least fifty people.

"Jesus," Cameron muttered. His stomach filled with acid.

"That's not what I thought you'd find to be the worst part," the other agent said as he opened a cabinet, showing off a board filled with images of Vivian. Pictures of her taken on her dock as she sunbathed. At summer camp while she sailed with her campers. At school while she taught.

And with Cameron while they kissed on the back porch.

Of course, in that one, his face had been replaced with Thor's.

"That's fucked up," Stormi said.

"No shit," Cameron muttered. He took a pencil and started lifting piece of papers on the desk. He read a few words on the pages.

Thor and Vivian…

Marriage…

Together forever…

Make her mine…

Do whatever's necessary…

Be the hero…

He soaked in as much of the room as possible, making sure that every detail was forever ingrained in his brain. He hated that he could do that. He didn't want this to be with him forever, but if he were going to catch Thor and put him away for a very long time...

And keep Vivian safe. This is what he had to do.

"What is he doing?" the other agent whispered.

"He's got a photographic memory. He's collecting evidence. The rest of us have to do it the hard way," Stormi said. "You might as well just stay out of his way."

Cameron tugged open one of the drawers and groaned. "I need gloves."

Stormi handed him a pair. "What did you find?"

"A folder with Oliver's name on it." He snapped on the gloves and lifted the folder. He flattened it on the table and started pulling the key information from the pages. Most of it was how Oliver was connected to the other players. Things that Simon—or Thor—wanted him to do. A check mark next to what Cameron assumed was a completed task.

Cameron's stomach churned. He couldn't believe the things that Oliver had done for his friend—not even a woman he was in love with.

Or maybe he was, but Annabel wasn't someone

he could be with. Still, he'd done all this to help Annabel save herself and her marriage.

Oliver was truly one of the good guys, and Cameron wished things had turned out differently. It broke his heart that Vivian would never be able to hug her brother again. Tears burned Cameron's eyes. He blew out a puff of air as he flipped over a couple of pages. "Thor was forcing Oliver to leave the game. He wanted Annabel back, and if Oliver didn't step away, Thor threatened to ruin Annabel."

"Is there anything there that indicates why he had the change of heart?" Stormi asked.

"Yeah. Me." Cameron carefully lifted an image of him and Vivian at the Boardwalk about a month ago. He remembered the night well. She hadn't agreed to go out with him, but she'd been warming up to the idea. "Thor's wanted Vivian for a while. He's been getting bolder and bolder with her. Showing up at her place unannounced. She's very nice to him, but she's been clear that she doesn't want to date him. But between her flirting with me" —he handed the picture to Stormi—"and the fact that I'm an agent, he needed to do something about Oliver. But I don't think he intended to kill him at first." He spread out a few more pages and quickly scanned them for the pertinent information and he certainly got an eyeful. "He writes that Oliver confided in him that he was struggling with his drug use and was having self-harm thoughts. He also writes here that Oliver told others, like Annabel, about his father being in a sex club. That he even saw the evidence."

"Does it say where?" Stormi asked.

"No. But some things in here don't jibe with what I know about Oliver in real life and what he told his therapist," Cameron said.

"Maybe Oliver was baiting him. Trying to get him to show his hand."

Cameron handed Stormi a piece of paper. "Thor found the videos in Vivian's closet. According to this, the plan was to make it look as if Oliver took his life over finding out about his father. But the plan developed only after Thor found out he was being played."

"Do we know if Oliver ever figured out that Thor was Simon?" Stormi asked.

"I can't tell from these notes. My guess is he didn't. Or if he did, it was within hours of his death."

"Check this out," one of the other agents said from behind the computer.

Cameron glanced over his shoulder. On the screen was a picture of Thor, badly photoshopped into an image of Vivian. Also on the screen were the words: *This is our summer. We'll be engaged by the end of it. Married by the end of the year.*

"It seems Oliver got in the way of Thor's plans to make Vivian his bride," Stormi said.

"Somewhere in here, there has to be a list of who murdered my first two victims," Cameron said.

"We need Kidd to look at his system," Stormi said.

Cameron nodded. "I don't want Vivian over here, but I think it's safe to say we don't need her sitting in front of a computer screen, waiting to chat with that asshole." He rolled his neck. "We need to issue a warrant for Thor's arrest. Get it out to every law enforcement agency in the area. We need to consider him armed and dangerous."

"I'm on it," Stormi said.

"Jacob and Katie offered for Vivian and her mom to stay there until we find Thor. I'm going to take them up on that. I think the Heritage Inn is too close to her house for comfort."

"I agree." Stormi continued to open and close drawers and cabinets as they searched the office for clues.

Cameron's mind kept going back to Vivian. No matter how hard he tried to focus on all the looming intel that surrounded him, all he wanted to do was go and wrap his arms around her, pull her close to his chest, and tell her it would be okay. He couldn't bring her brother back, but he could comfort her, and he sure as shit could bring Thor down.

But he needed to clear his brain first.

"Cameron, I found something that might be important," one of the agents said.

"What is it?" Cameron raced across the room to the agent in question.

"It's a safe." The agent waved his hand in front of a fake bookcase.

"Can you get inside that?"

"Of course. It just might take a little bit of time," the agent said.

"Do it, and then call me as soon as you know what's inside." Cameron had seen enough. His mind had enough intel. He didn't need more. Right now, he needed to go back to the Heritage Inn, collect Vivian, and drive her to Jacob's.

Then he needed to pick his brain for a few moments before heading back into the field.

"Stormi, I want you to get one of Tristan's men and head up to Camp Lookout. If Thor's there by chance, you know the drill. If he's not, find out as much as you can about him, what he's like there, and where he might be." Cameron turned on his heels and headed out the door. He took out his cell from his back pocket and quickly sent a text to Kidd, informing him of the situation. And then one to Vivian.

He should feel better that they knew exactly who they were dealing with, but he didn't, and he wouldn't until Thor was behind bars.

And that would happen today.

Vivian threw herself at Cameron as soon as he came through the door. "Kidd told me about some of the things you and Stormi found at Thor's house. I knew he had feelings for me, but that's just gross."

"You have no idea." Cameron wrapped his arms around her and squeezed tightly.

She welcomed the embrace. "Was my brother killed because of me?"

Cameron cupped her face. "No. His death is not your fault."

"I know. I mean, I understand I didn't cause it. But did Thor go after him because he had this sick, twisted idea of him and me?" Vivian hadn't had a chance to grieve for her brother, and she wouldn't until Thor was captured.

Kidd hadn't given her a lot of information about what Cameron had found. Actually, Kidd had beaten around the bush. What little he had told her hadn't made much sense, other than that Thor had this crazy idea that she would belong to him by the end of the summer.

Gross.

She shivered.

"Unfortunately, two unrelated things got caught in the same game." Cameron kissed her gently. "First, your brother wanted to help a friend. That's how he got caught in the game. And secondly, Thor's feelings for you had nothing to do with Oliver entering Thor's twisted world, which Thor never wanted you to see. That was made evident by some of the things he wrote in a notebook that he kept about you."

"That's really creepy."

"That's being kind." Cameron tucked her hair behind her ears and stared deeply into her eyes, cutting right to her soul. She had no idea why she'd been so standoffish with Cameron for so long. He was kind, considerate, and he genuinely cared about her and her wellbeing. He was one of the good guys, and she'd be lucky to have him as a boyfriend.

She knew there were no guarantees.

Look at Larry.

Another good guy who had made a horrible mistake.

More than one.

But her stepdad loved her mother, and she hoped her mom could somehow see past those mistakes and that she and Larry could work through their differences.

"What did Thor write about me?" she asked.

"I'll tell you on the car ride over to Jacob's." He handed Kidd something. "Thor has a relatively sophisticated system set up at his place, but I'm sure you won't have any problem cracking it."

"I appreciate your confidence." Kidd sidestepped Vivian and Cameron and stood in the middle of the doorway. "I'll be in touch."

"See you soon." Cameron pressed his hand to the center of Vivian's back. "We should get going. Jacob doesn't have that much time, and I need to get back out into the field."

"What about my mom?"

"Your mom and Larry are staying in the safe house with my agents."

"I don't like putting Katie's baby in danger. And why can't we all be together?"

"Because Thor can't be in more than one place at a time." Cameron pressed his finger against her lips. "And I'm well aware that he's had his followers doing things, but Kidd has his cyber team looking for any activity on the websites for people talking about Simon's games or orders from Simon. Besides, Thor wouldn't expect us to take your mom and Larry to a state trooper's house or you to the assistant district attorney's house. Trust me."

She palmed his cheek. For the first time since her father died, she trusted a man completely. She knew in her heart that Cameron would do whatever it took to make sure that everyone was safe. And not just because it was his job. Because he cared.

Honestly cared.

Of course, this was his job, and her brain reminded her that if this were any other case, and if she were any other woman, he'd still be giving it his all.

Just not all the special touches because he didn't have to drive her to the Bateman Estate, which wasn't a sanctioned FBI safe house.

"I do trust you."

"Good. Now, let's go."

She pushed her sunglasses up over her eyes and followed Cameron to his SUV. Her heart pounded erratically. She scanned the parking lot, looking for a camp van. Or Thor's car.

What did he drive?

Hell, she had no idea. She barely paid attention to the man unless she had to. He'd been a bit of a thorn in her side, and she only dealt with him when she had to. And, honestly, that had been more during the summer months than the school year. Thor had been easier to avoid in the winter—until she bought her house. Before that, she'd lived about twenty minutes south of the village, making it harder for him to simply stop by.

"Thor hasn't always been this interested in me." She stared out the window as they passed the beach at the south end of the lake. "But last summer, he started laying it on thick, and it only got worse when I moved into this house."

"When did you close?"

"I didn't move in until March, but I closed in February," she said. "He started showing up regularly in April. I honestly didn't think anything of it. Like I said before, I've known him forever, and he's been a decent friend."

Cameron reached across the front seat and took her hand. "If you saw what I just saw, you'd rethink that statement."

"So, why did he kill Oliver? That's certainly not any way to win my heart."

"No. It's not." Cameron squeezed her hand. "I believe it was a last resort. To protect his double life so he could still have you."

"I'm sorry, that makes no sense to me."

"If what I've put together in my mind is correct, Thor sees Oliver's death as a necessary evil to protect his interests. Because Oliver was coming after Thor as Simon, Thor felt like he had no choice. He had to put an end to Oliver. And he had to do it in such a way that it looked like Oliver ended his own life."

"But that's not what happened."

"Because he didn't anticipate me," Cameron said. "Nor did he consider that you and I would have feelings for each other." When he rolled to a stop at the corner by Cleverdale Country Store, he glanced in her direction. "And I do have some pretty strong ones for you."

She smiled. Her heart fluttered. "I've fought mine for you. Because of my father, I don't trust men."

"I don't blame you."

She tilted her head. "Really? Because I've been told that I'm being a little unfair to the male population."

"Not at all. Your father betrayed your mom in the most fundamental way. I don't blame you for being untrusting."

"But you expect my mom to forgive Larry." She shifted in her seat and studied his profile.

"I believe that's very different. Larry didn't cheat on his late wife. And he didn't cheat on your mom." Cameron made the turn onto Cleverdale and then into the parking lot of the corner store. "I will say that he crossed a line when he gave Oliver his wife's computer, but he had no idea how any of this was connected. But Larry's not an FBI agent. He had no idea what he was dealing with. Nor did Oliver. That was their only real mistake. Both of them should have come to me. Or Jacob. Or Katie."

"You really are Larry's fan," she muttered. In reality, so was she, but she was also in her mother's corner, and if her mom wasn't ready to forgive, then neither was she.

"It's not a matter of being a fan. I deal in facts, and while I know this is an emotional time, and your mom has every right to be mad, Larry was only trying to be a good friend to Oliver." Cameron reached out and ran his thumb over her cheek. "I'm not belittling your mother's feelings. Or yours. It's going to take time. I'm only saying that Larry isn't your father. Nor am I."

"I know that." She curled her fingers around his wrist. "Why did we stop?"

"Jacob's son Jonathan loves the home-baked cinnamon bread the owner of this store makes. I thought I'd pick him up some. I hope you don't mind."

"Not at all." She smiled. "You really are one of the good guys."

He leaned across the cab and brushed his lips over hers. "Promise not to tell anyone?"

"Your secret is safe with me." He slipped from the driver's seat and raced across the hood of the SUV

She let out a long breath and watched as he disappeared into the store. She would have to have a nice long chat with her mom after all this was over and they'd both had a little bit of time to process Oliver's death. Larry deserved to have his side of the story heard.

He'd also been looking for answers about his wife's betrayal and death.

The sound of the back door opening caught her attention. She twisted her head and gasped.

"Hello, Vivian. How are you this beautiful afternoon?"

"Thor?"

"In the flesh." He pressed a gun to the side of her head. "I wouldn't do anything stupid if I were you."

She swallowed.

"Now. We're going to sit here and wait for your boyfriend, and then we're going for a little ride, got it?"

17

Cameron stood at the cash register in total disbelief. The fucking nerve and balls of Thor to hop into the back of *his* SUV and think he could just get away with it.

Well, abso-fucking-lutely NOT.

He stuffed his money clip back into his pocket and took the loaf of bread. "Thanks." He sent a 9-1-1 text to both Jacob and Stormi and made sure he turned his tracking on. If Thor touched a hair on Vivian's head, Cameron would make sure he suffered.

Racing out to the vehicle, he paused about fifteen paces away and placed his hand over his weapon.

Thor was in the back seat.

With a gun pressed to Vivian's head.

Thor didn't want her dead. On the contrary. He wanted her all to himself. As his possession. But there was no way he wanted Vivian as part of the game. He would have wanted the person he took as a bride to be pure.

However, Thor *did* want Cameron six feet under. The only question was, how did he intend to make that happen? What was his game? Because Thor always had one.

From what Cameron had seen at Thor's house, and given everything he'd learned from Annabel, Sally, and Oliver, Thor didn't do his own killing. He wanted someone to do it for him so he could watch.

Why would this be any different?

It wouldn't.

The back passenger window rolled down.

"It seems you lost the spring in your step," Thor said.

Cameron rested his hand on his weapon as he inched closer.

"I wouldn't do anything with that gun but hand it to me, or she dies."

"You don't want her dead." Cameron caught Vivian's gaze. She looked more pissed than scared.

He wasn't sure if that was a good thing, or a bad thing. He unclipped his service revolver.

"Of course, not. But I'll do it if you try to pull anything. Now, give me the gun and get in the vehicle. I'll tell you where to go."

Cameron handed over his weapon and then slipped behind the steering wheel. He pressed the start button. "Where to?"

"Head towards Pilot Knob. There's a side street

about a mile up the road you're going to turn down. A friend of mine has a place there," Thor said.

"Does this friend have a name?"

"Not important for you to know." Thor continued aiming his weapon at Vivian.

That didn't sit well with Cameron.

He pulled out onto 9L. It would only take them ten minutes to get to the location. Shifting in his seat, he made sure that Thor had his sights on something else as he tugged out his cell and stuffed it into the seat. He had a bad feeling that Thor would leave Cameron in a ditch somewhere and take off with Vivian. If that were the case, he wanted to make sure she could be tracked.

And Stormi could do just that on his phone.

"Maybe not, but don't I deserve to know the plan since I'm not part of it?" Cameron kept glancing at Vivian, who stared straight ahead.

Her face had paled. Occasionally, her eyes shifted in his direction, but remained stoic.

"You don't deserve shit," Thor said with a dark tone. "You've done nothing but screw with my life lately."

"Really? What the hell have I done to you?" Cameron made the left-hand turn onto Pilot Knob. He drove the speed limit. Not a mile over or under. He didn't want to bring attention to himself, but he also wanted to give Stormi a chance to digest his quick text and develop a plan.

Not that he'd really given her much information to go on, only that he was in trouble.

"It doesn't matter," Thor said. "The world will be right again shortly."

"How?" Cameron wanted to reach out and take Vivian's hand. He wanted to tell her it would be okay, but he didn't trust that Thor wouldn't do something crazy like hit her—or worse. He needed to buy some time. He needed to be patient.

"The *how* isn't important to you, so shut up." Thor leaned forward. "Turn here and pull into the driveway of the third house on the left. Put the car in park and give me the key."

"Why would I do that?" Cameron rolled the vehicle to a stop in front of a modest home on the lake.

"Because you're getting out here, and we're leaving," Thor said.

Vivian turned her head; her eyes wide.

"I'm not leaving Vivian with you." Cameron slammed the gearshift into park and turned. "You'll have to kill me before that happens."

Thor laughed. "Oh, you're going to die. I'm just not going to be the one to do it." He pressed his gun closer to Vivian. "And while I'm not a killer and I love Vivian and don't want to hurt her, I will. So don't make me."

He scanned the area. It was a dead-end street with six houses. Four on the waterfront, and two up on the hill, overlooking the lake. It didn't appear anyone was around. But that didn't mean that someone wasn't sitting in their family room, looking down, watching the scene unfold.

The good news—if Cameron could really consider it that—was that Thor would want to watch him die. Hopefully, he'd want to catch the live show.

That meant Thor had to get somewhere where he could go online and watch, because Cameron doubted that he'd want Vivian to see.

"I don't understand something," Cameron said.

"I don't give a shit. Now, give me the keys."

Cameron reached into his pocket and set the key fob on the center console. He hoped his phone was well hidden in the seat. He needed Stormi to be able to track Vivian. She was what mattered right now, more than anything.

Vivian grabbed his hand and locked gazes with him. Tears filled her eyes.

"It's going to be okay," Cameron said. "Trust me."

"Get out of the vehicle." Thor turned the gun on Cameron. "Don't try to be a hero. She'll live if you do what I tell you."

Cameron eased from the driver's seat. "And what exactly is that?"

Thor opened the passenger door and stepped from the SUV. He kept the weapon pointed right at Cameron's heart.

If Cameron thought it would do any good, he'd take the bullet right now.

"You're going to turn and walk to that house and

ring the bell. They're expecting you." Thor climbed into the vehicle. "I'm going to drive away, and you're not going to stop me."

"Where are you taking Vivian?" Cameron's pulse increased. A dark sedan slowed at the top of the main road but then continued down Pilot Knob.

It wasn't his team.

He didn't like how this was going down.

"None of your business," Thor said. "But don't worry. I'm not going to hurt her. Not as long as my friend does what she's supposed to do, and Vivian here realizes that I'm the right person for her."

"I should warn you that every law enforcement agency is looking for you. There is no way you'll be able to go anywhere without getting caught." The longer Cameron stood there, the better chance his team had of arriving and creating a plan that didn't get anyone killed.

Or shot.

Except maybe Thor, because Cameron was damn tired of staring at the wrong end of a gun.

"Don't you worry about me or my little lady. We'll manage living off the grid for a while." He pulled the door closed, turning the weapon back on Vivian, who gasped. "Now, go. Ring that bell."

"This isn't over." Cameron turned. The hairs on the back of his neck stood on end.

Thor was either the dumbest man on God's green Earth.

Or the most brilliant.

The SUV's engine revved.

Cameron swallowed as he glanced over his shoulder.

"I'm not leaving until you enter that house," Thor said in an almost sing-song voice.

Cameron couldn't stall any longer. With a shaky finger, he pressed the doorbell and waited maybe thirty seconds before the door swung open.

"Babs Dillard?"

She stood at the threshold with a gun in her hand. "I'm sorry," she whispered.

Bang!

18

B*ang!* Cameron dropped to his knees at the doorway of some woman's house.

Vivian let out a blood-curdling screen. "What the fuck have you done?" She stared at Thor. "You bastard. And you think I'll go anywhere with you? You're crazy."

He pointed the gun in her face. "Do you want to die, too? Do you want me to send someone after your mother? Larry? Because that's what I'll do. I have people everywhere, willing to do my bidding."

She stuck her head out the window. The woman dragged Cameron's body into the house.

The tears in her eyes dried and were replaced with harsh rage. She turned her attention back to Thor, who pulled out onto Pilot Knob, heading north toward camp. "You'll never make me like you or want to be with you. If that's what your plan is."

"If that's the case, then Sally's dirty little secret will come out, and so will your father's. But it will happen in such a way that it will destroy your mom and Larry. They will become so shameful that maybe they will drink themselves into a car accident. Or drown in the lake. I'll make it happen. Look at what I made happen to Cameron."

"Fear is how you plan on keeping me? That's sick, Thor." She folded her arms across her chest and stared out the window. "You might as well just kill me now because I will never succumb to your wishes."

"That's my last resort, honey."

"Don't call me that." She swallowed the small amount of vomit that bubbled up from her gut.

Her brother was dead.

And if Cameron wasn't yet, he likely would be soon.

But she'd be damned if she'd put a nail in her mom's or Larry's coffin. She had to keep them alive. And that meant staying with this asshole. However, it would take some time before she could stomach playing along with his stupid game.

She blew out a puff of air. "I'm going to need some insurance and proof that my mom and Larry won't be harmed."

"You don't trust me?"

She glared. "You just had a man killed. Of course, I don't. But prove to me that you won't hurt anyone else, and maybe I'll come around."

"Now, who's playing whom?" Thor asked with a chuckle.

"It's not that I'm playing you. I'm working on a strategy for my mom's survival." She tucked her hair behind her ears as more of his plan developed. She knew that no one in the FBI would take what happened to Cameron lying down.

Jacob, Katie, and Jackson sure as hell wouldn't let it go.

"And I want to be able to see her again. Can you make that happen?"

"That might be harder, thanks to Cameron. They are going to spin this very negatively against me. And the media will say that I kidnapped you. I'm not sure how to change that narrative." He continued holding the weapon, aiming in her general direction. She was less worried about him shooting her, but she still didn't want to piss him off.

Jacob and Katie would be looking for her and Cameron shortly.

She had to buy some time.

She had to think like Cameron.

They drove past the main entrance of Camp Lookout and rounded the corner toward the waterfront and his cabin.

But they passed that, as well.

She noticed that the campground was eerily quiet.

That wasn't right.

There should be more people milling about.

Not a lot, but considering it was late in the day,

and a weekend, some of the lifer staff should be here, doing clean-up projects and preparing for the staff and campers.

"So, you just plan on waiting it out for a few years? Hiding out somewhere? We both have careers. What about my home? What about camp?" She pointed behind her at the bay they'd just passed where all the sailboats were moored.

"I'm prepared to start over." He turned into the last driveway where the main road ended, and the fire access road started. "I'm also prepared to have your mother join us. But not Larry. I'm sorry. He's not worthy."

She wanted to ask him what gave him the right to judge, but she realized that she'd made that call for her mom a couple of days ago when Cameron had been trying to tell her that Larry had his faults but wasn't a cheater.

He was simply trying to protect his family—and his late wife's memory from being tainted.

Something she—of all people—could understand.

As the SUV came to a stop where the access road ended, the world started to spin.

She closed her eyes and pinched the bridge of her nose. "This is a lot to take in."

"I know. I'm sorry that this is how we have to do things. Had Cameron not meddled in my plans, things would be different."

She snapped her gaze to Thor's. "But what about

Oliver? What about this Simon Says stuff? That is you, right?"

"I see Cameron has been filling your head full of crazy stuff."

"If you expect me to accept this so-called new life, I need you to be honest with me. Otherwise, put a bullet between my eyes and call it a day. Because you just had a man I care very much about killed. Not to mention my brother. The only thing that is keeping me wanting to stay alive is my mom."

"I know this is hard for you, but if you let your mind wander back to last summer, and then when you moved into your house, and some other times, we shared some special moments. We were connecting. You can't deny that. But then Cameron came into the picture, and he started mucking up the waters. If that hadn't happened, I know that you and I would be together right now, and this wouldn't have happened."

"And what about your game and my brother? Or are you going to say you didn't have him killed?" She twisted in her seat, leaning against the door. "And do you actually believe that I would be okay with your sexual exploits? The websites? The games? I'm sorry, Thor. But I find that disgusting. My father—"

"I know all about your father."

"And how do you know about him and what he did?"

"It doesn't matter," Thor said. "I'm sorry that you had to find out about my past. But that's over. I'm not doing it anymore."

She put her head between her legs and sucked in a deep breath. If she wasn't careful, she was going to lose her shit on Thor. What she really wanted to do was grab that fucking gun and turn it around on the bastard. "I don't believe you. You're a fucking liar."

He opened the SUV's door. "I'm not going to talk to you when you're like this," he said. "I'm going to prepare us for the hike we will soon be taking. You need to change your attitude. And then we can have a conversation. But until then, get out of the vehicle."

"You fucking shot me." Cameron gripped his side. Granted, the bullet had only grazed his stomach, but it still hurt like hell.

"I'm sorry. I had to make it look real. And I was under orders to video it. Thanks for playing along. Otherwise, your girlfriend might be dead."

"That still might be the case. If she thinks you killed me, she might panic." He glanced at his bloody hand. He had no way of reaching Vivian. No way of telling her that this was staged. That Thor's *person* had betrayed him. He could only hope that Vivian kept her cool until the calvary showed up. "Can I use your phone?"

"Sure." Babs handed him her cell. "I've got a first-aid kit. Why don't you follow me into the kitchen?"

"How did you get caught up in this shit?" he asked as if he didn't know.

"I've been trying to get Simon's attention since I last walked out of Agent Donovan's office. I heard he's the ADA now."

"He is," Cameron said.

"Once I got in on Simon's game, I stayed on the fringes until I found the right time to up the ante. That was when I learned that you were involved, and I jumped at the chance to be your executioner."

"I don't know if I should be terrified or flattered." Cameron took off his coat, folded it properly, and set it on the chair at the table. He took the fresh towel she offered and pressed it against his wound, which was a little worse than he'd thought. The bullet had more than grazed him.

It'd put a hole in his side.

He would need stitches, and it wouldn't be easy to stop the bleeding. He did his best to put pressure on both sides without groaning in pain.

"How did you know it was me? How long has he been planning this?"

"Ever since you started poking around those murders from a year ago."

"So, Thor ordered those?"

"Who's Thor?" Babs set a kit on the table and flipped it open.

"The true identity of Simon Says."

Babs face paled. "I've been talking with that sick bastard for a year now." She slammed the antiseptic cleaner on the table. "I've been playing his game and doing things that make me sick to my stomach. I can't believe my sister was into this shit, and that she took her own life for that bastard." Babs wiped away the fresh tears that rolled down her face. "Sometimes, I wonder if she did it because she hated herself so much."

Cameron reached out and rested his hand on Babs' forearm. "My partner is tracking the car that he drove away in. We're going to catch Thor. I just need to make sure we do it before he kills my girlfriend."

Babs nodded.

"Tell me exactly what his plan is and who the players are."

"I only know my role," she said. "And that was to video killing you and then doctor it so it looked like someone else did it."

"Who's supposed to take the fall for my death?"

"I don't know. I'm supposed to send the video to another player who has the tech background to do it. His or her screen name is *TheBenz*."

"Motherfucker." That had to be Ethan.

He knew Thor.

Vivian.

Oliver.

Ethan had inside information that would be valuable to Thor, and Ethan could potentially want revenge against Cameron.

Quickly, Cameron dialed Stormi's cell. "Come on, pick up."

"This is Agent Swanson."

"Thank God," he muttered.

"Cameron? Why aren't you at Jacob's? We lost your signal on Pilot Knob. We're about a mile from the camp."

"Pull over," he commanded. "I need an arrest warrant for Ethan. I need someone to come stitch up my side."

"What the fuck? Why?"

"I was shot. I'm fine. It's just a small hole," he said breathlessly. "Thor has Vivian. If you lost the signal to my cell, it means they probably went up the fire access road behind the camp. He was planning on having someone take the fall for my murder. I don't know who, but Ethan does."

"Jesus, that's fucked up. Kidd's calling Tristan right now."

"Good. He's been instructed to doctor a video that was taken of me being shot. I want Kidd to take that video and have it look like Thor did it. We're going to send it to him, via Ethan—"

"That's fucking dangerous when he's holding Vivian hostage," Stormi said.

"His plan is to go off-grid, but he's not going to do that until he knows his plan has been executed. That will give us some time to surround them, and the only way he's getting anywhere is if he drives back down Pilot Knob or tries to hike out of there. We're going to be ready." He grimaced as Babs pressed a bandage soaked with cold antiseptic against his bleeding flesh.

His eyelids fluttered and he gritted his teeth. "We don't have much time. I'm about five miles down the road. I'll have Katie pick me up on the way there. She's also good with a needle. I hope," he muttered.

"I really tried not to hurt you too badly," Babs whispered.

"I know. And I appreciate that," he said. "Stormi, what's the ETA on anyone picking up Ethan? I'm sure Thor is expecting to hear from him soon regarding this video."

"Tristan has a team a few minutes out. I'll let you know as soon as we have him in custody. In the meantime, we've called for backup, and I'm going in for recon. We'll stay in touch."

"You fucking better. I'm not losing Vivian."

"I'm not going to let anything happen to your girlfriend," Stormi said.

"You better not."

19

Vivian sat on a rock at the first clearing about a mile from where the main road ended and sipped the water that Thor offered. He acted like all of this was normal.

That, somehow, she'd manage to forgive him for what he said he *had* to do so they could have the life that they *deserved*.

Oh, and he promised he'd give up *the game*.

She gulped the tasteless liquid, only the nasty flavor of betrayal hit her belly. Thor had been her friend. Her colleague. What the hell had happened to him to make him into this monster?

She shivered.

He sat at a picnic table with his laptop, staring at the screen with a crinkled forehead. He did that whenever he was frustrated. It'd always driven her nuts when they worked on the campers' skill-class schedule. Every summer, he had to be in control. He had to do things his way. And when it didn't work out, he got that scrunched-up look on his face.

It wasn't attractive.

And now, it made her sick to her stomach because she knew he was waiting for something that had to do with his stupid Simon Says game and Cameron.

Tears filled her eyes.

Could he really be gone?

Just because he'd been shot didn't mean he was dead.

She stiffened her spine. She wasn't doing this. No way in hell would she sit here and wait for this asshole to decide her fate. Disappearing would be worse than dying where her mother was concerned. Whatever happened to her, the people who loved her deserved closure.

And so did those whose lives Thor destroyed.

Thor's gun rested on the table next to the computer.

She needed that weapon if she were going to turn the tables. She could go over there, rub his shoulders, pretend to be on his side. But he wouldn't fall for that. He'd know she was up to something. Only fools in movies and television shows thought that the person being held against their will would change their tune so quickly.

Thor was too smart for that.

She stood and inched closer. "What are you doing?"

"It doesn't concern you." He glanced in her direction. "There are those protein bars you like so much in the backpack if you want one."

"I'm not hungry." She continued strolling in his direction with her hands clasped behind her back. Her gaze went from her feet to the sky and back to his computer. She wanted to see the screen, but she didn't want to appear too nosy.

"You're going to need eat something. We will eventually be doing some hiking."

"I really don't have good shoes for that."

"I've taken care of that," he said. "You have everything you need." He smiled. "You never have to worry again."

She laughed. Not a sarcastic ha-ha laugh but a full-on belly laugh.

"I don't see what's so funny."

"You do get we're going to fugitives, right? We're always going to be worried and looking over our shoulders, wondering when we're going to be caught."

"No. That's where you're wrong."

She stood directly behind him and peered over his shoulder. "How is that possible? Cameron told me about what he found in your house. His people were there. They know you're Simon Says. More than just Cameron knows about your games and what you've had people do."

"That doesn't make me a criminal." He shook his head. "I've never hurt anyone. I've never forced anyone to do anything. If they feel that way, it's on them."

"You just forced Cameron to go into that house by holding me at gunpoint. How is that not hurting someone? Not to mention whoever was behind that door killed for you." A cold sensation washed over her skin as if she'd stepped inside an icebox. "You even said yourself that your people will do whatever you want. You're holding something over their heads in order to make them do these things."

"Oh, you disappoint me." He twisted on the bench. "I'm only pushing people to do what's in their true hearts. They go to these websites because there is darkness in their souls. They need to explore that. It's not my fault."

Rage filled her like an erupting volcano. "My brother's heart was pure. The only reason he went there was to help a friend."

"Are you sure about that? Because he struggled when he found out about your dad." Thor lifted his hands, rubbing one index finger over the other, making a *tsk tsk* sound. "You shouldn't have kept that from him."

"You took those videos from my house."

Thor nodded. "But your brother found them a long time ago. It unleashed that legacy that was already there." He reached out and took her hand.

She jerked away.

He let out a short chuckle. "Your brother played this game for a long time, and he enjoyed it. Which is why I kept him in the game for so long. Besides, I don't think he really wanted to go. Every time I upped the ante, he did it."

"You're a sick man," Vivian said under her breath. "I'm not going anywhere with you today."

"Don't make me do this the hard way."

"I'm not making you do anything. I'm simply not going anywhere with you. I'll never want to be with you. I'll never care for you. I'll always resent you for what you did to my brother. To my boyfriend. And to all those innocent people. So, you might as well take that fucking gun and put me out of my misery because that's what being with you would be. Fucking miserable." She lunged at the table and made a play for the weapon.

Thor jumped to his feet and shoved her to the ground. "Are you fucking kidding me?" He reached for the gun and pointed it at her as she lay on her back, elbows digging into the hard earth. "Don't be stupid."

"Pull the trigger," she said, venom lacing every single syllable. She'd never hated anyone. Not even her father. She resented him for betraying her mother. For destroying their family.

And then for being a coward.

But part of her loved the man who'd been her daddy. No one could take that away. He wasn't evil. He had an addiction.

Thor was Satan.

He exploited people's weaknesses for his own sick, twisted pleasure.

"Do it, asshole. Or don't you have the fucking nerve?" She blinked. She really didn't want to die, but she wouldn't run either.

He leaned closer, pressing the metal against her temple.

Her heart beat so fast, she figured the crickets could hear it.

"It's not that I don't have the nerve. But I love you. However, for the last year, something has always gotten in the way. First, it was your mother's dating and you buying a house. Then it was you moving and problems with your brother and then your mom's wedding. Of course, we can't forget Cameron, who fooled you with his charm. You just need a little time to see me for who I really am."

"Having Cameron killed did that."

He stood upright, lowering his weapon. "I'm going to get back to my computer. As soon as I'm done, we're heading out. Don't make me go to plan B."

"And what's that?"

"Drug you."

"If you do that, how do you plan on getting me up Black Mountain?"

He laughed. "We have options for how we get there, and that's all I'll say about that." He sat back down in front of the computer, resting the gun on his lap.

Well, if he had a second game plan, she'd come

up with one of her own. Because there was no way she would hike any farther. Not with him.

"What the fuck is she doing?"

Cameron groaned as he took the binoculars from Katie. "Looks like she's tired of being held hostage and wants to fight back."

"I've always known she had spunk, but I was honestly worried about how she'd handle herself in a situation like this." Katie pushed herself into a sitting position. "I can't believe she made a play for the gun."

Nor could Cameron. "She's desperate and thinks I'm dead."

"That might not be a good thing."

"I know." Slowly, Cameron stood. He surveyed the area. It would take at least fifteen more minutes before the SWAT team was in place. The goal was to take Thor alive, but they had a sniper in position if it came down to it.

"Your boss is going to be pissed that I'm here," Katie said. "So, it's probably best if I take a step back."

"Agreed. I appreciate you stitching me up."

"I enjoyed it," she said with a beaming smile.

He laughed. "Of course, you did."

"Jackson and I will be at the clearing if you need us."

"I appreciate it." Cameron rolled his neck as he

made his way to where Stormi and Kidd were perched about twenty-five paces to the north. "Are we ready?"

"We are," Stormi said.

Cameron wasn't completely on board with this plan, but they were nearly out of time. "Okay. Send the video and then stumble on down."

Stormi pinned the mic on Kidd's shirt.

Cameron brought the binoculars to his eyes once more. "She'll recognize you right away, and she'll have a hard time hiding that," he said. "Try to come up on them so she'll see you, but he won't see her face."

"I know," Kidd said. "We've gone over this five times."

Cameron wanted to remind Kidd that he'd be ramming the plans down his throat if that was his girl down there but opted to keep his mouth shut. They all knew what was at stake, and he trusted them with his life.

Kidd pulled out his tablet from his knapsack. He tapped the screen. "It will take a couple of minutes for it to hit his inbox." Kidd handed Cameron the electronic device. "Follow my script, and you'll be fine."

Cameron nodded. "Let's take this asshole down."

Kidd tapped the mic. "Testing."

"Loud and clear," Stormi said.

Kidd shouldered his backpack and headed down toward the clearing.

Cameron placed his hand on his service revolver. He blew out a puff of air and kept his focus on Vivian.

"He's going down," Stormi said.

"I know. But if Vivian has even a single bruise, you're going to have to stop me from beating the shit out of him."

Vivian knew something was wrong when Thor started mumbling obscenities and pounded his fingers against the keyboard.

"He's going to regret crossing me," Thor mumbled.

"What's going on?"

"Nothing that concerns you." Thor slammed his hand against the table. It vibrated, sending his water tumbling to the ground. "This has to be some kind of stupid joke." He set the gun back on the picnic table, and his fingers flew across the keyboard in angry succession.

Maybe she had a second chance. She leaned over and picked up the water bottle. She stood three feet behind him, to the left. When she straightened her body, she swallowed a gasp.

There stood Agent Kidd.

"Excuse me," Kidd said. "Sorry to bother you, but my dog ran off." Kidd held up an empty leash. "Have you seen any dogs running through here in the last half hour or so? He's a—"

"No. Sorry. We haven't." Thor quickly took the weapon and tucked it behind his back. "We're a little busy getting ready for a camping trip, and I forgot to do some things at home." He pointed to the computer. "My wife here isn't real happy with me about it, and I'm struggling with my hotspot."

"Oh. I work in IT. Maybe I can help," Kidd said.

"Don't you need to go look for your dog?"

Kidd smiled. "It's not the first time he's run off." He pointed over his shoulder. "I live in the last house on the main road. I had to call the cops because some idiot parked his car in my driveway." He pointed at Thor. "That wasn't you, was it?"

"No. We're in the public parking lot. We have a permit and everything," Thor said as he slammed his computer shut. "Honey. I did what I could. We should get going if we want to get to our spot by sunset."

"If you see my dog," Kidd said, "he's an American Bulldog and answers to the name Coop. Please give me a call." Kidd reached into his pocket and handed Vivian a card. She glanced at it.

Step behind me.

"We sure will." She tucked the card into her back pocket. Her legs felt like bricks as she jumped behind Kidd.

He raised his weapon. "I'd put yours down. You're surrounded."

"I'm not going to do that," Thor said, holding his weapon high. "You see, she's not my only hostage."

"Actually, she is." Cameron appeared on the hill behind Thor.

"Oh, my God." Vivian tried to move around Kidd, but he wouldn't let her. "I thought you were dead."

"So did I." For a split second, Thor lowered his weapon as his gaze shifted from Kidd to Cameron.

Kidd shoved Vivian to the ground and tackled Thor.

She jumped up and raced across the open field, lunging at Cameron and wrapping her arms—and legs—around his body.

He groaned, stumbling backward.

"Oh, shit." She unclasped her ankles and let her feet hit the ground. "How are you not dead? Didn't you get shot?"

He lifted his bloody shirt. "I did. But it's a flesh wound." He cupped her face. "I'm fine." He brushed his soft, sweet lips over her mouth, and she melted into his arms.

She never wanted to let go, and when he pulled back, tears filled her eyes. She blinked. The severity of everything that'd happened hit her heart like a jet hitting Mach one. "What does he mean he has another hostage?"

"I want you to know that everyone is safe and—"

"Just tell me." She sucked in a deep breath.

He nodded. "The reason you haven't heard from

Lilly is because this asshole had one of his so-called players kidnap her. He's been blackmailing Ethan to continue the game in order to get her back."

Vivian snapped her jaw shut. The blood in her veins boiled. She glanced between Cameron and Thor, who had been hoisted to his feet and hand-cuffed and was currently hurling insults at Kidd.

Two could play that game.

"You fucking asshole." She turned on her heels and marched over to Thor with her hand fisted and her arm cocked and ready for a fight.

"Vivian. Don't do it," Cameron called. "Oh, hell. Go ahead."

"Who the fuck do you think you are?" She stood only six inches from Thor. "Don't answer that," she said, swallowing her breath. "You're a sad, pathetic excuse for a man. You couldn't get anyone's attention, so you had to hide behind a computer screen to build yourself up. But look where that got you." She looked him up and down. "You're going to prison. For a very long time."

"No. I'm not." Thor laughed. "They think they have me, but there are so many holes in their case, it's sad."

"That's where you're wrong," Kidd said. "Your players are turning on you left and right. They are all too happy to testify against you."

Cameron inched closer. "And we're going to give them immunity if they do."

Thor's smile disappeared.

Vivian lifted her hand and then dropped it to her side. "You're not worth the sore knuckles."

Cameron slipped his arm around her waist. "Get him out of here," he said. "Lilly's okay. I promise you that. She's completely unharmed. And Ethan is cooperating, though I'm more than annoyed. He should have come to me."

"And my mom and Larry?"

"Perfectly safe." He leaned in and kissed her cheek. "I'm sorry you thought I was dead."

"Yeah. That sucked." She stared at him as they started walking toward the main road. "How did you know where I was?"

"I left my cell in the SUV. Stormi can always track my phone when we're working."

"I'm not sure how I feel about your work wife knowing where you are at all times."

"That's just when I'm working." He smiled. "But I'll let you track me one hundred percent of the time."

"Does this mean we're in a relationship?"

"I thought you'd never ask."

20

THREE WEEKS LATER...

Cameron curled his fingers around the wood railing and stared down at the dock. Vivian and Lilly were still deep in conversation.

"Maybe we should go." Jacob leaned against the railing.

"No," Eva said as she and Katie stepped out onto the deck with a tray of food and more wine. "We had no idea that Lilly was going to crash this party."

"I feel so bad for that poor girl," Katie said. "She's going through a lot."

"She sure is." Cameron kept his focus on Vivian and her friend. Some things didn't sit right with Cameron when it came to Ethan's story. It wasn't that Cameron thought he was lying, but it felt like he was still holding back.

"I know what it's like to be in Lilly's shoes," Eva said.

"She's a strong woman." Cameron turned and faced Vivian's mother. "How are you doing?"

Eva handed him a glass of red wine before sitting at the table. "I'm doing great now that I know my daughter is dating you. Don't they make a cute couple?" She turned to Katie.

"I've been saying that for months," Katie said.

"Cameron might be the smartest one in any room, but he's a bit slow when it comes to women."

"Aren't you all so funny?" His cheeks heated. "I'm happy about Vivian and me, too, but you know what I was asking."

"Are you tired of me living here?" Eva batted her lashes. "Am I getting in the way of you sleeping over."

Katie laughed. "Eva, you crack me up. But you also know how to change the focus from yourself to someone else."

"She's right. Have you talked to Larry lately? Because I ran into him at the—"

"Why is everyone such a Larry fan," she said with a heavy dose of sarcasm.

"Because he's not a bad guy," Cameron interjected.

"He's no Ethan, that's for sure," Eva mumbled. "I've known that young man for a long time, and I never would have thought he'd cheat on Lilly. But I didn't think my first husband was such a shit either. And to be honest, hearing about some of the things Oliver did…" Eva shook her head. "I have to wonder if he also had the same tendencies my late husband did."

"No. I don't believe that." Cameron sat at the table and took a slow sip of his wine before snagging a couple of pieces of cheese from the snack tray.

"I don't either," Jacob added. "I can tell you from everything I've learned from the case, he was doing whatever he could to help his friends. It wasn't just Annabel. There were others. He got caught up in something he couldn't control and was in over his head."

Eva let out a long breath. "He went to Larry for help, and I feel like Larry should have told me."

"You're right. He should have." Cameron rested his elbows on the table. "Eva, I have no right to tell you what to do or how to feel. I know you didn't want anyone to know about your late husband, but we do."

"And that doesn't change how we feel about you." Katie reached out and took Eva's hand. "You've always been so sweet and kind to me. Even when the world thought my uncle was a murderer and they treated me like a freak. You didn't."

"We're not the sum of our families' mistakes," Eva said.

Cameron arched an all-knowing brow. "I've seen some pretty crazy shit during this case. People like Ethan. Annabel. Your husband. It's an addiction. They need help, not our judgments. Yes. They hurt the ones they love. And maybe you can't ever come back from that—I know I'd personally struggle to forgive someone who did that to me. However, Larry didn't do that. He lied to you about his wife and you—"

"I know. I lied about my late husband, too."

Cameron nodded.

"But he made a huge mistake when it came to Oliver, and now he's gone."

Cameron's eyes burned. It had only been two days since they'd had the celebration of life, and he still got choked up every time he thought about it. "I don't know if Larry telling you or not would have changed the outcome for the better or for the worse." Cameron lowered his chin. "Thor's a sociopath. He doesn't have the ability to feel empathy. The moment he felt threatened was the moment he put this crazy plan to get rid of me and take Vivian for his own into motion. You knowing might have only made him move that timeline up. That might not have been good for my team."

"Perhaps you're correct." Eva pushed aside her glass.

"Larry was only trying to protect the people he loves. We all make mistakes when we do that," Cameron said.

"You can't be only twenty-six, young man." Eva stood. "Tell my daughter I went home."

"Home as in to Larry?" Katie asked.

"Yes. If he'll still have me," Eva said. "I'll come collect my things tomorrow."

"Will do," Cameron said. "Tell Larry we said hello."

He leaned back in the chair and sipped his wine. "Vivian is going to be quite happy her mom decided to give Larry a second chance."

"He's a good man," Jacob said. "A little misguided in his actions, but the bottom line is that he meant well. I'm not sure I can say the same for Ethan."

"I feel really bad for Lilly," Cameron said. Ethan was a habitual chat room user. While Ethan had agreed to see a therapist, and Lilly had agreed to couple's therapy, Cameron didn't hold out much hope for their relationship.

But who was he to judge?

"I think we all do." Katie nibbled on a cracker. "Vivian told me that Lilly believed she thought Ethan had been cheating on and off for years but never said anything. I don't think I could ever stay with someone who did that." She reached out and took her husband's hand. "I can forgive a lot of things, but I'm not sure I could forgive what Ethan did."

"It certainly is a tough one," Jacob agreed.

The wood under Cameron's feet vibrated.

He glanced over his shoulder and smiled. "Hey, beautiful." It had only been a few weeks since they'd officially started dating, but he felt as if he'd found his person. It was too soon to say that he was in love. That would be crazy.

But he certainly knew he could absolutely fall head over heels for Vivian if given the time.

Vivian rested her hand on his shoulder and squeezed. "Where's my mom?"

Considering that Lilly was standing right there with puffy eyes, he wasn't sure how to tell Vivian the good news. Lilly might not see it that way.

"She went out for a bit," he said. He'd explain it all when Lilly left. "Do you ladies want more wine?"

"I could do a little more," Lilly said as she took a seat next to Katie. "How's your little boy?"

"He's becoming quite the little handful." Katie held up her phone, showing off a picture.

"He looks just like Jacob." Lilly's voice had an overwhelming sense of sadness to it, but it also had a certain edge that Cameron wondered about. Where had it come from? And why?

"What's going to happen to Ethan?" Lilly fiddled with her fingernails. "He told me his deal hasn't been settled."

"You're correct," Jacob said. "It hasn't."

Lilly lowered her head and sniffled. "He's cooperating. What more do you need from him?"

Vivian rested her hand on Cameron's thigh and squeezed. "Lilly. It's okay. Tell them."

Lilly swiped at her cheeks. "I just want to know why everyone else is getting immunity and my husband is being left out to dry."

Cameron exchanged a quick glance with Jacob. "That's not really what's happening."

"Lilly," Jacob said. "Ethan lied to us. He withheld

information. And when you were kidnapped, he obstructed justice. It's not that we don't want to work with him, but he's still trying to negotiate. We need total cooperation, and we believe he's still not telling us everything."

"He's not," she said. "But he's trying to protect people. You have to understand that others are still caught up in that insane world of Thor's that don't want to be pulled into this. Ethan's trying to do right by them as well as put Thor away, but you're not giving him any wiggle room because he lied to you when I was kidnapped."

"Lilly," Vivian said. "Tell them."

"It's not their business." Lilly let out a long sigh. "And it shouldn't have any bearing on their decision."

"We need as many people as possible to come forward. Others have given us names. Why won't Ethan?"

"My husband has lost his job. He's lost the respect of his family. He could lose me. But he's lucky. He has money. He'll survive. Others are going to lose everything if this comes out. They can't afford that."

Jacob leaned forward. "What if I could work out a deal with many of them so they could remain anonymous? Then all they'd need to do is tell their stories to the judge and no one, other than me and the judge, would ever know who they are."

"You can do that?" Lilly asked with wide eyes.

"Yeah. I can," Jacob said. "I have twenty witnesses

so far who are willing to testify. The more I have, even anonymously, the better. But I need Ethan. He played a key role in the final game. Without him, my case falls apart, and that could put Thor back on the streets and on the internet. We don't want that."

"No, we don't," Lilly mumbled.

"Why are you and Ethan revisiting this?" Cameron asked, slightly annoyed. He'd thought this was a done deal. "Why does Ethan have cold feet?"

"It's not that. But since we learned I'm pregnant, and many of these people have families—children—he's worried about what coming forward will do to them. He's trying to do the right thing, and I'm trying to salvage what's left of my sanity, not to mention holding onto a thread of my marriage."

Cameron had to give Lilly kudos for her candor. Her life moving forward, especially during the trial wouldn't be easy. If she stayed with Ethan, it would be a thousand times worse.

Add having a baby on top of that…

Lilly was stronger than he'd ever given her credit for.

"Why didn't he just come out and tell me all of this?" Jacob said.

"Because he thinks you're out to get him. And frankly, so do I." Lilly squared her shoulders and brushed her hair from her face. "He might have lied to you about a few things, but he's one of the few people who remained on the fringe of Thor's game. He didn't ever meet anyone. And he never played in the game until he was forced to when he got caught." Lilly held up her hand. "And, yes, I'm aware that he might not have come clean with me about his extracurricular activities had all of this not happened, but that's my problem, not yours. And we're in therapy. It's my decision if I choose to stay with him, and the jury is still out on that matter. But I am willing to fight for my child's father. In the end, he did what you needed, and he's still willing to do that. To the bitter end. But as I said, he has the money to start his life over. Others don't. Can't you give the guy a break?"

Cameron had to admit, she had a point. He could only hope that Ethan was willing to put his money where his mouth was.

"Yes. I'm willing to do that," Jacob said. "But he's got to start being honest with me and not sending you to have these conversations."

Lilly nodded. "I'll tell him that."

"Good." Jacob stood, taking his wife's hand. "We need to get going. I promise I'll do what I can, but he needs to come to me. If he does that, I'll make sure he gets full immunity."

"I should get going, too. Ethan is waiting for me." Lilly nodded. "Thank you. I know he wants to work with you; but understand he's willing to go to jail to protect these people." She placed a hand on her stomach. "I'm being selfish. But regardless of whether I stay with him or not, I don't want the father of my baby going to prison if I can help it."

"I can understand that," Jacob said. "Tell him to come see me first thing in the morning."

"I will do that," Lilly said.

"Let me walk you to your car so we can talk a little more." Jacob waved his hand toward the path around the front of the cottage.

Cameron watched as Jacob, Katie, and Lilly disappeared around the side of the house. His heart broke for Lilly. But she was strong. She'd make a good life for herself and her baby in spite of everything, and regardless of whether Ethan was a big part of her life or not. Cameron knew that much for sure.

"So, I've got some news," Vivian said.

"Oh, really? What's that?"

"I'm not pregnant."

He tilted his head. "That's good news. Though I do want to have kids someday."

She patted his hand. "Someday. Just not today."

"Agreed." He sipped his wine and ate some cheese while he turned his attention to the lake. He could see a life with Vivian. A good one. With a dog. A couple of kids. The whole ball of wax.

"You're deep in thought," Vivian said in that sweet voice of hers that made him believe that everything would be okay.

"I was just thinking about Ethan and his decision to try to protect the anonymity of some of those people. While I don't think I could ever stay with a man who did that to me, at least Ethan won't be creating a secret legacy for his child. A mistake that my mother and I made when we buried that secret with my father."

Cameron took Vivian's hand. "You're not responsible for Oliver's death."

"I know. But I can't help but think that if my mom and I had been open and honest about his infidelities, then maybe Oliver and even Larry would have felt comfortable coming to us and talking about it. I mean, in some cases, it's not a choice, it's an addiction. And I hope that Ethan gets all the help he needs."

"So do I," Cameron said. His part in the investigation was over. Not only that, but he'd given his notice. In a couple of weeks, he'd no longer be a federal agent. It had been a good run, and he was proud of the things he'd accomplished. But it was time to do something else.

Though he'd yet to tell the world that, including Vivian.

"It's my turn to talk to you about something." He adjusted his chair and caught her gaze. "It's kind of serious."

She tilted her head. "You've got my attention."

"This case has taught me a lot of things about myself. Mostly that while I'm good at my job, being an FBI agent isn't what I want to do with the rest of my life."

"Really? What is it that you want to do?"

"I want to help people. I want to solve problems. I want to make a difference. But I'm not sure being an FBI agent is the way to do it, so I gave my notice."

Vivian smiled. It was one of those sweet smiles that conveyed the kind of love and support that a true companion would give to their loved ones.

Did she care that much about him? God, he hoped so.

"What do you want to do instead?"

"Katie and Jackson offered me a job, and I accepted."

Vivian leaned closer and kissed his cheek. "That's amazing. You'll make a great private investigator."

"You don't think I'm crazy?"

"Not at all," she said. "I totally believe in following one's heart, dreams, and gut. And if all of those are telling you to take that job, then so be it."

"It means I'll be looking for a place to live up here."

"You've got a place to crash for a while. And if it takes a long time and we're still together, maybe we skip that part."

"What are you implying?" he asked.

"Absolutely nothing, and absolutely everything."

He couldn't believe they were going down this road this early in the relationship. Then again, nothing about how they'd gotten together was normal, so why should living together be any different? "I will take you up on that offer."

"I thought you might."

"I'm glad you did." He kissed her plump lips. "I really care about you."

"I know you do," she said softly. "I feel the same way about you."

"I'm in big trouble," he said.

"Why is that?"

"Because I think I'm falling in love with you."

"The feeling is mutual."

EPILOGUE

END OF THE SUMMER... A FEW MONTHS LATER...

Cameron paced in front of the dock in front of Vivian's home—no—the home he shared with Vivian. "Come, Coop."

Their two-month-old American Bulldog wagged his tail happily and came running, only to stumble over his two large front paws.

Cameron laughed. "You silly dog." He bent over and patted the dog on the back. "Don't you ruin this for me." He handed him a bone filled with peanut butter in hopes he wouldn't go running off into the trees where a bunch of eyes were on him, waiting.

Impatiently.

He glanced at his watch. Vivian had mentioned that she might be a little late. Something about stopping at the drug store. A car whizzed by. It wasn't Vivian.

Cameron went back to pacing and thinking. Thor's trial had concluded yesterday. He'd been sentenced to life in prison without the possibility of parole. Justice had been served. Ethan had come through by gathering enough players willing to come forward and tell their stories to the judge with the promise that their privacy would be protected.

Ethan and Lilly's relationship status was still unsure, but Cameron could see a big change in Ethan—for the better—and Lilly was glowing, enjoying her pregnancy and doing her best to ignore the haters.

He stuffed his hands into his jeans' pockets. That had been the hardest thing for him to get used to in his new job.

No suits.

No ties.

But at least he still got to strap on his weapon. He liked that he got to keep that.

And he loved his move to Lake George.

Of course, the icing on the cake had been falling in love with Vivian.

The sound of tires on pavement caught his attention. Vivian's car rolled to a stop in the driveway.

Coop popped his head up. His ears flopped.

Vivian went into the house. She'd get the note to meet him down at the waterfront. It was only a matter of minutes.

This had better go off without a hitch, or there would be hell to pay. He took the bottle of wine and poured himself a glass then sat in the Adirondack chair with his dog at his feet and waited patiently for Vivian.

He waited.

And waited.

Perhaps this wasn't the best plan.

"Hello, honey," Vivian finally said.

"I thought you didn't get my note." He raised his glass. "Want some?"

"I'll stick with water for now." She plopped down in the chair and bent over to pet the dog, who didn't seem to care that Mommy was home.

Meanwhile, he poured a second glass, praying his hands didn't shake.

But they did.

At least, he didn't spill the red liquid.

"Cheers to a new school year, and let's hope my students aren't full of teenage angst," she said with a laugh as she tapped her water bottle to his wine.

"Like that's possible."

"So, how was your day?" she asked.

"I had to case out a store with Jackson, and then I had to get in a car with Katie. I don't know what was worse."

"You'd think Katie would change her driving habits with her husband being the assistant district attorney and now that she's a mom, but she thinks she's a race car driver or something."

"I swear I thought I was going to die." He held up two fingers. "Twice."

She raised the glass to her lips and sipped. And then she tipped her head back, closed her eyes, and sighed.

Well, that didn't go as he'd expected.

"Don't you want to hear about what I'm working on with Jackson?"

"Sure." She turned her head and blinked, her blue eyes sparkling in the sun.

His lungs deflated, and he couldn't take in another breath. For a man with a photographic memory, he couldn't remember a single word from his well-thought-out script. Not one. His mind was a complete blank. He had no idea what to say.

"Um. We went to a jewelry store."

She arched a brow. "You're working a case that involves a jewelry store? That sounds like it could be interesting."

Cameron's heart pounded so hard, it hurt his chest. His throat went dry. He opened his mouth, but nothing came out.

"Are you okay?" Vivian asked.

He reached for his tie to loosen it, only he wasn't wearing one.

"This is not going the way I planned," he managed to croak out.

"What are you talking about?"

Quiet laughter erupted from the trees.

"Is someone here?" She leaned forward, squinting to try to get a better look.

It was now or never.

He stood and reached into his pocket, finding the ring. He pulled it out, and the damn thing slipped from his fingers and fell to the ground. "Fuck," he mumbled.

"What was that?" She bent over and pressed her hands into the grass.

"I'll get it," he said.

More laughter. This time louder. And it sounded as if they were getting closer. Jerks. They weren't supposed to show their faces until after he'd popped the question.

And she answered.

With a yes.

They'd better not be getting this on video. He cringed at the thought.

He dropped to his knees and started patting the ground.

Coop jumped up onto him and licked his face.

"Get down." He lifted the puppy off his lap and set him aside.

"Found it," she said triumphantly. She held up the ring. "Oh, my," she said as she fell back in the chair. "This is a diamond ring."

"It's an engagement ring," he corrected, taking it from her hand. "I had this big thing planned, but I screwed it all up." He slipped it onto her ring finger. Thankfully, it fit perfectly. "I love you, Vivian. I want to spend the rest of my life with you."

"Are you proposing to me?"

"I'm trying to," he said. "And I really suck at it. But will you marry me?"

She cupped his face. "Yes." She planted her lips

on his mouth in an aggressive, sloppy kiss that belonged in the bedroom.

Clapping. Shouting. Laughter filled the air.

She jerked her head back. "Mom? Larry? Oh, my. Jacob and Katie?"

A few of her friends from work, and Jackson and Shannon, plus a few neighbors filled the front yard.

"Please tell me someone got all of that on video," Vivian said.

"I'm hoping they all saw how I fumbled that and took pity on me." Cameron stood, helping her up and put an arm around her waist. "I don't ever need to see that."

"Too bad," Jacob said. "I think we all videoed it."

"Oh. I'm already loading it to social media," Eva said.

"Are you still recording?" Vivian leaned into him, wrapping both her arms around his shoulders.

"No," someone said.

"I need someone to start recording again," Vivian said, staring into his eyes. "Please?"

"On it." Jacob raised his cell phone.

"Me, too," Larry said.

"I love you, Cameron" she said. "I'm amazed at your timing. I mean, you've always been intuitive, but did you know?"

"Know what?"

"You really don't have any idea?"

Her mother gasped. "No way," she whispered.

"No way, what?" Cameron turned his attention to

the audience. All of a sudden, he felt like he was standing outside in his boxers. "What's going on?"

"You know how we always have this little problem about using birth control?"

His eyes went wide. His cheeks heated. He couldn't believe she was bringing up their sex life in front of her parents. Their friends. "What does that have to do with—oh." He swallowed.

Everyone laughed. Hard.

"Are you pregnant?"

"That's why I was late in getting home. And why I didn't come down here right away. I thought you might have figured it out when I didn't have wine."

"I didn't even think about that," he mumbled. "Are you sure?"

"We need to have it confirmed by the doctor, but I can show you the pregnancy test if you want."

"That won't be necessary." He lifted her off the ground and twirled her around.

Coop barked.

"That was the best-worst proposal ever, and I wouldn't have wanted it any other way," she said.

"We're getting married. And having a baby," he said. "I couldn't be happier."

"Thank you for being patient and for always being there for me." She smiled.

"I know trust was hard for you, and while I can't promise you that our life together won't have its ups and downs, I can promise that you will always be able to trust me."

"Can I trust that you'll mow the lawn tomorrow?"

He laughed. "Yes, dear."

Thank you for reading SECRET LEGACY. Please feel free to leave an honest review!

Grab a glass of vino, kick back, relax, and let the romance roll in…

Sign up for my Newsletter (https://dl.bookfunnel.com/82gm8b9k4y) where I often give away free books before publication.

Join my private Facebook group (https://www.facebook.com/groups/191706547909047/) where I post exclusive excerpts and discuss all things murder and love!

And on Bookbub: bookbub.com/authors/jen-talty

ABOUT THE AUTHOR

Jen Talty is the *USA Today* Bestselling Author of Contemporary Romance, Romantic Suspense, and Paranormal Romance. In the fall of 2020, her short story was selected and featured in a 1001 Dark Nights Anthology. She is currently contracted to write in the a brand new series with Kristen Proby's Lady Boss Press, as well as Susan Stoker's *Special Forces: Operation Alpha* and Elle James's *Brotherhood Protectors.*

Regardless of the genre, her goal is to take you on a ride that will leave you floating under the sun with warmth in your heart. She writes stories about broken heroes and heroines who aren't necessarily looking for romance, but in the end, they find the kind of love books are written about :).

She first started writing while carting her kids to one hockey rink after the other, averaging 170 games per year between 3 kids in 2 countries and 5 states. Her first book, IN TWO WEEKS was originally published in 2007. In 2010 she helped form a publishing company (Cool Gus Publishing) with *NY Times* Bestselling Author Bob Mayer where she ran the technical side of the business through 2016.

Jen is currently enjoying the next phase of her life… the empty nester! She and her husband reside in Jupiter, Florida.

Grab a glass of vino, kick back, relax, and let the romance roll in…

Sign up for my Newsletter (https://dl.bookfunnel.com/82gm8b9k4y) where I often give away free books before publication.

Join my private Facebook group (https://www.facebook.com/groups/191706547909047/) where I post exclusive excerpts and discuss all things murder and love!

And on Bookbub: bookbub.com/authors/jen-talty

facebook.com/AuthorJenTalty
instagram.com/jen_talty
bookbub.com/authors/jen-talty
amazon.com/author/jentalty
pinterest.com/jentalty

ALSO BY JEN TALTY

Candlewood Falls

RIVERS EDGE

Legacy Series

Dark Legacy

Legacy of Lies

Secret Legacy

With Me In Seattle

INVESTIGATE WITH ME

SAIL WITH ME

FLY WITH ME

Club Temptation

SWEET TEMPTATION

The Monroes

COLOR ME YOURS

COLOR ME SMART

COLOR ME FREE

COLOR ME LUCKY

COLOR ME ICE

It's all in the Whiskey

JOHNNIE WALKER

GEORGIA MOON

JACK DANIELS

JIM BEAM

WHISKEY SOUR

WHISKEY COBBLER

WHISKEY SMASH

Search and Rescue

PROTECTING AINSLEY

PROTECTING CLOVER

PROTECTING OLYMPIA

PROTECTING FREEDOM

PROTECTING PRINCESS

NY STATE TROOPER SERIES

In Two Weeks

Dark Water

Deadly Secrets

Murder in paradise Bay

To Protect His own

Deadly Seduction

When A Stranger Calls

His Deadly Past

The Corkscrew Killer

Brand New Novella for the First Responders series

A spin off from the NY State Troopers series

PLAYING WITH FIRE

PRIVATE CONVERSATION

THE RIGHT GROOM

AFTER THE FIRE

CAUGHT IN THE FLAMES

The Men of Thief Lake

REKINDLED

DESTINY'S DREAM

Federal Investigators

JANE DOE'S RETURN

THE BUTTERFLY MURDERS

The Aegis Network

THE LIGHTHOUSE

HER LAST HOPE

THE LAST FLIGHT

THE RETURN HOME

THE MATRIARCH

The Collective Order

THE LOST SISTER

THE LOST SOLDIER

THE LOST SOUL

THE LOST CONNECTION

A Spin-Off Series: Witches Academy Series

THE NEW ORDER

Special Forces Operation Alpha

BURNING DESIRE

BURNING KISS

BURNING SKIES

BURNING LIES

BURNING HEART

BURNING BED

REMEMBER ME ALWAYS

The Brotherhood Protectors

Out of the Wild

ROUGH JUSTICE

ROUGH AROUND THE EDGES

ROUGH RIDE

ROUGH EDGE

ROUGH BEAUTY

The Brotherhood Protectors

The Saving Series

SAVING LOVE

SAVING MAGNOLIA

SAVING LEATHER

Hot Hunks

Cove's Blind Date Blows Up

My Everyday Hero – Ledger

Tempting Tavor

Holiday Romances

A CHRISTMAS GETAWAY

ALASKAN CHRISTMAS

WHISPERS

CHRISTMAS IN THE SAND

CHRISTMAS IN JULY

Heroes & Heroines on the Field

TAKING A RISK

TEE TIME

A New Dawn

THE BLIND DATE

SPRING FLING

SUMMER'S GONE

WINTER WEDDING

Witches and Werewolves

LADY SASS

ALL THAT SASS

www.ingramcontent.com/pod-product-compliance
Lightning Source LLC
Chambersburg PA
CBHW052147010525
26066CB00011B/292
9781638270171